IN THE CITY of the
DISAPPEARED

Also by Tom Hazuka
The Road to the Island

IN THE CITY of the DISAPPEARED

a novel

Tom Hazuka

Bridge Works Publishing Company
Bridgehampton, New York

Published in the United States by Bridge Works Publishing
Company, Bridgehampton, New York. Distributed in the United
States by National Book Network, Lanham, Maryland
For descriptions of this and other Bridge Works books visit the
Web site of National Book Network at www.nbnbooks.com.

FIRST EDITION

The characters and events in this book are fictitious. Any
similarity to actual persons, living or dead, is coincidental and not
intended by the author.

Library of Congress Cataloging-in-Publication Data

Hazuka, Tom.
    In the city of the disappeared : a novel / Tom Hazuka.— 1st
ed.
        p. cm.
    ISBN 1-882593-31-6 (alk. paper)
        1. Chile — History—1973–1988—Fiction. 2. Americans—
Travel — Chile—Fiction. 3. Peace Corps (U.S.)—Chile—
Fiction. I. Title.
PS3558.A95 I95 2000
813'.54—dc21   99-055391

10 9 8 7 6 5 4 3 2 1

Jacket design/illustration by Eva Auchincloss
Book design by Eva Auchincloss

Printed in the United States of America

Dedicated

to the memory of

John T. Hazuka

Para todos mis amigos chilenos—sobre todo Veronica Inostroza y Hugo Buitano—y para los desaparecidos que nunca conocí.

For all my Chilean friends—especially Veronica Inostroza and Hugo Buitano—and for the *desaparecidos* I never met.

IN THE CITY of the
DISAPPEARED

1

The black body and the white body leaped high in the January heat, arms extended, and two pairs of palms slapped the volleyball at the same instant. The ball tipped the top of the net and dinked to the ground on the black body's side, sending up a puff of dust. Groans and laughs from the other players.

"Game!" shouted Phil Dwyer, who had served the point. "Damn, Lewis, you be havin' terminal White Man's Disease if you can't outjump Harry the honky!"

Lewis Briggs grinned as he wiped the sweat from his glasses with a corner of his shirt. His skin was the color of coffee with plenty of cream in it. "I don't want to give him a complex," he said.

"It's about time *you* ate one for a change, sucker," Harry Bayliss said. "Besides, you needed some dessert after that gourmet Peace Corps lunch." Lewis rolled his eyes.

They had been in Chile for less than a week; it seemed surreal to Harry that ten days ago he was at Stumpy Dixon's crowded apartment in Queens, counting down the seconds as the gaudy Times Square ball dropped to start 1978. This was their third day of

Spanish classes at the Peace Corps training center in Santiago. Most of the sixteen members of their training group got together for coed volleyball after lunch; it was already routine. Lewis was the only non-white face among them. He and Harry were alone in the advanced Spanish section. No matter that Harry had graduated from St. John's, while Lewis had gone to Yale, or that Lewis's father was a doctor in Minneapolis while Harry's dad worked for the Post Office — Lewis wasn't a snob or otherwise an ass as far as Harry could tell.

It was scorching hot, too hot to stay indoors all day studying Spanish. When Harry had left New York for group orientation in Miami, it was ten degrees with windchill diving below zero. Miami had palm trees and Spanish — Cuban, mostly, not the Puerto Rican he usually heard in New York — but Chile still was an abrupt change of worlds. On the bus to Santiago from the airport he saw a *Tome Coca-Cola* billboard and felt both scornful and reassured. He saw a two-wheeled donkey cart and snapped a picture. He laughed with proper irony at a wrought-iron factory sign that read "American Screw (Chile)". Everything was new, and that was welcome.

Harry gulped some water and strode through the building to the front yard. He squinted against the sun. Along the stuccoed wall next to the street ran a narrow canal, murky and swift, that had swept away his Frisbee on the first day. Beyond the wall, across the quiet street, was the army's *Academia de Guerra* — War Academy — with armed sentries in towers at each corner. A billboard painted with a red, white and blue Chilean flag proclaimed the military motto: *Por La Razon O La Fuerza* — "By Reason Or By Force".

Harry was looking for Jean Hargrove. She had quit after the first volleyball game, and he expected to see her on the shady bench beneath the grape arbor. Instead he found Katie Perkins, a cheerleader-type who had earned his animosity by bringing her guitar to the welcoming party on Saturday and boring a captive audience with a slew of lame folk songs. Harry could play rings around her on guitar, but he didn't spend his life looking for a stage. She had even tried to turn it into a hootenanny — "Come on, guys, let me *hear* ya!" — though few of the Chileans knew or understood the words, and most of the Americans were trying to forget them. Now Katie pretended not to see him walk by, and he couldn't have cared less.

But Jean was something else. She was from Los Angeles — "Redondo Beach, actually" — and to a kid from New York who had never been farther west than Pittsburgh California was exotic, another planet. They'd hit it off right away in Miami, when she ordered for him at a macrobiotic restaurant and a herbaceous bale arrived that he actually sort of enjoyed.

"I love your green eyes," she'd said in her soft, southern California accent. "And your hair's that pretty color Crayola calls burnt sienna. You should let it grow." Her sun-bleached blonde hair reached halfway down her back. She smiled at him, eyes as blue as robins' eggs, face tanned "from my Dad's going-away present, a ski weekend at Mammoth".

Harry swallowed a botanical mouthful. "I will. I only got it cut for the military types down there." He chuckled, but it was a nervous laugh. "For all I know they beat up on longhairs."

"For all we know they beat up on everybody." She

3

fed him a forkful of her tofu concoction. Her smile made it more than tolerable.

Classes didn't start for ten minutes, so Harry decided to see if Jean had gone to the little store up the street. It had two wobbly tables under a eucalyptus tree, and yesterday a handful of the trainees had stopped there for a drink after school. Jean had good-naturedly handled the laughs when she ordered a Coke by asking for *una caca* instead of *una coca*.

Harry stepped off the broiling lawn into the shade of the tree-lined road, and for a moment delighted in the cool transition. Then the cool melted. Two soldiers marched toward him with Jean trapped between them, each gripping one of her arms. The one on the left dangled her Nikon camera from the same hand that carried his rifle.

At a trot, Harry reached the entrance to the base seconds before they did. The soldiers halted. Jean tried to sound calm, but there was no mistaking the fear in her eyes.

"Harry, these guys grabbed me and they've got no sense of humor."

"Is there a problem, *señores?*" Harry had studied Spanish all through high school and college, while Jean knew only the few words she'd picked up since they arrived.

The soldier held up the camera. Dark half moons stained the armpits of his green camouflage uniform, and sweat trickled down his forehead. *"Es prohibido sacar fotografía de instituciones militares!"*

"What'd he say, Harry?"

"You can't take pictures of army bases."

"Are you serious? Tell them I didn't know. Tell them I'm sorry."

The soldier scowled and ripped open the camera. A foot of film trailed from the cannister, which he crumpled and jammed in his pocket. Jean swallowed hard. The terror in her face mixed with disgust.

The soldier grinned at her helplessness. "Maybe next time you won't take our internal security so lightly, Miss America No-Bra." Jean's red tank top was tucked into faded Levi's. The soldier still holding Jean snickered. The camera hung slack like a broken jaw.

Harry stepped forward. "You have no right —"

The camera crashed on the pavement, not thrown, just dropped, as if by accident. Jean stiffened and her mouth opened, but no sound emerged. Harry froze at the soldier's words.

"No *right*? Should we go inside for questioning to find out what my rights are, gringo spy?"

"How long have you worked for the CIA?" taunted the other one. He shoved Jean away. She knelt to pick up her camera and snapped it back together. It rattled like a lightbulb with a shattered filament. She glared at them and set her jaw, but said nothing.

Harry felt a knot growing in his chest. "We're not spies," he said. "We're Peace Corps volunteers."

"Same thing." One soldier smirked. The other hawked and spat skillfully on Harry's foot, the slimy gob slithering between the exposed toes in his sandals. Harry had never felt so powerless.

Jean's face contorted. "I just wanted pictures of the brown hills, because they remind me of the hills at home in summer. What do I care about a stupid army base?"

"May I be of service here, *señores?*" It was Fernando Ruiz, Harry's instructor; Lewis followed a step behind. Fernando spoke deferentially, almost servilely. "These students are late for class. Is there any difficulty which I could help to clear up?" He manufactured a smile.

"You, nigger, get away!" said the soldier who had dropped the camera. "This doesn't concern you."

Lewis hesitated, looking to Fernando for help that didn't come.

"Now, nigger! Are you deaf?"

With a final glance toward Harry, Lewis retreated. Fernando's solicitous expression never wavered as the soldier detailed the crime, and he never addressed the Americans except to tell Jean what she already knew now about the ban on photographs. He apologized profusely; he promised it wouldn't happen again. The soldier's spit oozed between Harry's toes.

"But he broke Jean's camera!" he said in Spanish.

The guilty soldier fondled his rifle. "Broken law — broken camera." His finger twiddled the trigger. "Obey the law and nothing gets broken."

Fernando thanked the soldiers for their patience and understanding and hurried his students away. Not until they were back behind the wall, where the soldiers couldn't see him, did Harry kneel to clean his foot. He gagged and dunked his sandal in the scummy canal. He needed time to think through what had just happened, to figure out what it meant, but Fernando wouldn't excuse them from class. "You're not in the United States anymore, Harry. You must learn to live here in Chile. Now let's discuss what happened as if we had imagined it all, so you can practice the past subjunctive."

But Harry's mind drifted. He kept wondering how

Jean was coping in her beginner's Spanish class. He kept hearing the crunch of camera on asphalt and the mocking words of bullies with guns. Two years in Chile seemed impossibly long, stretching out in front of him farther than he could imagine. I'll be twenty-five when this is over, he thought. He had joined the Peace Corps to help people who needed it, to travel, have adventures and live in a different world for a while. He had prepared himself to live without luxuries — the "mud hut" existence. He hadn't prepared himself for curfews and martial law. "The Toughest Job You'll Ever Love", the Peace Corps ads said. Harry thought of his father, suffering with inoperable bone cancer. Teach kids to play baseball and save the world? Right. What am I doing here? Dad was always with *me* when I needed him. He felt like a defector begging for asylum. His fingers drummed on the desk. Flies buzzed at the window.

"This is sick, Fernando," Lewis said. "They smashed Jean's camera and called me a nigger. No way I'm going to pretend we imagined that. Forget it — tell us about the *golpe.*"

Golpe de estado, Harry thought. *Coup d'état.* Interesting we don't have words for it in English.

Fernando looked at his two students, then at his watch, cleared his throat twice and shuffled some papers. Suddenly his resistance crumbled. He leaned toward them like a conspirator.

"1973 was a terrible time. *Entienden?* Inflation, shortages, riots in the streets. I'll never forget my girlfriend coughing and crying, running away from tear gas while still holding an election sign that said 'No to civil war! Chile wants change without blood!' "

Fernando tried to smile. "I had already dropped my

sign." He mopped his face with a checked handkerchief. "Chileans got so desperate that many welcomed a military takeover, anything to end the chaos. You must understand, Chile has a long history of democracy. But then, overnight, dictatorship. Six P.M. curfew, tanks in the streets, people jamming foreign embassies to plead for asylum, innocent civilians kidnapped and *desaparecido*. Do you know what it's like to be waked at dawn by machine gun rat-tat-tat somewhere close, too close? Of course you don't. I wish I didn't. Now, over four years later, Pinochet has the gall to claim the armed forces don't want power but have a sacred duty to govern and prohibit politics until Chile is ready for democracy again."

"Who decides when that is?" Lewis asked.

"The same ones who decide everything in this country. The ones with the guns." Fernando picked at a scab on his knuckle. It began to bleed. "Not a word to my boss," he whispered. "He supports Pinochet. In fact, not a word to anyone — I need this job. You understand how it is."

Harry wasn't at all sure he did.

That night the waitress at Bar Budo brought Jean a new glass of wine, and Harry a second gin and tonic. They sat at a sidewalk table. Headlights flashed by on busy Avenida Pedro de Valdivia, and exhaust fumes tainted the sticky air. An enormous orange moon shone through the smog.

Jean's foot brushed his calf. She looked at Harry, eyes bright and shell necklace white against her throat. "What a sky. One glass of wine under that moon and my camera's no big deal any more. I'm healthy. They didn't hurt me. My parents will send me another camera by diplomatic pouch and all I lose are some souvenirs."

"Yeah," Harry said. "No way I'd pay what it costs here for that camera. Triple the U.S. price is what the third world pays."

"How does anyone afford it?"

"Seen many Chileans with Nikons around their necks?"

Her foot rubbed harder. "We'll win in the end," she said. She sipped her wine, eyes glistening above the glass. Harry grinned in spite of himself.

"Did you really play pro baseball, Harry?"

"Sort of. I mostly rode the pine in A ball in upstate New York last summer. They released me after six weeks. I didn't have a chance."

"They didn't give you a fair shot?"

"No, the other guys were too good."

Jean laughed. "So you joined the Peace Corps to coach baseball."

"Actually," Harry said, leaning close as if to tell a secret, "disco drove me out of the country. But now I see there's no escaping the madness." Wretched disco music was blaring from the bar.

Smiling, she pushed him away. "Will you be serious for a second?"

"No, I didn't join the Peace Corps to coach baseball. I didn't even know there was such a thing. English major, I figured they'd send me to teach English someplace. But when my recruiter mentioned this job I jumped at it, especially since Peru is so close."

"Peru?"

Harry bit the flesh from his lime slice. "As a kid I

9

wanted to be an explorer almost as much as a big leaguer. I read all the books about Troy and Atlantis, Easter Island, the Maya and Aztecs. But the Incas were best of all. Cuzco, Sacsayhuamán — and especially Machu Picchu. I'd dream about it. I even had pictures of Machu Picchu on my wall next to Mickey Mantle and Yankee Stadium. My brother thought I was a weird little snot. What did you want to be?"

"A nurse, then a surfer, then a lawyer for a few misguided weeks, and finally I decided on being rich and famous. So I graduated from UC Santa Barbara and signed a lucrative contract with the Peace Corps."

"We do make the big bucks, you have to admit."

Jean looked him in the eye. "To tell you the truth, mostly I just felt like doing something wild."

Their eyes locked. "That's the best reason I know," Harry said. "My last semester of college, people I'd never seen except in jeans were putting on suits and hustling interviews with every company they could find. It was depressing. No way I'm ready for that."

Jean shrugged. "I guess the Peace Corps is for people who can't handle the normal way. Misfits."

"Misfits who want to travel. I've got to get out West someday. I've never been farther from home than Daytona one Easter break. Not counting Miami."

"Or now. Hey, I've never been back East."

" 'Back East?' How can it be 'back' if you haven't been there before?"

"Well, why do you say 'out West'?"

"Maybe the East is backward and the West is far out."

She groaned. "You sound like my dad, dumb jokes

and all." She looked up at the moon. "What's *your* father like?"

Harry thought back to the August before, the muggy afternoon the biopsy results came in. He had gone to the park to shoot baskets, running hard to clear his mind until he knew for sure: forget the adventure and helping others, forget the Peace Corps. Dad needs me. But when the old man found out he blew up, said Harry was no son of his if he let them both down and stayed home.

Harry almost told her. But his throat tightened. "He's a great guy. You'd like him."

Jean folded her hand over his and stared into the night. She chewed her bottom lip. Men at the bar debated World Cup soccer as if lives depended on it.

"I can't believe they broke my camera today. It seems so far off already."

"Not far enough," he said. No asylum, he thought. Thinking of Lewis's pained face when the soldier ordered him away, for the first time Harry admitted to himself that part of him was relieved to be thousands of miles from home, where he didn't have to watch his father die.

2

That Saturday Harry stood at the window of his room on Calle Marathon, fingerpicking his guitar as he looked out at the National Stadium. The *cordillera* behind it, off to the east, was invisible except for a few peaks poking above the scum-gray smog. The summer haze grew thicker and darker every day, and Chileans told Harry nothing would change until rain washed it away.

He had practice in twenty minutes, his first encounter with Chilean *béisbol*. Ray Clark, who'd been coaching baseball with the Peace Corps in Santiago for a year and a half, had phoned him the night before to say practice started at ten A.M., *hora inglesa*.

"Say what?"

Ray laughed. "English time, rookie," he said in a southern accent. "It means on the dot. As opposed to *hora chilena*, which is anywhere from five minutes late to maybe nobody shows up at all."

"Sounds pretty disparaging to the Chileans."

"Hey, they made it up, not me. See you *mañana*."

The National Stadium was a bleak concrete oval, part of an enormous complex of playing fields surrounded by a high cinder-block wall. Harry tried to imagine being in his room over four years ago, in the fall of 1973, listening to the crackle of gunfire in the stadium, wondering who was being murdered by Pinochet's soldiers, wondering if you were next. The sky must have been clearer then, in September after the winter rains, fresh snow covering the mountains. Would he have heard the screams of the prisoners? He heard the soccer crowds roar, whenever the home team scored a goal.

Guitar still hanging around his neck, Harry picked up an aerogram from his concave bed and read it again. Ten days here and already the second letter from home, the first one mailed before he'd even left the States. He'd sent a postcard from Miami, and written back once in Chile. Not bad, he thought, considering how busy he was and that he'd spent two miserable days in bed with cramps and vicious diarrhea. That's when he found it was possible to be so vegetated you could look at the ceiling for hours at a time and not be bored. But it was a piece of cake compared to his dad's chemotherapy.

The letter was a hybrid, half from each parent. Half as far as space went, that is; Mom fit in more words with her smaller handwriting. Her part was mostly news: a massive blizzard practically shut down New York, Harry's brother Dave was dating an N.Y.U. graduate student, Karen O'Connell was doing great in law school — you are keeping in touch with her, Harry, aren't you? You could do far worse than marry a lawyer, you know.

Dad talked about the Mets' prospects for 1978, predicted Denver would upset Dallas in the Super Bowl ("I know it won't happen but I hate the blankety-blank Cowboys too much to pick 'em"), and asked if Harry had scouted any potential big leaguers yet. "And don't listen to your mother's matchmaking — if she was any good at it, she wouldn't have got stuck with me!"

Harry dropped the aerogram back on the bed. Not a word about Dad's cancer, or the treatment. Maybe that was good news, but more likely they were just sparing him the details. Suddenly Harry realized that he held back from them, too. He had written about training, and some of his impressions of Chile, but left out anything he thought would really worry them. He described the curfew, the beggars and the *barrio* shacks — but not the soldiers who broke Jean's camera or the murders in the National Stadium. And certainly not the *desaparecidos*, the people who had simply disappeared.

He opened his door. A moronic TV variety show blared from Señora Cabezas' bedroom. She was half-deaf, or pretended to be. His stomach grumbled from the skimpy breakfast she'd fed him, a day-old roll and some tea; he'd nab a piece of bread on the way out. The Señora lay in bed, propped on pillows, covers loosely pulled up to her breasts. She wouldn't dress until lunch at two. She was a prune of a woman with rotten teeth who claimed to be fifty but looked a decade older, whose life was dedicated primarily to complaining about her husband, a stoop-shouldered man in photographs who had been discourteous enough to die of a massive heart attack and leave her all alone. Harry didn't blame him. On the day Harry arrived she informed him she was only taking him in for the rent money, and insisted that he buy batteries for his little cassette player instead of wasting her electricity. Her son lived two hours away in Valparaíso, and never came to visit.

"*Hasta luego, Señora,*" he said as he passed her room. "*Qué?*"

"I'm going."

"Where?" Her eyes never strayed from the boobery on the screen. She dragged on a Belmont cigarette; an ashtray full of lipstick-stained butts rested on her lap.

He had told her twice about his plans for the morning. "To baseball practice across the street."

"*Verdad*. Be a good boy and put on some water before you leave? My tea is cold." She smiled fawningly, like a five-year-old wheedling a favor. Her teeth were gummy brown nubs. "*Gracias, mijito.*"

Harry hated it when she called him *mijito*. He was not her "little son," and when she said it he thought of his father. With a match he lit the gas stove under the kettle and went outside. A blue and white city bus lumbered by, battered and creaking and spewing black exhaust fumes that stung his nose and eyes. He held his breath and dodged traffic as he jogged across the street in the middle of the block. A few steps from the stadium compound, he realized he had forgotten to steal the bread.

A ferret-faced man with sleepy eyes stopped him at the gate, but waved him through when Harry said he was going to baseball practice. Then Harry thought of something. "Where's the field?" he asked. The gatekeeper squinted at him, cigarette smoke jetting from both nostrils, and pointed a cadaverous finger toward a far corner of the grounds. All Harry saw were soccer fields.

And more soccer fields. Striding double-time on an uneven dirt road, sure that he was late, he passed half a dozen grassless soccer fields, all of them occupied. Bright-shirted weekend athletes yelled instructions. On his left loomed the stadium, gray and solid in the rippling heat. Stadiums are supposed to be vibrant and alive, he thought, but this one is a place of death. This is where soldiers hammered Victor Jara's fingers one by one, for leading prisoners in revolutionary songs to keep up their spirits. Then they smashed his guitar in front of his face and shot him. Harry thought of his sweet old Martin guitar, inherited from his grandfather, and what it would feel like to see it destroyed. Jara's songs were banned in Chile and Harry had never heard his music, but already two people had told him the story of his death. His murder was a symbol, they said — soldiers trying to silence a popular voice that sang of love, and the struggle for equality, and of rich men, many of them foreigners, who made fortunes from the sweat of workers barely earning enough to keep their families alive. Harry was ashamed to admit that he didn't remember hearing about the *golpe* when it happened. He had been a freshman in college, and slaughter in a skinny country on the bottom side of the planet meant nothing to him. He flexed his fingers and made two hard fists, imagining a hammer crushing his knuckles like walnuts.

Suddenly cowhide cracked on aluminum. Beyond the last soccer field, two men chased a baseball that skipped by them on a sun-baked outfield of dried weeds. The infielders yelled at them to hurry. The center fielder finally trapped the ball, then heaved it ten feet over the cutoff man's head.

"*Huevón!*" screamed the shortstop. "Big Balls! You suck!"

The center fielder flung down his glove. "Jump next time, you drunken runt!" The left fielder mocked both their ancestries and lit a cigarette.

The next batter slapped a grounder that rolled

through the first baseman's legs and out past the right fielder, who stood with his back to the diamond watching a soccer game. His teammates' cries woke him up, and guessing wrong he sprinted in the opposite direction from the hit. When he saw his mistake, he sulked and walked after the ball while the batter gleefully rounded the bases, running the last ten feet backward to home plate. The team at bat heaped abuse on the outfielder, who flipped his hand in the air, palm down, in the universal Chilean gesture of disgust or annoyance. The insults were so graphic and inventive that Harry started laughing too — until reality hit, and his stomach sank. Two years of his life teaching these characters to play baseball? In the shadow of that stadium?

Looking at the dead grass on the parched earth, he walked toward the dilapidated stands on the third base side. *"Vamos, gringo!"* shouted voices from the bench. Harry waved, wondering how anybody could know him, and felt silly a moment later when he saw the cries were for the man tapping his bat on home plate. Harry sat on the wooden bleachers and a sliver jabbed his ass.

"Home run, Ray!" cheered a thin-armed boy standing a few rows above. He was about ten, with skin the color of peanuts and ragged cotton pants fastened with safety pins. The kid crouched in an unorthodox hitting stance, right elbow low and close to his body, hands practically touching his ear, then took a vicious batless swing and had to hop to keep his balance. "Like Ray!" he said. "I am good like Ray!"

Ray set himself at the plate in the same strange style, Popeye forearms bulging, fat end of his bat tracing tiny circles in the air. The fielders were all swung around toward left and playing insanely deep. The pitcher looked like he wished the mound were a lot far-ther away. He hung a curve that spun over the outside corner like flying meat wearing a "hit me" sign. Ray waited on it and creamed a line drive over first that hit foul by a foot. The ball rolled all the way to the soccer field, where a goalie examined it as if it had dropped from outer space. Harry was impressed — that ball was smoked, and to the opposite field no less.

"You see?" said the boy. "You see?" His face glowed with the adulation that at his age Harry had reserved for Mickey Mantle, and for his father when he'd crush home runs for Sullivan's Pub in city softball games. "That's *my* dad," he'd say. "He plays third base and went three for four today and let me drink some beer from his can."

The fielders moved even farther back, and more straightaway. The pitcher bounced a fastball in the dirt past the catcher all the way to the rickety backstop, then through a hole in the rusty chicken wire. Immediately the kid jumped off the bleachers and ran after it, while the hitting team taunted the pitcher as if he'd just blown the World Series. Ray grinned at them and put a finger to his lips. He bunted the next pitch down the line and sprinted to first almost by the time the third baseman touched the ball, but the would-be all star threw anyway and chucked it into right field. Ray coasted into second. The fielders traded excuses and insults. Harry's stomach dropped. Two years was a long time.

"*Bueno*, Ray!" The boy waved, and when Ray waved back the kid grinned like the sun. He looked at Harry and Harry returned the smile, warm inside at what base-ball and heroes can mean when you're ten years old.

Ray moved to third on a groundout and scored on a fly ball. He plopped down on the bench, and was strapping on his catcher's shin guards as Harry walked over.

"Ray? I'm Harry Bayliss." He stuck out his hand.

Ray's grip was like a wrestler's, and the shoulders straining the seams of his baseball shirt told Harry he could have squeezed a lot harder if he'd wanted to. He looked about twenty-five, though his thick brown beard made it hard to tell for sure. Harry was 5'11", though taller than a lot of liars who said they were six feet, and when Ray stood up they saw exactly eye to eye.

He wiped his sweaty forehead with his sleeve. "Rough party last night?"

"What do you mean?" Harry had stayed up late reading and thinking and talking himself out of making a collect call home, but if that was enough to make him look hung over he was hurting worse than he thought.

"You're two hours late, bucko. The kids finished practice at noon. Didn't I say ten o'clock? Maybe my English is down the commode."

"Sure you did. I don't know —" Then it registered. Out of habit he'd set his clock radio alarm, and the different South American electrical current caused it to run slower. It lost about an hour and a half every eight hours. "I screwed up," he said as Ray put on his chest protector. "I set my electric alarm and it lost time."

"This country could stand to lose some fucking time." A bandy-legged guy too macho to wear a batting helmet sliced air for strike three and the last out of the inning, and heaved his bat so far the on-deck batter had to dance to keep his ankles intact. Ray spat in the dust. "Pathetic. Let me catch this half-inning and we're out of here. I've got some friends I want you to meet."

Ray's team bitched at losing their catcher and

squabbled over who would take his place. "The game'll break up soon anyway," Ray said as they left the field, the kid from the bleachers tagging along. "You won't catch *these* guys skipping lunch."

If they're so bad, how do you stand this job? Harry decided it was too early to ask that question.

Ray tousled the boy's hair. "Go home and take care of your mother," he said with a smile, and off the boy ran. Though Ray's Spanish was grammatically perfect, he had the same southern accent as he did in English. Ray watched the boy for a moment, then nodded toward the stadium. "I reckon you've heard about that place."

"Enough to make me wonder about teaching sports in this country. Give the people games and song festivals, to take their minds off curfews and censorship and *desaparecidos*."

"Sounds like you got it all figured out, Rookie."

"I've got nothing figured out. I'm just trying to find out where I stand."

"I'll tell you where you stand. In a military dictatorship with one A.M. curfew. Bars closing that early is grounds for revolt right there."

"I'm serious, Ray. How do we live with ourselves? I don't want to help those bastards."

Ray kicked open the door to the shack behind the field that held equipment and coaches' lockers. He sat on a stack of dirty bases and unlaced his spikes. Harry leaned against dented lockers. Despite the tin roof it was cooler inside, out of the sun.

"Listen. Should we two suffer because Truman nuked Japan? Should Chileans hate all Americans because the CIA and Kissinger helped overthrow Allende?

You think it's fair to deny kids the chance to play ball because of the goddamn government they live under? You tell *me*. All I know is me and the kids have a good time, and good times are in short supply for a lot of them. Beyond that? You come up with some answers, let me know."

Harry certainly had no answers. Doing the right thing had seemed so simple when he filled out the Peace Corps application. He thought of the boy in the stands, and wondered how it felt to be that special in someone's eyes. "That one kid acts like you're Babe Ruth," he said.

"That's Juan Perez, my best pitcher. The kids call him Barata, the Cockroach. He lives in a *callampa* with his mother and five sisters. *Callampa* — that's Chilean for slum. You'll hear the word a lot." The lockers rattled when Ray tossed in his spikes. "Barata's father was a labor union leader. Disappeared in the *golpe*."

"Jesus." Harry tasted the dust in the air.

"It's not *me* — Barata just needed a big brother and I was convenient. It's kids like him that make this job worth it."

"You don't work much with adults?"

"You shitting me? If I did I'd have bolted long ago. Only the kids matter."

"That makes me feel better," Harry said.

"Give it time," Ray said.

They caught a *liebre* — a green microbus — that turned right on the broad Avenida Grecia and rolled past the National Stadium. Hundreds of children milled around inside and outside the iron fence, laughing and roughhousing, oblivious to the smog, many with no memory of life before the "state of seige" that President

Pinochet renewed every six months. With Barata's smile on his mind, Harry wondered how many of these kids had heard shots during the revolution, and how many of those shots had cut down friends or members of their families.

3

They transferred to a *liebre* for La Reina, a *barrio* of comfortable houses with red tile roofs, surrounded by walls and well-kept lawns and gardens. Harry saw no apartment houses like the one where he lived. Like in New York City, it didn't take long to change worlds here. The bus crossed a wide canal of sluggish gray water and headed toward the mountains on a shady, tree-lined avenue.

"Marisol's hot shit," Ray said. "She loves a good time. Her old man's dead, but he used to be a big deal actor and writer so she knows all these poets and artists. Some of them are pretty fucked up but at least they're not boring."

"How do you know her?"

Ray twirled his Atlanta Braves baseball cap around on his index finger. "Through another volunteer who lived with Marisol's mother during training. Now I'm porking Marisol's sister."

"Older?"

"Younger."

"Sounds complicated."

"It's worth it. Hey, where you from?"

"New York. Long Island."

"So that's why you talk so weird."

"*I* talk weird? Where are you from?"

"Macon, Georgia, my man, a redneck born and bred. My parents are Yankees from Ohio, but I try to keep that a little-known fact in Macon. The Civil War — oops, I mean The War of Northern Aggression — ain't quite over in those parts."

"Where'd you go to college?"

"Florida State. We had some damn good teams. And the babes . . . man, Tallahassee is beaver heaven. This is our stop."

Harry knew Ray was a fine ballplayer if he had played for Florida State. They walked down a driveway that dead-ended in a waist-high picket fence. A dachshund scrambled off the front porch of a small brick house and ran yapping to the gate, toenails clicking on the flagstone walkway. Harry heard someone strumming a guitar, and a woman's voice singing softly in Spanish.

"Beautiful song," Harry said.

"*Te Recuerdo Amanda*, by Victor Jara. The *milicos* smashed his fingers . . ."

"I know."

Ray raised his eyebrows and opened the gate. The dog leaped to their thighs again and again, like a frenzied toy no one knew how to turn off. They followed the music; Ray peeked through lilac branches into a picture window.

"Ray!" The music stopped, and Harry could hear other voices. A sandy-haired woman in her late twenties opened the door. She was barefoot, with floppy bangs and a dashiki, and laughed and kissed his neck when Ray

24

gave her such a hug that he lifted her off the floor. The dog scooted inside.

"Harry Bayliss, this is Veronica Huerta, Marisol's sister." Harry wasn't sure about Chilean greeting etiquette yet, but she solved the problem by taking his hands and kissing him on the cheek. "I'll get you some wine," she said. "Marisol and Lalo went to buy more."

"Introduction time," Ray told Harry in English, as they entered the group with full glasses. A round of handshakes and kisses and some minutes of talk later, Harry had them straight.

They were mostly in their early- to mid-thirties. Mauricio, a long-faced poet with big ears, constantly stroked his graying beard as if checking for cracker crumbs. His wife Mona knitted a sweater almost unconsciously, following all the conversations yet rarely speaking, and even more rarely laughing at her husband's jokes. Portly Alfredo, the oldest at forty or so, had buck teeth and a growing reputation as a short story writer; he'd recently won a national literary prize. But Ray told Harry outside the bathroom later that his home life was purgatory and his Catholic wife refused to divorce him. Carmen wore her midnight-black hair in a windblown style, a careful chaos. She and Veronica were actors on a children's TV show.

"We're underpaid but need the exposure," Carmen said. "And the star makes a fortune and doesn't bother to learn his lines, so we look bad. But we're lucky to be working at all — jobs in the arts hardly exist here since the *golpe*. Not like in the *Estados Unidos* where artists are millionaires."

"*Can* be millionaires," Harry said. "My brother Dave's a freelance writer in New York, and he barely —"

25

"Forget running!" said a man's voice outside. Something bumped against the front door, then it opened and the dog sped out again. "You bloody gringos are too busy staying healthy to enjoy being alive. You'll be dead soon enough anyway. And the rednecks say you people are lazy!"

A woman laughed. "It's against the law to work hard in Chile on Sunday. We're a very Catholic country, you know." She walked in as she finished the sentence, wearing a black Waylon Jennings and Willie Nelson T-shirt. Her dark hair, parted in the middle, fell in thick curls to her shoulders and hid the hand on her neck of the man with her. He carried a straw-covered five-liter jug of red wine. A step behind, in nylon shorts and running shoes, came Lewis.

"Hey, Harry."

"You two know each other?" said the guy with the wine. He was tight and wiry, eyes blazing with energy like Harry's image of Jack Kerouac, crazy for anything. "Are you another dupe sent by the capitalists to save us poor Third World losers? Why not help the blacks in your own country first?" He gestured toward Lewis. "This clown's down here jogging in the sun while his people freeze their asses off in Harlem."

Ray jumped up from the couch where he'd been sitting thigh to thigh with Veronica. "Come on, Lalo, we're low on wine. How about uncorking that jug? Harry, you haven't met Marisol. Marisol Huerta, Harry Bayliss — the new baseball coach I told you was coming."

"For Christ's sake," Lalo sneered. "*Another* one? Lovely, that's just what this country needs."

Ray rolled his eyes. "And the shy, retiring wallflower over there is Lalo Garcia."

"*Mucho gusto,*" Harry said. He kissed Marisol's cheek and turned to Lalo, but he was at the table twisting in a corkscrew.

Marisol laughed. "That's OK. Forget him and kiss me again instead." She kissed him on the mouth. Harry was already glad that he had come. Marisol seemed charged from the inside, a quiet vitality that felt good to be near. He laughed too.

Veronica began picking a pretty instrumental on the guitar. "Do you know this song?" Marisol asked him.

"No."

"It's by Victor Jara."

"*Another* one?" Harry said, loud enough for all to hear. A grudging smile appeared on Lalo's face.

"He has many." She sipped her wine, a dreamy, unseeing look in her eyes, as if she were watching a memory. "He was a good man, though sometimes very sad."

"You knew him?"

"I met him. You meet everyone when your father is famous. And you learn fame means nothing — even less than money."

Harry thought of his father, sorting mail in the post office year after year. The job's never done, Dad used to say. It gets to you sometimes. There's always more where that came from.

"It must be interesting to have a famous parent," Harry said.

"To me he was my father, not a famous person. Nothing else matters but love and your friends. Cheers." She clinked her glass to his.

Sparks flowed with the wine through Harry's body, delicious electricity. He sat in a wooden rocker and Marisol knelt on the rug beside it, leaning on the arm of the chair. She was looking at Lewis, across the room talking Spanglish with Alfredo and Mauricio. "Now Lewis is staying with my mother, which makes me laugh. She always takes in a Peace Corps boarder, but she had half a heart attack when she saw his dark skin. He won her over quick, though." Her eyes scanned Harry's face. "How old are you?" she asked.

"Almost twenty-three."

"Twenty-two. I'm thirty. My daughter is five. My father died at fifty-eight. I don't care how old anyone is, as long as they don't act too young or too old to be depressing."

Harry was captivated. "I never thought of it like that before," he said, filling both their glasses. "*Gracias, mijito,*" he heard for the second time that day, and this time he liked it.

"We drink a lot of wine, but I think not too much. I'd better check on Lalo. He's a bad cook and might burn the chicken, but I'll splash on wine to keep it juicy."

"Is Lalo your husband?"

Marisol hesitated. Harry worried that he'd said something wrong.

"No, he's a neurotic artist. And a very good one." She winked and went out through a sliding screen door to the patio. The wine was giving Harry that perfect afternoon buzz, the kind he knew would put him to sleep by dusk if he didn't keep drinking. Just like he knew the high wouldn't stay perfect if he *kept* drinking. Veronica played a soft melody on the nylon strings. The smell of grilling meat set Harry's belly growling. He thought of that morning's paltry breakfast and envied Lewis's luck to live with these people.

"I've never even *been* to Harlem," Lewis said. "All the

times I took the train from New Haven to Grand Central, not once did I let my ass out at 125th Street. I'm no ghetto guy."

Mauricio sniffed. "Lalo can bark about the socialist revolution till the cows come home, but meanwhile he lives rent-free at his parents' second house. Some Che Guevara."

"You don't understand," Alfredo said. "Lalo's art speaks for him."

"His mouth speaks plenty, too."

"Who isn't afraid to express himself fully in this *mierda* of a country? I am, and my stories suffer for it. Lalo's art subtly depicts the horror. To do more would be suicide. He draws what most of us hardly dare to think."

"Sure," Mauricio said. "Using symbols only the educated can understand. How many of his precious proletarians does that reach? When's the last time you saw a 'worker' in an art gallery? And I'm sure when he was there he had one of your books under his arm."

Alfredo lit a cigarette, and blew a smoke ring that drifted over his head like a halo. "Is it better to be arrested and reach nobody?" He looked straight at Harry, who hoped it was a rhetorical question. Alfredo smiled like Mona Lisa with a Marlboro. "Lalo was tortured — beaten up and shocked with electrodes on his balls. Would *you* forget that kind of barbarity? Would *you* forgive it?"

Mauricio folded his arms and sulked. Veronica's fingers left the strings, and the room fell silent. The dog whined and scratched at the door, but nobody moved. "Should have kept my damn mouth shut," Lewis said under his breath. Mona's knitting needles clicked like a telegraph. Harry gulped his wine, wondering if Lalo had heard anything from outside.

"Ready!" Marisol called from the patio. "Get it while it's hot." She stepped into the room. "Who died while I was gone? Have something to eat and liven up. And poor Matador wants company." She let in the dog, who beelined across the room and dove into Ray's lap, doubling him over.

"Now I know why you call him Killer," he squeaked, and the tension melted in laughter.

Harry felt better the moment Marisol came in. She impressed him as someone who could fix things, instinctively do the right thing. He wished he could say the same for himself. She put a Rolling Stones album on the ancient portable record player, a one-peso coin taped to the tone arm.

"Do you like this band?" She had put a flower in her hair, a big daisy.

"Very much."

"My favorite song is 'You Can't Always Get What You Want,' but many of the words I can't understand. You must translate for me."

Was she being ironic? Something told him Marisol wouldn't bother.

"I like your flower," he said. She took his hand and led him outside.

He filled his plate with chicken, potato salad and *ensalada chilena* — tomatoes and onion in oil with spices. They ate bread with hot chili sauce called *ají*. Harry dipped sparingly.

"You don't like *ají?*" Marisol asked. She dunked a

chunk of bread and scooped enough to make her eyes water. "We Chileans are all part masochist."

Carmen sat next to him on the lawn. "Do you have a girlfriend in the States, Harry?"

"Figures you'd ask that," Veronica said.

"I'm just curious."

"So was my cat that had seven kittens!"

Carmen blushed, and Harry felt his own cheeks reddening. "Not really. In college I dated this one girl pretty often. She's in law school now."

"Wonderful!" Lalo said. "Exactly what your country needs, more lawyers! Baseball isn't your national pastime, lawsuits are."

"Why do you always slam the U.S.?" Harry said. He wasn't being defensive. He really wanted to know, and expected to hear about Yankee imperialism and how the CIA helped overthrow Allende.

"Because I love it," Lalo said. "It's the best country in the world, not to mention the one most ready for the socialist revolution — though it doesn't seem so on the surface. I know, I've lived there. I got an M.B.A. at Penn State and worked in New York for two years."

"For an advertising agency," Mauricio said. "Some Communist."

"Socialist," Lalo corrected. "But I am first and foremost an artist, and like everyone else in this sad world artists are addicted to eating. And in that soul-sucking materialistic society, garbagemen earn more than most artists." With an eye on Harry he added, "Despite Carmen and her deluded dreams of stardom."

Mauricio's teeth ripped into a drumstick, and he talked as he chewed. "Garbagemen should be better paid

31

than most artists. At least they haul away junk rather than create it."

Lalo set his plate on the grass, the food hardly touched. He glared at Mauricio, then pointed at Harry, Lewis and Ray in turn. "Okay, democratic gringos. Did you all vote in the last election?"

Lewis and Harry nodded. Ray shook his head. "I remembered too late to get an absentee ballot."

"No excuse, democratic gringo. Well, we had an election here three weeks ago. A vote of confidence for motherfucker Pinochet. Mark the black circle for No, mark the red, white and blue star for Yes. No publicity or campaigning allowed for the opposition. Official results? Eighty-something percent Yes. Bullshit. I personally know twelve people who voted No at the same box I did, but the final count at that station was nine No votes. And who knows how many others voted No there?"

"What do you expect?" Marisol said. "*They* count the ballots."

"Nothing!" Lalo sprang to his feet. "Nothing! Just like I don't expect to see Jaime Rodriguez or Tito Quiroz again! Dragged out of their houses and disappeared! Thin air! Nobody knows anything!"

"*Silencio!*" Carmen hissed. She glanced around warily, but there was no way to tell how far the words had carried beyond the little rectangle of bricked-in yard, and who, if anyone, had heard. "Use your head for once, will you?"

"For what? To kiss their murderous military pigasses?" Lalo flung up his arms, eyes wild. Spittle flew from his lips and caught in his beard. Harry's foot tapped the ground, but not in time with the music because the record had stopped, and his throat was dry when he swallowed some wine. Lalo scared him. He had never seen such hatred pour out of a human being. What did his eyes look like, what did he yell when strapped naked in a chair, watching a soldier reach for his testicles with a live wire? And the soldier — was he a frightened kid reluctantly following orders, or did he grin and dig the wire into the skin, holding it there for a long instant after his commander told him to stop?

Mauricio threw a fork that bounced off the house and clattered on the cement. "If I hear your fucking stories one more time I'll puke! I knew Jaime and Tito, and had other friends killed besides, and three-quarters of the rest of them had to run from Chile and I haven't seen them in over four years. Do you think you were the only one to suffer? Will your big talk change anything? Monday you'll put on a tie and go to work helping capitalists sell people shit they don't need, just like me. We'll hate it and we'll do it. Don't give me your noble crap and don't look to me for sympathy."

Lalo's eyes narrowed. "You will never understand," he said, spitting out the words like spoiled wine. He emptied his glass in a gulp, banged it down on the table and stalked off.

Marisol shook her head, hesitating, obviously torn over what to do. "*Mierda*," she said finally, and hurried after him. Mauricio rolled his eyes and gnawed on a hangnail. Carmen toyed with her hair, winding it around her fingers. Harry wanted to help but didn't know how, a feeling he'd already experienced often in Chile and knew he'd never get used to. All he knew was that he didn't want Marisol to go.

"He's been through a lot," Alfredo said.

"The dirty deed calls," Ray whispered to Harry, and he and Veronica disappeared into the house. They didn't leave her room for the rest of the afternoon. Partly because the wine made his fingers itchy, partly to escape the tension, Harry took his glass inside and picked up the guitar Veronica had been playing. It was a small, wide-necked classical guitar, so different from his grandfather's steel-string Martin dreadnought, but it felt good in his lap. Any guitar felt good when the world didn't. The same notes waited at the same frets for his fingers to find. Music was logical, it made sense and was beautiful besides, and the instrument was a friend that sang as sad or pretty or loud as his heart wanted it to. He took out the extra pick he always carried in his wallet, right behind one of the emergency condoms he'd bought in Miami. The rubber was already wearing a ring in the leather.

He sat on the couch, fretting the chords of the new song he'd written for Jean. On the opposite wall was a colorful oil painting of steep green hills dotted with houses and cut by snaking switchback roads, with a funicular in the foreground and a ship-filled harbor in the distance. He went over for a closer view and read in neat printing, *Valparaíso '68, LALO*. Beneath it hung a pen-and-ink drawing of naked figures swirling in a black vortex, contorted and elongated with gaping, twisted mouths as if screaming. "Lay-Low '74, New York City" was scrawled on an upside-down woman's skeletal white torso. A strange uneasiness gnawed at Harry: it was impossible to tell whether the creatures were rising from the maelstrom or being sucked down into it.

"Pretty weird, isn't it?"

Harry flinched. He hadn't heard Lewis come up behind him.

"Sorry. I walk softly and carry a little stick. You play guitar?"

"I try." Harry always let people listen and decide for themselves how good he was.

"I play harmonica. Let's jam sometime. Marisol's mother says I can have people over anytime."

"Good thing, because the witch I live with is a hypochondriac and a miser."

"Be glad she's not your girlfriend." Lewis's smile disappeared. "Listen," he said. "What do you make of Lalo?"

Harry had been asking himself the same thing. Was the guy a hero, a role model or a self-centered jerk? Was it possible to be all three at once?

"I don't know. Interesting as hell, screwed up bad over the torture, but who wouldn't be?" Harry remembered the soldier's slimy spit seeping between his toes, and began to understand the rage, the feeling of utter helplessness as a uniformed stranger drew the electrodes toward your crotch. "He must have some brutal stories."

"Believe me, he does. I've heard a few." Lewis straightened the Valparaíso painting. He checked the other frame but left it alone. "Lalo does more than tell stories, though. We have to watch our asses. Drugs and politics are the two things Peace Corps kicks you out for, no questions asked, and Lalo's fairly heavy on both angles. Just so you know, okay?" He offered his hand.

Harry shook it, a warm wave spreading inside at the closeness he was starting to feel for Lewis. "Thanks," he said. "Hey, I have a basketball. Want to shoot some hoops after classes tomorrow?"

"I suck at basketball. Always dribble the damn thing off my foot. But I'd be psyched to play hockey if you can find a rink."

"I doubt there's a rink in this country. Anyway, I kind of like my teeth where they are."

"In Minnesota we call that being a pussy."

Harry grinned. "Funny, in New York we call it common sense."

Lewis clapped him on the shoulder. "I'm off to study Spanish, digest that lunch and finally get in my run. Later — and keep in mind that stuff about Lalo, okay?"

"See you Monday." Through the picture window Harry watched Lewis head down the driveway and out of sight. Basketball might not be his game but the guy was lean and muscular, definitely in shape. Harry sat thinking with wine and a guitar, sunlit leaves and flowers before him, the lilting rise and fall of Chilean Spanish behind. Home seemed very far away, and nothing was simple any more.

Suddenly Marisol turned the corner, walking up the cracked concrete driveway with her head down. As she neared the fence, Harry saw she was crying. He dropped the guitar on the couch and rushed outside.

"Marisol, *qué pasa?*"

She fumbled with the latch on the gate and he opened it for her. She looked up at him, her face twisted, and he saw the angry red patch on her cheek.

"Did he hit you?"

Marisol covered the mark with one hand and closed her eyes. Harry reached for her. He wanted to comfort her, to bring back the vitality that had shone from her only minutes ago, and now was gone. Seeing that change was far worse than her sadness alone.

"Lalo hit you, didn't he? The bastard hit you!"

"No," she said, mouth pressed against his chest so he could barely hear. "That wasn't Lalo. Sometimes he isn't Lalo anymore." He felt her fingernails through his shirt. "How could the *milicos* do that to him? How *could* they?"

Again, Harry didn't know what to do. He held her tight, his feelings toward Lalo more confused than ever. Marisol's fingers dug into his back. Her body quivered.

"I hate them," she said through clenched teeth. "My God, how I hate them."

Harry hugged her and waited for help.

4

Over the next weeks Harry tried to understand the swirling emotions at Marisol's, until finally he realized it was impossible. He didn't have the knowledge yet, didn't have a context. The experience that wrenched apart these people's lives had occurred at the start of his freshman year in college. While Chileans were dying or fleeing into exile, Harry was chugging beer at parties, gratefully watching the Vietnam War wind down, and daydreaming about spring and that first perfect day back on the baseball field. Like most Americans, he had paid scant attention to a revolution half a world away.

Harry fought not to pass judgment, but Lalo slapping Marisol was unforgiveable. Yet the man fascinated him — he had never seen that kind of intensity before, except in movies, and most actors overdid it to the point you couldn't help but remember they were just acting. And they didn't really hit people. Wondering if he even had the right, Harry wrote a song for Victor Jara. He used the key of A-minor — for power, he hoped, and mysteriousness, not for sadness. Although it was a start, sadness got you nowhere.

Sitting on the creaky bed in his room, he worked

out a tricky fingerpicking flourish to end the song. He played the ending a dozen times, getting it down, getting it right. He looked up. Through the dirt-streaked window he saw the National Stadium. Again he wondered about the song. Was he showing off with that slick ending? Should he keep the music stark and simple? It was unnerving, bizarre: Harry only knew Victor Jara's songs secondhand, played by other people. Because his music was banned, Harry still hadn't heard the man sing. He remembered the look — incredulity melting into fear — from the record-store clerk his second day in Chile, when he'd naively asked where the Victor Jara cassettes were. The questions multiplied when he decided on a title for his song: "Sadness Gets You Nowhere". How much life had Harry Bayliss lived to give the world advice?

He liked the song, though. It sounded good, no matter how he answered the questions. And sometimes that helped when he had no answers at all. He almost sang it the next time he was at Marisol's, the following weekend, but couldn't convince himself. There was a smaller group that day, just Marisol and Veronica, Ray and Lalo, and Harry only played at all because Ray dropped the guitar in his lap and told them all how good he was — though the guy had never even heard him. He played half a dozen of his other songs, trying to ignore Lalo, who alternately stared at him like he was a laboratory specimen or gazed off as if bored, and didn't join in the applause.

Harry left late, and was waiting in the dark, dying street for the last bus before curfew. Footsteps scuffed closer on the sidewalk. Harry stiffened, ready for ugliness.

"You're good," he heard in unaccented English. "Don't let the bastards make you forget that." And without slowing his pace, Lalo turned the corner and was gone.

His skin electric, for a frozen moment Harry watched the place where Lalo had been.

"*Gracias,*" he shouted after him into the night. "*Gracias, amigo.*"

The next Saturday was an anniversary: one month in Chile for Harry's Peace Corps group. Marisol said that Valparaíso was wonderful, so that morning Harry and Jean took a bus to the Pacific. It was a two-hour ride, through the farmland of the central valley and over the coastal mountains to the ocean. "The geography's so much like California it's creepy," Jean said. To Harry the trip was an exotic adventure. Exploring in South America! Not exactly Hiram Bingham discovering Machu Picchu, but exciting enough. And to be doing it with a wonderful woman he didn't even know existed five weeks ago. . . . Halfway there, they were holding hands.

They figured it was crazy not to visit Viña del Mar, the famous resort city a couple miles north, but after an hour of playing tourist they wanted out: Lalo was right when he warned Harry the place was plastic, a "sandbox full of capitalist cat shit". The prices were ridiculous, the beaches jammed with toasting bodies, though only an occasional maniac was swimming. The Humboldt Current kept the water frigid year-round.

They got out of Viña, riding a bus along the coastal road, a thin strip between the ocean and steep hills, houses clinging to their slopes although this was earthquake territory. They rode to the last stop, down by the docks. What a difference — Viña was a playground, Valparaíso a hardworking port. The smell of rank fish and creosote filled the salt air; garbage bobbed in the filthy water. There were ships from all over the world — Greece, Yugoslavia, Australia, some languages he couldn't recognize. Sweating stevedores in oil-stained clothes gawked at Jean, and Harry didn't blame them.

"Careful, Harry," she said as they strolled along the wharf. "Some of these guys are really checking you out."

"Very amusing," he said, glad to be the one walking with her, holding hands in the sunlight. Their rubber sandals slapped the pier. Swooping gulls fought for scraps, and one stood motionless on a post, eyeing them like a bouncer at a rough club.

"It's like San Francisco," she said. "All hills. Come on, let's take that box thingie to the top."

"The funicular."

"Is that Spanish for 'box thingie'?"

Harry got brave and curled an arm around her shoulder. "You got it," he said. "Literal translation."

The old wooden crate creaked and moaned its way down. Jean and Harry got in. As they climbed, the harbor spread out before them, sparkling blue, no garbage visible from this distance. Boats from everywhere floated offshore; gaudy Viña curved off toward the north. It was delightful, yet strangely disconcerting, and Harry couldn't imagine why. Then it hit him: the scene was from Lalo's painting, ten years before. A vision of Lalo and Marisol, a decade ago, maybe in love, shot into his mind. They might have sat just like this, in this same car.

Jean leaned over him to see better, resting her chin

on his shoulder. One breast nestled against his side. Harry pretended not to notice.

At the top the car jerked and thudded to a stop. They started walking and wandered for miles, no agenda, exploring wherever whim took them. The sun was strong but a breeze swept up from the ocean and dried the sweat on their skin. They couldn't stay on high ground, and had to keep descending one hill and climbing another. The roads, some of them only rutted dirt, were roundabout switchbacks, so they kept mostly to the narrow foot trails worn straight up and down into the slopes.

They were puffing when they reached the top of still another path. A handful of boys played soccer with a ragged rubber ball, their field an eroded dirt road at a twenty-degree angle. A barefoot kid with scabby legs miskicked and sent the ball bouncing down the hill. He sprinted after it but stubbed his toe on a rock and tripped, scraping to a stop on his belly.

"Ouch!" Jean said. The boy was howling but his playmates just yelled at him. The ball kept rolling.

"What are they saying, Harry? Why don't they help him?" Her Spanish had improved tremendously, but there was only so much anyone could learn in a month. And the obscenities these kids were throwing around weren't heard in too many classrooms.

"Basically that he's the world's biggest candy-ass, and if he doesn't hurry up and get the ball they'll give him something to *really* cry about." Harry looked around at the crude wooden shanties. Only haphazard struts prevented them from tumbling into the valley. This was the poorest *barrio* he'd seen yet. "You have to be tough to live here."

"Will people treat *us* like that when we screw up? That cute little guy's the smallest one, and they don't cut him any slack at all. We'll be just like him when we start out." In March she would leave for a hard life in a rural southern town, teaching basic health practices and hygiene to *campesinos*, while he stayed in Santiago. Harry respected her for her commitment and felt a little guilty, as if his job were too soft to be a real Peace Corps assignment. And he'd be working in the shadow of the National Stadium.

"Check it out," Jean said.

The boy scrambled to his feet. Dirt and blood formed a muddy red paste on his knees. *"Vayanse a la mierda*, sons of whores!" he screamed, and tore after the ball, lodged under a rusted Ford Fairlane well down the hill. He stumbled once and nearly lost his balance, but didn't go down, then trudged back up the road with the ball under his arm. He passed a pregnant teenage girl lugging a mesh bag of groceries, two toddlers fighting to keep up behind her. The soccer game began again.

Harry and Jean walked on, quiet now. Daylight faded. The sun blazed red as it sank into the ocean, and soon the first stars glittered in the burgundy sky. They stood on the crest of a hill and watched the night happen.

"It blows me away," Jean said. She leaned against him. "All that plastic wealth in Viña and this poverty right next door. And we can choose either world."

"What choice? We're here to work with people who need help."

"Sure. But we can take vacations. We can afford to eat in Viña if we want. And most of all, we know it's not forever. Two years and boom, homeward bound, *adios* to the shacks on the hill. And don't think the people in the shacks don't know it."

Harry kissed her forehead. He'd come to Chile hoping for simple answers in a simpler society, but already his life was more complicated than ever. Yet the entanglements made him feel alive. Getting cut after six weeks of pro ball was laughable compared to living in a patched-together shanty, or being tortured, or having your friends disappear. Here in Chile he might actually be able to make a difference, and he couldn't wait to try.

They took a crazy route down through backyards and over plank bridges, sliding on slick mud trails, a rock in each hand to scare off snarling dogs. When they finally found their way out of shantytown, the night was as black as the ocean. Near the waterfront, occasional streetlamps oozed thin yellow light. They walked the narrow, winding streets by the docks, past bar after seedy bar and grimy seafood restaurants with tattered curtains. A cool, salty breeze drifted off the ocean. The last vendor at an outdoor market packed unsold melons into crates. Moldy husks and squashed fruits and vegetables littered the pavement, smelling of sweet decay not quite rotten.

They tried El Viaje, a little dive with yellowing, decades-old travel posters covering the walls: the Pyramids, the Parthenon, the Roman Coliseum encircled by a flotilla of tail-finned land yachts straight out of *American Grafitti.* Two broad-shouldered men with furrowed faces and tattooed forearms sat on bar stools drinking *aguardiente,* smoke curling from their hand-rolled cigarettes as they bantered loudly in a language that sounded like it had no vowels. The heavier one squinted at Jean as she passed, and grunted something that made his buddy snort and spray firewater all over the bar. Harry and Jean took a table in the most distant corner. It wobbled, even with two matchbooks under its gimpy leg. The red-and-white checked plastic tablecloth had half a dozen cigarette burns.

They ordered *congrio* and a carafe of white wine. Stains on the old waiter's white shirt advertised most of the menu. He poured the wine before Harry had a chance to wipe out his glass.

"Salud," the waiter said. The moment he left, Harry and Jean took napkins and cleaned their silverware under the table.

"Are we Ugly Americans, or what?" he said.

"I'd rather be an Ugly American than get double dysentery. Zero fun." Jean flicked her hair back away from her face. She glanced at the soccer highlights on the black-and-white TV behind the bar.

"Do you miss the States, Harry?"

"We've only been here a month."

She turned away from the television, back to him. "That doesn't exactly answer the question."

"Yeah, sure I miss it. My family, everything. But the trade-off's worth it. Being here, doing all this new stuff." He paused. "Meeting you."

The waiter brought the food, cigarette dangling from his lips. Harry watched the long ash as it threatened to fall on the plates. But it hung on.

One eye shut, Jean watched Harry through her glass. "I miss home, too," she said. "But new friends help fill the empty spaces."

Harry refilled their glasses. "To new friends, then," he said.

"I will definitely drink to that."

They left El Viaje happily high and glad to be alive. Harry crooked his arm and Jean took it. Her walk was bouncy, jaunty. "All that hiking today and I'm still jazzed," she said. She clenched his arm and he pulled her close.

They hiked across town to the bus terminal, to check the last departure for Santiago. Harry went to the window. The sallow gnome in the cubicle looked like he lived there, with a half-eaten *empanada* on a greasy hunk of butcher paper and an ashtray with an olive pit and a belly-up cockroach, antennae feebly waving good-bye.

"Nine-fifty," the gnome said, and replaced his nose in his *El Ratón Mickey* comic book.

"The *last* one?"

The gnome bit into the *empanada;* brown juice dribbled down his chin. "You calling me a liar, or just incompetent?"

The cockroach was rallying, its legs squirming. *"Muchas gracias,"* Harry said.

"The *last* one?" Jean said when he told her. Harry was sure his face showed as much disappointment as hers did. The station clock read 9:41.

"Hey, what luck not to get stranded," she said.

"Good luck or bad?"

Jean stared at her day pack, toying with the zipper.

"I guess we'd better get on," he said.

The bus rolled away on time. It was a smooth-running old Mercedes. From the bench, Jean and Harry watched it turn a corner and disappear.

"Oops," she said.

"I didn't want to deal with a two-hour ride, then have Señora Cabezas' ugly mug waiting for me."

"Why leave the shore when the weather's beautiful?"

"It's hot as hell back in Santiago."

"Not to mention the smog."

"Not to mention," Harry said, "it's way too early for this day to end."

Jean grinned and tugged him toward the exit.

Suddenly the night was young again. Back by the water, music poured from the open doors of cafés. Some were clean and inviting, others hard-edged and angry, full of loud men looking for trouble and women who'd already found it, at tables covered rim to rim with empty beer bottles. He watched Jean taking it all in, on her face a wondering smile that matched his own.

His arm was around her. "*Amiga*," he said, "what would you say to a little more wine?"

Her arm squeezed his waist. "I'd say you're a mind reader."

They found a liquor store on the corner, *Botillería Los Zapatos del Pescador*. "The shoes of the fisherman," Jean translated. "It's a sign, Harry." For luck they bought a bottle of *Gato Negro*, a smooth red wine that came with a little plastic black cat hanging on a string around the bottle neck. Jean tied it to her necklace, next to the single white shell on her throat. The fat man behind the counter ogled her — out of the corner of his eye, but it was still ogling. When Harry asked, he licked his lips and pulled the cork for them.

"*Norteamericanos?*"

"*Sí.*"

"I have a cousin there — in California."

"I'm from California," Jean said.

"*Verdad?* Maybe you know Vicente Hernandez. He lives in Los Angeles, or was it San Diego?"

"I don't think so. California *es muy grande.*"

The man shifted his bulk on the stool and lit a Belmont with the butt of his last one. "I knew that," he said. He watched the smoke curl toward the ceiling. "Long time in Chile?"

"A month."

"*Un mes. . . .* You like it?"

"*Sí.*"

For an instant pride shone in his face, then he shook his head. "Chile used to be good, now *es una mierda.* Goddamn *milicos.* Are you Mormons?"

Harry held up the bottle. "Do Mormons drink wine?"

"Not in public." The man shrugged and studied his cigarette. "*Buenas noches,*" they said as they left. He grunted a response but didn't look, just watched the smoke curl off the cigarette.

They had a bottle of wine and a decision to make. They gravitated toward the water, but the streets down there were darker than ever, too dark, as if they were hiding something no one wanted to find. Two weaving drunks whistled at Jean and shouted slurred remarks in a language Harry was glad he didn't understand. The docks were for the daytime.

But the night was too fine to lose. "Come on," Jean said, and together they climbed back toward the funicular.

It had stopped running, and the door was locked. They were on the edge of the city, the downtown part anyway, with the port below them and the shanties above. But the hills were strangely dark. Harry was about to comment on that, when halfway through a drink from the bottle he realized many of the shacks had no electricity. He felt like a naive, pampered gringo that what should have been obvious was so alien to his universe.

"*Peso* for your thoughts," Jean said.

Harry gazed up at the black hills. "Sadness gets you nowhere," he said. "That's what I was thinking." He felt her at his side and passed the bottle, a deliciously illicit sensation like they were sharing some rainbow secret.

It's winter in New York, Harry thought.

"I don't think it gets you anywhere either," Jean said. She nestled her head on his shoulder. Harry stroked the black cat at the hollow of her throat. He had no idea how long they stood there, leaning against the funicular, slowly working on the magic of that wine. Starlight glimmered off the bottle each time they tipped it up to drink. By the time they started down the hill the bottle was half empty, and a faint sliver of moon was rising over the ocean.

They stopped at the first *pensión* they found, on a quiet but gloomy side street. Three hefty women wearing gobs of makeup leaned out of the first-floor window like extras in a Fellini film, holding pudgy babies, laughing loudly and drinking wine mixed with Fanta orange soda in plastic tumblers. They offered to share.

"No, *gracias*," Harry said, glad he had an excuse to turn down that vile stuff. He held up the bottle, then pointed it toward the peeling sign: *PENSIÓN EL BARCO BLANCO*. "Are you ladies the owners?"

"No," said the heaviest one. "And we're not ladies either!"

They giggled hysterically. "Knock," said the one missing both front teeth.

Harry gave a polite rap with his knuckles. Nothing happened.

"The old fart's deaf as a bat!"

"Give it a good poke, *hombre*. Pretend it's a woman."

Giggles turned into guffaws. He pounded with his fist. A few seconds later the latch clicked. Harry hesitated, then pushed open the heavy door. The dim hallway was empty and undecorated, and smelled like a cellar. "*Arriba*," said a tired voice. It belonged to a man's stooped silhouette on the second-floor landing.

"I'll wait here," Jean said. "It's too embarrassing to show up like a derelict dragging a wine bottle."

"Something tells me this guy's used to worse than that." Gripping the rickety railing, Harry took the creaking stairs two at a time.

The man still held the rope he had rigged to open the door from upstairs. "My wife is dead," he said. "Stairs are for young people." Harry followed the bent back and thought of old man Haggerty from home, who everybody said got hunched over from carrying his money in his shirt pocket.

"Only one room left."

It was a windowless box reeking of mothballs. The bed sagged beneath a mustard-colored spread worn threadbare in patches like a mangy dog. Harry could tell it squeaked without testing it. He asked the price, knew he was being taken, and paid without haggling. The man stuffed the bills in his polyester shirt pocket and didn't offer a receipt.

"How is it?" Jean asked when he returned.

"Kind of like a mud hut. Perfect for Peace Corps types."

The women implored them to stay, holding up a wicker-covered five-liter *garrafa* of wine to show they had plenty. "Maybe *mañana*," Jean said.

"I didn't catch it all," she said on the stairs, "but those women are sisters and have five kids between them. None of them are married, and two are pregnant again."

"And they're drinking like that? And smoking?"

Jean shook her head. "Was it my place to say something? Would it do any good?"

Harry had no answer. Outside the bathroom in the hall Jean hugged him and gave him a fierce, desperate kiss. He knew it was as much for the uncertainty of the job that awaited her as it was for him. The landlord stuck his head around the corner and stared like a pervert at a peepshow. Before Jean could notice, Harry hustled her into the room and slid the bolt. Without saying a word they clung to each other, groped clothes to the floor and lay naked, intertwined on the lumpy bed of a sleazy hotel in a city where desperate people's shacks huddled in the shadows just beyond. And Harry saw how terribly easy it was to forget the part of the story where people play their whole lives on soccer fields pointed downhill.

Sometime deep into the night he woke to find Jean stroking his hair. He smiled in the darkness. Their noses touched.

"I'm really glad we came to Valparaíso, Harry."

"I'm even gladder that we stayed."

She got up and fumbled till she found the light switch by the door. A single bare bulb hung from a cord over the bed. Jean stood naked and tanned among the clothes strewn on the floor. She stretched like a diver, arms extended overhead, her body lean and taut, and Harry was tempted to pull her right back under the covers. She wriggled into her panties and dressed quickly.

"Back in a flash. Will you still be here?" She touched his lips and went out.

Hands behind his head, Harry stared at the ceiling. Unpainted strips of plywood covered the cracks between sheets of plasterboard. He checked his watch — their second month in Chile was nearly two hours old. He felt wonderful, and silently thanked his father for putting him there.

Then he thought of the shanties covering slope after slope, waiting in the dark for the next earthquake. And the sisters downstairs, their unborn children drinking wine with orange soda, smoking cheap cigarettes.

The toilet flushed across the hall. It was his turn next.

5

They didn't tell anyone about Valparaíso, but it seemed like within a few days the whole world knew. "Better me than you," Lewis told him. "This just proves women are crazy. But I suppose *something* decent had to happen in your sad-ass life." And he bought Harry a beer.

Not that Jean and Harry cared what people thought. Harry worried that sex would skew their friendship, maybe even wreck it, but nothing really changed. A week passed without them making love again. Opportunities were scarce; living with Chilean families was like a time warp to high school — without a car. And that was okay. It was enough to see Jean every day at class, and occasionally take a weekend trip or snatch a furtive hour in one or the other's bedroom. Missing out on chances to have sex wasn't what mattered. What mattered was reading in the Sunday *El Mercurio*, buried on page twelve, that another "leftist" labor organizer had been found murdered in Santiago, this one floating naked in the fetid Mapocho River, throat sliced ear-to-ear like a smile.

The image haunted Harry all through practice that

morning: a faceless man with dripping head lolling back, ripping away. And the man with no face was Lalo.

Ray hollered in English. "I know you'd rather be porking in Valpo but wake up or a line drive's gonna knock your Yankee teeth out." From the parched and cracked pitcher's mound Barata grinned at his hero Ray, though he couldn't have understood a word.

In the equipment shack later, Ray peeled off his sweaty T-shirt and put on a clean one. "Coming to Marisol's, Rookie?"

The idea sounded good, sounded great in fact. The soccer crowd roared in the National Stadium. Harry's eyes followed the noise.

"I don't think so," he said. "Not today."

"Heading back to Valparaíso, studly? Hey, don't forget to lock up. I'm outta here."

Harry sat in the shed alone, on a stack of dusty bases. Despite the shade it was blazing under the tin roof. Minutes passed, and more minutes. A strange lassitude came over him — suddenly nothing seemed harder than to know what to do next. It wasn't too late to go to Marisol's. It's never too late, he told himself. But the throat-slit man from the paper would not go away. In Harry's brain, arms strained to pull the corpse from the river; bright blood painted the filthy water.

He clicked shut the rusty old lock and started walking, not aimlessly, exactly, but without direction — anywhere as long as he'd never been there before. He left the side gate and began the long loop around the Stadium compound. Across Calle Marathon he could see his room in the gray cube of the apartment building. The curtains were open.

"It's never too late," he said out loud, but that was

naive bullshit and he knew it. Ask the guy in handcuffs as the knife bites under his chin.

Harry headed north across wide, congested Avenida Grecia, the stifling February air thick with exhaust, his only goal to leave the Stadium behind. Many blocks passed, some noticed, some a blur lost in thought. And the thoughts kept returning to Lalo, to Marisol, to Lalo's painting of Valparaíso in the good days, the innocent days. But good days according to who? The people in the shacks on the hills? The shacks were there under Allende, and now under Pinochet, and who knew if they would ever go away. Harry felt like such a kid, such a beginner. Ray called him Rookie as a joke, but it was the truth.

He noticed a brightly colored sign from over a block away, but couldn't make out what it said until he got fairly close. The hand-painted black letters on a blue background were hard to read: El Oasis. Luxurious but crooked palm trees, painted by someone with more imagination than talent, framed the name. Chalked on a battered blackboard hanging from a nail, the menu offered *almuerzo* — lunch — for only fifty pesos. Harry realized he should be hungry by now. He went in, the sign creaking overhead in the breeze.

The restaurant had no windows, just a wide door that stayed open, leaving the flies free to come and go. They mostly came. Harry chose a table near the door, as far as possible from an ancient console television blaring a Venezuelan soap opera: macho studs with slicked-back hair and pillow-breasted women with supercilious attitudes and sagging faces, whose acting was as spontaneous as a cue card. Most of the tables were empty. A teenage boy with Indian features took Harry's order and brought him a bottle of carbonated mineral water. Harry checked his cloudy glass and decided to drink from the bottle. He inspected the silverware and surreptitiously cleaned it with waxy squares of paper that passed for napkins and were as absorbent as a duck's back.

As he poured oil and vinegar on a meager salad, a tiny woman with a weathered face emerged from the kitchen and sat at the table next to him. She also had Indian features, like people in Peru and Bolivia. Her black hair hung in a thick braid far down her black dress, almost to the yellow knot of her apron strings. She crossed her legs and stared out the door at the torpid side street. *"Le gusta?"* she asked blankly, her face expressionless.

"Sí," Harry answered, mouth half full. *"Delicioso."* A fly lit on a slice of tomato and he shooed it away.

"Bueno." She gazed into the street again. *"Norteamericano?"*

"Sí."

"Americano," she whispered. She watched the waiter take away his empty plate and replace it with a steaming bowl of *cazuela*. A chunk of smooth, dark chicken floated in the broth. "Hector," she said. The waiter stopped.

"This is my son Hector," she said.

"Harry Bayliss. *Mucho gusto.*"

Hector nodded, his face impassive. *"Igualmente."*

"Americano," she said. Hector nodded again and left. Harry blew on a spoonful of soup.

The woman spoke to the street. "We almost went to the *Estados Unidos*. My children and I. Everything was ready. We even had the green money, five thousand *dolares* that we saved for many years. Then our house burned down. Money, passports, photographs — gone. Thank God no one was hurt. I would trade all the money in the world for the safety of my children." Her face collapsed and she began to sob, her fingers digging at a rumpled handkerchief. "I was married at twelve and had my first baby at thirteen. I know." Her head sank to the table. "*Mi pobre* Reynaldo. How could they do it to you?"

"*Mamá!*" A chunky girl about fifteen appeared from the kitchen and rushed to her mother, who sat hunched over the table, shaking her head and crying into her tightly folded arms. Harry sat helpless, hands in his lap.

"Come, *Mamá*, come with me." The girl guided the woman to her feet as the melodramatic music of the soap opera gave way to a detergent commercial, mothers in ecstasy as stains floated off their children's clothes. "Pardon us, *señor*," the girl said. "My mother, we are not —"

A shadow filled the doorway. "*Qué pasa?*" demanded a deep voice. A compact, athletic man strode into the restaurant. "*Mamá!*"

"She's okay, Miguel," the girl said, leading her away. "She just got upset, don't make it worse."

"Jesus, Mary and Joseph." The man crossed himself and drooped into his mother's chair, tossing a newspaper onto the table. MORE BOMBINGS IN SANTIAGO, screamed the red headline of *La Tercera*.

Harry's soup was lukewarm. It had seemed impolite to eat while the woman was talking, then when she started crying he forgot about food. Hector approached with the main course, but wheeled around at the sight of the full bowl of *cazuela*.

"Bring him a new bowl," the man ordered.

"No, no, this is fine," Harry said. "And I'll take that plate now, thanks."

Hector set it down and hurried back to the kitchen. "My brother," said the man. "A good boy." He lined up the paper with the corner of the table.

"*Norteamericano?*"

"*Sí.*" Harry was starting to feel Chilean, but his looks were a disappointingly immediate gringo give-away.

"We almost moved to the United States."

"Your mother told me."

He rolled his eyes. "I should have figured. *Me llamo* Miguel." They shook hands. He was maybe thirty, with straight black hair and high, strong Indian cheek-bones under deep-set dark eyes. He looked like the Aztec warriors on those velvet paintings in Mexican restaurants.

"Let me buy you a beer, *amigo.*" Harry protested, but Miguel waved off his words and went behind the counter to pull a couple of cold ones from the belly of a dinosaur Philco.

"I own a newspaper kiosk," he said. "Not bad, but business fell off when they moved the bus stop to the next block."

"Does your mother run this place by herself? What does your father do?"

Harry instantly regretted the question. Miguel stared at the sunshine. "We lost everything in the fire. *Mamá* did not trust traveler's checks." He shrugged. "But we still had cousins in California and we needed money. So in 1975 my father left *Mamá* in charge of the restaurant and went to Argentina where he could earn more. In two years he would come back, then maybe we would have enough. The next year the soldiers took over there." His voice faltered. "They disappeared him. He used to write every week. Now for two years we have heard nothing. Nothing. Please eat. Don't interrupt your meal. I'm sorry, I'll leave you in peace."

"No, stay, please." Harry ate a few bites. "You're not interrupting. I appreciate the company." The man obviously needed to talk.

"Then in August I went to play two Polla Gol cards but found I only had money for one. The card I didn't play won. I would've split six million pesos with one other winner. Perfect with the third baby on the way."

Instead you spend your days in a metal box, Harry thought, waiting for your third child to arrive. Before he could ask when the baby was due, Miguel touched his arm.

"I wish I'd never saved the card I didn't play." He rolled the paper into a cylinder; smudges of newsprint stained his hands. "Missing doesn't hurt much unless you know you came close. *Otra cerveza?*"

"No, *gracias.*" Harry's bottle wasn't half empty. Having Indian features in Chile was a disadvantage. Harry had heard plenty of prejudiced remarks about *los indios.* He shooed a fly off his fish.

"Flies," Miguel said. "They don't give up." A fat one landed on the newspaper and jerked its wings over the headline. Miguel snatched it with one hand and flung it down hard on the table top. The fly bounced once and buzzed in frantic circles on the green formica, then lay still. Miguel flicked the corpse on the floor. "Bombings," he said, tapping the word with a forefinger. "Bad business."

Harry checked; no one was in earshot. He leaned forward. "I think the government explodes most of those bombs, not the leftists. It keeps the people scared and gives an excuse to maintain the state of emergency. You notice that almost nobody ever gets hurt."

"Nobody gets hurt!" Miguel snapped open the paper and shoved it at Harry. "*Animales de mierda*," he said, and spat out the door.

The close-up showed bricks and rubble, crisscrossed by broken boards and a smashed television antenna. From beneath the debris, absurdly framed by what was left of a window, poked a lifeless human hand. The thumb rested barely an inch from a jagged shard of glass, as if the owner's last wish had been to avoid further mutilation. LEFTIST BOMBER DIES IN EXPLOSION proclaimed the blood-red headline.

Harry's guts roiled. Miguel's eyes, sleepy and defeated until now, burned with an intensity that reminded Harry of Lalo. His nostrils flared.

"Do you believe that this, this" — he scanned the article with his index finger — "this schoolteacher was a Communist bomber?"

"No, Miguel, I don't. But it's *possible* that he was. We can't be sure."

"You can never be sure of anything in this goddamn country! That's the way they want it!"

"Miguel!" Hector warned from across the room. The other customers — there were only four, three men at one table and one at another — stared at them. The lone man, frail and grandfatherly with five days' worth of grizzled beard, raised his glass of white wine to them and drained it in a gulp. Hector, his eyes pleading with his brother, turned up the volume on the television. Miguel spat again on the sidewalk. He shook his head at the floor.

"He is a good boy but he is afraid," he said. "They

have made good people afraid. My father was not afraid." He paused, absently rolling wet rings onto the paper with the bottom of his bottle.

"We're all afraid sometimes," Harry said.

The fire was gone from Miguel's eyes as if doused with water, leaving sizzle and smoke. "But I sell lies every day," he said. He gazed dully at the roughed-up newspaper. "This poor guy is on the front page, but when my brother Reynaldo lies half-dead pissing blood in the hospital because some *milicos* beat the crap out of him, no one knows. That's not in the papers I sell. That's not news. It's not news unless they want us to know about it."

Harry's teeth were clenched. He felt Miguel's frustration, a seething hatred mixed with total impotence to set matters right.

"Why?" he asked.

"Because most people will do what they're told and think what they're told, that's why."

"No — why did they beat up your brother?"

Miguel's voice quavered. "He'd just gotten out of school for the day. He's only sixteen, for God's sake! Some kids yelled at a group of *milicos* on the other side of the street, then ran when the soldiers came after them. Reynaldo had done nothing so he kept on walking, minding his own business. They jumped him from behind and punched him unconscious. They pounded his head on the sidewalk and kicked him when he was down. He lost four teeth. Of course no one dared to help."

"Didn't he try to explain?"

Miguel's look was almost pitying. "How long have you lived in this country, *amigo*?"

61

He shook Harry's hand and left to go sell newspapers. Harry drank from his beer, but it was too warm to finish. He paid for his half-eaten lunch, Hector handing him his change without a word, and without meeting his eyes. He took a bus downtown and wandered around. It was cooler under the shade trees of Providencia Park, an oasis of green along the Mapocho River that looked like pictures of Paris.

Museo de Historia Natural, said the sign on a big stone building. Harry put his shoulder to the heavy door and went in. A lively crowd gathered around the star attraction, a young Indian boy six hundred years old. Under climate-controlled glass he huddled wrinkled and stiff, eyes shut tight against the mountain cold that had killed him and preserved his flesh. Harry stayed in the museum for hours, studying the mummy from every angle, and studying the sweating people in shirtsleeves who had paid to come see him.

6

Harry's fingers tapped the window of the Peace Corps office reading room. Outside two squirrels chased each other in the garden, trampling daisies. "I don't get it. What could Castle possibly want to talk to me about?"

Lewis didn't look up from his *Time* magazine. Peace Corps volunteers received the international edition of *Time* free, and often the trainees would bus downtown to the office to read it. "Probably to give you the gold-plated *Gringo* Award for speaking such good Spanish. Relax, will you? Stop acting like a neurotic New Yorker."

It can't be Dad, Harry thought, or they'd have told me on the phone. Rosita the secretary had called that morning to say Steve Castle wanted to see him after classes at 4:30. So far as Harry knew, the Peace Corps Country Director hadn't invited anyone else for a personal visit to his office, and they had been in Chile for almost ten weeks. Their swearing-in ceremony as volunteers was only three days away.

"You'd make a good Freudian proctologist," Harry said, and picked up a *Time*. The words swirled in an article on disco fever and his armpits were gluey with sweat. The minute hand of the wall clock trickled down toward the six.

Castle greeted him at his office door. He was a tall, handsome man with prematurely gray hair. A ring of flab slouched over his belt. He gave Harry a hearty handshake and broad smile, like a politician, and Harry had no clue if he was sincere or not.

"Park yourself." Castle gestured to an armchair pulled up close to his desk. Harry sat and tried to look smooth. His shirt stuck to his back.

Castle lit a meerschaum pipe, and his smile melted. "I'm not going to sugarcoat this. Unless you can come up with some very good answers to some questions, I have no choice but to initiate termination proceedings. In fact the decision has already been made, on the basis of the evidence now in our possession."

Harry's heart went wild. His throat was a dry sponge. He caught himself leaning forward with hands clasped between his knees. Recalling his body language from college psychology class, he forced himself to sit back with unfolded arms.

"Have you been smoking pot?" Castle asked out of the corner of his mouth, not removing his pipe.

"What? Here in Chile? Absolutely not." Harry's brain raced. Could Castle possibly know about the one time he had taken a few hits, at Marisol's when Lalo passed around a joint? No way — he and Lewis were the only Americans there. A sudden suspicion of Lewis shot into his brain. He squashed it.

"We have compelling evidence that you're lying."

Harry remembered goofing with other trainees on the questions at the Armed Forces physical they had to take: Have you ever used illegal drugs? Are you or have you ever been a member of the Communist Party? Have you ever had a homosexual experience? Who would be idiot enough to say yes, they wondered.

Castle stirred his nearly spent tobacco. A plastic cube held snapshots of his kids and tired-looking wife, and one of Castle grinning over a hooked rainbow trout, flopping in the net.

"The evidence is wrong. I'm not that stupid." Harry was talking much too fast. His voice sounded unnatural even to him. "Where did this so-called evidence come from?"

"Señora Cabezas complained about you from the very first week. Coming in late, disturbing her —"

"She waited *up* for me! I didn't ask her to do it. I didn't *want* her to do it. On top of that she made it seem like a favor, lecturing me when all I wanted to do was go to bed. I was always quiet."

"I got a frantic call from her early one Sunday morning. Got me out of bed. You'd gone to Viña on Saturday and never returned."

"That was my fault — though I *did* tell her I might be staying over. Then I missed the bus."

"By sheer coincidence did Jean Hargrove miss that same bus?"

"Leave Jean out of this."

"Calm down, son. I want to hear your side." Castle pulled out a loose eyelash, checked his fingers to make sure he'd got it, and flicked it to the floor. "I'm not enjoying this any more than you are. Jean *is* part of this. Señora Cabezas reports that on several occasions you two spent hours behind closed doors in your room."

The miserable hag was playing games with his life! No wonder her son never visited.

"Does the junta have a law against friends visiting?" Harry hated the tremor in his voice. Castle smiled knowingly, as if to say yes, I understand the baser urges of the human animal. "I was at Jean's house far more often than she came to mine. Did her family ever complain?"

"Well, no."

"Because they're good people, not sickos looking for warts on everything."

"Señora Cabezas reported the odor of strange smoke in your room, especially when you were with Jean."

"Jean happens to like incense, and so do I. That's all I ever burned in that room. It beat breathing the pollution of Cabezas' cigarettes."

Castle tapped his pipe on an ashtray in the shape of South America, emptying the bowl. "In essence," he said, "you're claiming this woman wants your balls in a jar for no reason. Put yourself in my place. Would you swallow that? You knew the ground rules when you came here, and agreed to abide by them. You also knew the consequences for not doing so."

"In other words, you don't believe a word I've said." Have some compassion! Harry wanted to scream. I'm *me*, not some statistic who supposedly broke one of your precious rules. Be a man, not a mindless bureaucrat who makes me walk the plank to cover your ass. Watching Castle's gray eyes bore into him, Harry realized how much he wanted to stay in Chile. He was fascinated by its complexity and looked forward to his work with kids like Barata. It sickened him to think of never seeing Jean again, or Marisol. Or even Lalo — maybe especially Lalo. Chile had repression and curfew and police with machine guns, but now Harry wasn't afraid of the change. He welcomed it.

And what would his father think if they threw him out?

"Your version of the events is interesting, Harry. But you have to remember that I have the reputation and image of the Peace Corps to consider, not to mention that of the United States. There's more at stake for me here."

Harry tried not to panic. "More at stake for *you*? I'm the one about to get kicked out for some old witch's lies! Talk about erratic behavior — she probably hates me because I won't sit in front of the TV with her ten hours a day. She hates me because I won't be her son!"

Pride couldn't keep tears from sliding down Harry's cheeks. He smeared them off with the back of his hand. Frustration gnawed his guts; he began in some tiny sense to understand Victor Jara in the National Stadium, watching soldiers smash his guitar to splinters before advancing on him with a hammer.

Castle shuffled some papers on his desk. He cleared his throat. "You're obviously sincere in your denial, and the reports from the training center *have* been excellent concerning your progress and cultural adaptation."

It sounded like quotes from *A Handbook for Bureaucrats*. Harry waited for the inevitable "but".

"But you must understand my position. The organization is bigger than any one individual and its goals are more important. One bad apple can spoil the whole bunch. Unfortunately sometimes it's not what you are but what people think you are that counts."

Is this the Peace Corps or Albania? Harry leaned forward. "How can you convict me on the basis of one person's word? Why haven't other people noticed it? Why don't my teachers see I'm a drug addict with 'erratic behavior'?"

"That's precisely why I tend to believe Señora Cabezas. Who else would regularly see you at night, away from classes where of course you'd try to maintain a clean image?"

His reasoning was so warped Harry was stunned. Castle chewed on his unlit pipe stem. "This is not an easy decision for me, and I've lost some sleep over it."

Harry wiped clammy palms on his pant legs. It would be bad enough to pay the price for something he *did*, but he had never set foot in Señora Cabezas' house stoned. A one-way plane ticket Stateside — the infamous Braniff Award, something Peace Corps volunteers joked about. The organization over the individual, Castle had said. That sounded like Communism — the CIA's pretense for helping Pinochet and the military shoot down the democratically elected Marxist government in 1973.

"At this point in time, I'm inclined to give you another chance." Castle's tone was brighter now, and a smile flickered at the corners of his mouth. He exuded self-satisfaction, as if expecting Harry to kiss his feet in gratitude.

"You won't regret it," Harry said. Relief jellied his muscles.

"Most don't get a second chance — you certainly

won't get a third. Straighten up and fly right. Keep your nose clean."

Harry's knees shook when he stood up.

"Good luck," Castle said. He didn't offer his hand.

"Sure," Harry said, and walked out too drained to even be angry.

You *did* get a second chance, he realized. And justice barely played a part in it. Plenty of innocent people never get a chance at all.

Harry flexed his unbroken fingers. His hands were trembling and he shoved them in his pockets. How long was I in there? Did that just actually happen? It didn't seem possible, that jolt out of nowhere, yet at the same time nothing in the world was more real to him right then. That's life, he thought — full of sudden somethings ready to strike. You can't get away from it. Drunk drivers. Soldiers with guns. Cancer caught in a routine checkup.

But love — love can happen, too. Forget that and you're dead.

"What's the deal with those hands in your pockets, Opie? Shufflin' off to see Aunt Bea in Mayberry?" Lewis slapped Harry on the arm with a rolled-up *Time*.

"I've got two words for you: let's drink."

"What are we celebrating? Bayliss takes the *Gringo* Award in a landslide?"

"Try the Braniff Award."

Lewis's jaw dropped. "You're shitting me. No way."

"Like I said — let's drink."

They did, bottles of ice cold Kaiser with six percent alcohol at the first dumpy café they ran into. Lewis heard the whole story, shaking his head, interrupting for clarification or to abuse Castle in ever more inventive and vile language. By the second beer they were laughing, loving life. Harry had done it. He had beaten the odds. It was like drawing one card in poker and filling an inside straight.

"You didn't dodge a bullet, man. You dodged a friggin' MX missile."

"Guess I'm just living right."

"So. . . ." Lewis's face grew solemn. He hesitated, as if searching for the right words to say something really important. "I don't know, I just keep wondering. . . ."

Harry stopped laughing. "What? What is it?"

"Who do you think gets on top — Castle or Señora Cabezas?"

Lewis cracked up. Harry shuddered. "You evil bastard. Don't give me nightmares."

They ordered *hamburguesas* and a couple more Kaisers. Lewis spooned a thin layer of *ají* on his burger. "Easy on this stuff, pansy-man. I don't want to have to carry you out of here."

"The first burger I ordered in Chile," Harry said, "I slathered on a ton of *ají*. Nearly incinerated my mouth. I thought it was ketchup."

"You are one lame-ass honky."

"You think that's bad — I didn't learn about *ají* till a few days later. I just thought Chileans made spicy burgers. I even put more on, trying to cover up the taste."

"Good thing you don't need brains to be a baseball coach."

"A *real* good thing. So what do you want for dessert, Uncle Tom — Oreos?"

Lewis grinned. "I should kick your sorry ass."

Harry grinned back. "Call first and book yourself a hospital room."

They clinked bottles. "Hey," Lewis said. "Let's go to my pad. Isabel says I can have company anytime, even dregs like you."

"Cool." It *was* cool, living in a nice house with a classy lady like Isabel — Marisol and Veronica's mother. She always seemed to have a smile, and loved to read books and talk about ideas. While *salchichas* — hot dogs — were about the best Harry could expect from Señora Cabezas, Lewis was an excuse for Isabel to cook meals she would never have made just for herself: broiled *corvina* filets; *congrio; lomo a lo pobre.* Isabel didn't waste her days in bed watching bogus Venezuelan soap operas.

Riding in the back seat of the *liebre* up glitzy Providencia Avenue, Harry fought jealousy all the way. How much sweeter would the last nine weeks have been if he had lucked out like Lewis in a great living situation, instead of getting stuck with Señora Cabezas? Good thing his Spanish was already fluent because he hardly ever talked to her. That was the whole point of staying with Chileans, to speak Spanish and get to know the people, but she was so repellent it defeated the purpose. All of the fifteen other members of their training group lived with pleasant families — Harry had caught the shaft, that's all. Bearded bad. And to top it off, the bitch almost got him the Braniff Award!

Lewis waved his hand in front of Harry's face. "Earth to Bayliss. I knew you were a wuss but I didn't know three beers would put you in a coma."

Harry couldn't help smiling. It felt good to goof

around with Lewis, the way Harry and his brother Dave used to. "I was thinking," he said.

"I thought I smelled something."

"I'm serious, you tube steak. Why should a loser like you get Isabel, and I have to live with Cabezas? There's no friggin' justice."

"Same reason soon you'll be sharing Ray's apartment here in Santiago, while the rest of us drag our butts off to the sticks. I mean, *baseball*, my man! Talk about hitting the damn lottery. If you think life gave you a shit sandwich, I'll trade and eat yours. You take my place and go to San Isidro. I'll stay here and teach kids the hit-and-run."

"I know it'll be hard, living out in the *campo*. But —"

"You're whining about justice, bucko? Look, you got Jean. I don't want to hear it."

"OK, OK, I'm an asshole."

"Damn straight. With whipped cream on top."

Lewis was right. Everything he said was true. Harry did have Jean. But not for long. In a couple of days she'd be gone, riding the train eight hundred kilometers south to a hard life in a new world he wasn't part of. Who knew when he'd see her again? The only thing sure was it wouldn't be soon. Harry thought again of how bizarre it was: a group of strangers from all over the U.S. gets tossed together in Miami, then flies nine long hours to Santiago, with nothing necessarily in common outside of an itch to join the Peace Corps. And you bond, at least most of you do, at least somewhat, because this is a tough time, a huge change, and you're in it together. Americans outside of America. But not as tourists — you're going to live here, and you hope you fit. Then ten weeks pass, and the group breaks apart. Just like that. Together one day, apart the next. Togetherness — if there *is* any — remains only in the mind.

Harry remembered Jean's sleeping head snuggled on his shoulder in the cramped Braniff DC-8, somewhere in the night high over the Andes. He thought of her remark in Valparaíso, how in two years they'd be returning to the States, "and don't think the people in the shacks don't know it".

"Look at it this way," Lewis said. "We're all going to be sad leaving our families next week. You'll be jumping up and down to bolt from Cabezas."

The bus turned right off Providencia onto Tobalaba and along the polluted Canal San Carlos to Avenida Principe de Gales — Prince of Wales Avenue. Now every passing block moved them farther from the frenzy of the commercial district and into the pleasant residential area of La Reina. Tidy brick and stucco houses, red tile roofs, plenty of trees and shade to relieve the mid-March heat. Harry still found palm trees exotic, though they grew all over Santiago. At least he knew now — after naively asking his teacher Fernando when coconuts were in season — that these palms weren't that kind. If they kept riding, another few miles up Principe de Gales they would be almost to the Peace Corps training center — and the army base where the *milicos* had smashed Jean's camera. But instead they walked to the front of the bus.

"*En la esquina, por favor,*" Lewis said. The driver dropped them at the corner, then pulled into traffic while still making change for a woman who got on.

"Insane system," Harry said. "In New York you gotta have exact change. This is asking for an accident."

"Bumper cars, man. More exciting that way."

They jogged across the street, and Lewis unlocked the heavy iron gate to Isabel's yard. She insisted that people call her Isabel, not Señora Huerta. Julia the maid called her Señora Isabel, but Harry supposed that was to be expected in the Chilean class system, just as Julia addressed Isabel with the formal and respectful *usted* for "you", and Isabel responded with the informal *tu*. Señora Cabezas' first name, which she had never invited Harry to use, was Flor. Yeah right, he thought. Some "flower" she is.

Lewis locked the gate behind them. "People live behind walls in this country, don't they?"

"Not Marisol," Harry said.

"Even she's got a little wooden fence. Anyway, I mean in general."

Harry had noticed what Lewis was talking about but it had never really sunk in. Almost every yard in Santiago was surrounded by a wall, an iron fence, or both. You saw that in the States, too, but nowhere near to this extent. U.S. fences tended to be just in the backyard, maybe to keep a dog from running off, not around the entire property. And never did they use the Chilean security technique of embedding sharp shards of broken glass in concrete on top of a wall. Harry hadn't seen glass often, but when he did, he noticed. It glittered in the sun like some evil kaleidoscope. Low-tech razor-wire: chance it over that stuff and your blood would be running down the wall.

Isabel's Spanish-style house had a small, shady yard front and back and a six-foot stucco wall with a rounded top — no broken glass. Wrought-iron bars were bolted over the windows. To the left of the front door, a slim cactus with delicate white flowers snaked up through the bars almost to the roof.

"Overachiever," Lewis said.

Harry touched a sharp thorn with his fingertip. "Notice it's to the *left* of the door. Must be a Communist cactus."

Lewis shrugged. "It's on the right if you're leaving."

"Oh yeah. How do you say 'duh' in Spanish?"

"Beats me, but you better find out. You're going to be using it a lot."

"Not as much as 'OK, señorita, if you really ask politely you can share my bed tonight'."

Lewis rolled his eyes. "Yeah, with me. While you curl up in a horny ball on the floor."

As they went in the house, Harry thought how strange it was that politics had become so important to him in Chile. In the States it would never have occurred to him to make a comment (admittedly a lame one) about a Communist cactus. Left and right were just directions, not code words for Allende's elected Communist government and the soldiers who bloodily overthrew it. But politics was hard to escape in Chile, though officially it didn't even exist. No elections; Pinochet was dictator, period. Yet the very lack of political writing or discussion called attention to its absence, made people notice. Citizens who had rarely bothered to vote now chafed at losing that right. Joni Mitchell sang it, Harry thought. You don't know what you've got till it's gone.

The house was quiet. Lewis tried the double doors to the patio. Locked. "I guess no one's home," he said.

They checked the kitchen and found a note on the table, held down by a ceramic saltshaker.

"Dear Luis,

Your dinner is redy. Please to be making it hot on the fire. I am visiting. Isabel"

"What's with the English?" Harry asked.

"She likes to practice once in a while."

"I'm impressed."

"You mean Señora Cabezas doesn't leave you notes and tasty food?"

"Remind me to murder you later."

Lewis took a bottle of Undurraga red from the wine rack in the dining room. "I'll replace it later. Isabel hardly drinks anyway."

"I'll buy it," Harry said.

Lewis popped the cork. "There's a first time for everything."

The wine went great with the *estofado de vaca,* thick stew with chunks of beef and vegetables. "Meat's supposed to be bad for you," Harry said with his mouth full. "Shows how much Cabezas loves me because she hardly gives me any."

"She's just playing hard to get. I mean it, if you play your cards right I think you could get over with her."

Harry set down his spoon. "Well, I *was* hungry."

"She's probably an animal in the rack."

"You're a frigging deviant. You should be committed."

"I am committed — to saving the world through the Peace Corps."

"Man, I finally get a good meal; don't make me sing *la canción del buitre.*"

"The song of the vulture" was Chilean slang for vomiting. They laughed hard but not long, because laughter interfered with eating. But behind the fun and the feast, and the relief that he had dodged the Braniff Award, Harry felt sadness lurking. Training had become dull and routine after ten weeks, full of endless lectures by Peace Corps bureaucrats about policy (mostly saying what you couldn't do), mixed with occasional interesting talks on Chile by U.S. Embassy officials. But now training was ending, and the impending separation weighed heavily. No more Jean, no Lewis — just like that. Harry was unsure about his future in Chile. What sort of job would he do? And he knew Lewis was nervous, too. Probably more so because, like Jean, Lewis was heading alone to unknown territory far off in the rural south.

For the first time since they had known each other, Harry and Lewis sat in silence. No matter how true it was, two twenty-two-year-old guys weren't about to say how much they'd miss each other. Or that they were scared.

Harry refilled their glasses right to the midpoint. "OK, PCV-to-be, is that *vaso* half empty or half full?"

Lewis grinned at the allusion. On day one of staging in Miami, their group leader Bethany had only a single object on the table in that Howard Johnson's conference room: a glass of water filled to the midpoint. She paused, then slowly scanned their faces; obviously she had rehearsed this. "Some people might see that glass as half empty," she told them, nodding just a little too self-righteously. "A Peace Corps Volunteer sees it as half full."

Lewis took a hefty sip, then raised his glass as if for a toast. "Well, Mr. Castle, I do believe this sucker's *less* than half full. And soon to be bone dry."

Harry drank as much or more, and clinked glasses. "You're our kind of guy, Briggs. The Peace Corps needs derelicts like you."

"I knew a Yale degree would come in handy sooner or later."

Soon they were debating whether the *bottle* was half full or half empty; quite a few laughs later there was no doubt it was empty.

"I wish I had my ax," Harry said. "We could finally get around to playing the blues."

"Marisol's got one."

"Yeah, but it's a classical guitar. Nylon strings."

"Boo hoo, you wimp. Would Blind Lemon Jefferson hold out for steel strings?"

That's all Harry had to hear. Besides, going to Marisol's never seemed like a bad plan. "We're there," he said. "Grab your harp and let's roll."

Halfway out the door Harry stopped. "Wait a minute."

"What's up?"

"I better call Cabezas, tell her I'm staying out."

Lewis whistled in mock appreciation. "You *are* a good little boy."

"Bite me. The last thing I need is her calling Castle."

"Hey, I know how jealous she gets, worried you're steppin' out on her."

"You're a sick dog. You need treatment."

Harry made a quick call. Fortunately Señora Cabezas was home. When the hypocrite started whining how she would miss him, he cut her off and hung up. Better that than burning her ear with what he really wanted to say.

It was only a ten-minute walk to Marisol's. They went a block out of their way to stop at a nameless corner *botillería* for wine — one bottle for Marisol, and a replacement bottle for Isabel. When Harry insisted on paying, then came up a few pesos short, Lewis ragged him into oblivion.

"I just have one question. Were you born worthless or did you have to practice?"

They sauntered up the sidewalk, trading banter they knew was idiotic, but who cared? It was fun, and better than worrying about tomorrow, which did no good anyway. Whatever was going to happen they would find out about soon enough. Tonight was for laughing at the stars, passing around a bottle, enjoying your friend's company while he was still there.

Lewis pulled out his harmonica and blew sweet blues with one hand, bottle swinging in the other. Harry took both bottles to free Lewis's hand to play vibrato, and the notes bent and wailed and cried out in the night. Then disappeared, who knew where.

The music stopped. "I can't believe we didn't get our act together to play until tonight," Lewis said.

"We *haven't* played yet."

Lewis tapped out the spit on his palm, then slipped the harmonica back in his pocket. "Not music, anyway," he said.

Harry's fingers itched for the six strings, nylon or otherwise. This was going to be fun, jamming with a guy who knew what he was doing. They turned down the pitted concrete driveway to Marisol's house. Her ancient 2CV Citröen sat alone at the end of it. As they approached they could see a light on in the living room, straight ahead, but heard no music, saw no one. They hesitated at the gate of the waist-high wooden fence.

"What time is it?" Harry whispered. He rarely wore a watch but was glad other people did.

Lewis checked his wrist. "Can't see," he whispered back. "It's got to be around eleven."

"Is it too late?" Harry had expected to find visitors, so lateness hadn't been a factor. Showing up uninvited was no problem. It was the Chilean way to drop by unannounced and enjoy spontaneous company. Mauricio had said, that first afternoon Ray brought Harry to Marisol's, *"Los gringos saben ganar dinero, pero no saben vivir,"* and Harry couldn't deny it. Most Americans *were* better at making money than at living life.

They froze at the sound of Marisol's voice.

"I will *not* have you tell me how to live my life!" Her words were angry, not loud.

Lalo's were both. *"Por la puta madre,* leave your fantasy land, woman! Stop pretending everything is all right!"

"Of course it's not all right. But you're the one living in a fantasy land, responsible to no one but yourself. I owe it to Panchy to make her life as normal as possible."

"I'm responsible to my country. The real country, not this *mierda* of a Chile we have now."

"Lalo, we all want Pinochet overthrown. But get this through your head. My child comes first."

Lalo slouched into the living room, where they could see him. He stuffed his hands in his pockets and threw back his head to stare at the ceiling. Except his eyes were closed.

"So," he said, "it's over between us."

Marisol was still out of sight. "Don't say that. You're my friend forever. But as lovers . . . Lalito, you don't want to be a father."

"I could try."

"You won't change. And what you do is important. You're braver than the rest of us put together. But I've already lost one husband. I couldn't go through that again. I couldn't let Panchy lose a father."

"So the bastards win."

Long seconds passed. Harry realized he was holding his breath.

"They only win if we let the hatred destroy us," she finally said. "But no matter what I'm a mother now, and my daughter comes before some 'revolution' that might never happen. I'm sorry, but there it is."

Lalo's shoulders trembled. He squeezed his eyes shut tighter. Savagely he wiped away tears with his sleeve. "Fuck this shit," he said in English, "fuck all of it" and stalked out of view.

Harry tensed, ready to rush in if Marisol needed help. But instead the deadbolt slid. The front door flew open as Harry and Lewis dove behind the Citröen. Crouching low, heart pounding against the bottle clutched to his chest, Harry expected to hear the door slam. But it never closed at all. Lalo fumbled at the gate latch, cleared his throat and spat. Under the car Harry saw shoes stop on the other side, one toe tapping so fast it seemed to be shivering.

"Fucking headbreakers." Lalo sniffled as he scraped

a match twice, three times. It fell burning on the concrete. He exhaled heavily, like a sigh. Cigarette smoke tainted the air. Harry had a feeling Lalo was waiting, hoping Marisol would call him back.

"*Rompe*fucking*cabezas*," they heard, and fast footsteps scuffed off into the night.

Harry and Lewis's eyes met from a foot away. "Damn," Lewis whispered. "What was *that*?"

Harry had no answer. He set the bottle on the driveway, and raised himself far enough to peek through the driver's side window. The door to the house was wide open. Somewhere inside, he faintly heard Marisol crying.

"Jesus, Lewis, do you hear her? We have to do something."

"Like what? Go in and embarrass her? Say we heard it all? That shit is private, man."

Harry sat down with Lewis, their backs to the rust-speckled car. "We'll wait awhile, then knock. Like we were just showing up. Cool?"

"Sounds like a plan." Lewis took out his Swiss Army knife and twisted in the corkscrew.

"Quiet when you pop the —"

Marisol's door clicked shut. Lewis touched a finger to his lips, then gently eased out the cork. "*Salud*," he mouthed silently, and handed Harry the bottle.

Harry sipped and passed it back. He was thinking about what would happen in a few minutes, whether Marisol would be glad to see them, the acting job that all three of them would undoubtedly do, pretending nothing was wrong in hopes that would make it true, knowing that it wouldn't.

Suddenly music poured out the window, a scratchy record of the Stones' "(I Can't Get No) Satisfaction". It wasn't real loud — Panchy was surely sleeping — but it was loud enough. Harry smiled. This was a good sign. They got up and went around the car to the fence and leaned against it, transfixed.

Framed by the window Marisol was dancing alone, arms flailing, black curls whirling around her face. She was a superb dancer, but this was more than dancing; it was desperation, it was a ceremony, an exorcism maybe. Harry knew he wouldn't think that if he hadn't heard the scene with Lalo. But he had. And he wished he were in there dancing with her.

"One more song," he said. "Then we go in."

Without taking his eyes off her Lewis tipped back the bottle, swallowed. He chewed on his upper lip. "I don't know, man," he said. "This is weird."

Harry took the bottle. "*I'm* going in."

Still staring at her, Lewis nodded. "*Officially* weird," he said.

Harry was bopping a little to "Satisfaction"; it was impossible not to. As the last notes faded, Marisol's face was obscured by a curtain of curls. She stood statue-still, shoulders slumped, her expression completely hidden. Suddenly she pushed her hair back with both hands, revealing tear-stained cheeks and a huge smile. Just as suddenly she disappeared from the window. The music stopped; the living room went dark. Ten seconds later, cracks of light seeped through the shutters in her bedroom.

Lewis nudged Harry's shoulder. "I think that's a sign."

Harry stared at the living room, where the light had been. "Let's get out of here," he said.

They wandered the quiet streets of La Reina, saying little, solemnly trading occasional swigs from the bottle. In a small park full of tall palm trees they saw two ragged boys, maybe ten years old, sleeping huddled together on a piece of cardboard under a bush. Quietly they walked past, so as not to wake them. A few blocks later they crossed the street to avoid a swaying drunk arguing with the air.

"A toast to our role model," Lewis said, waving the bottle. They drank to the gallows humor, but not without wondering.

It was not a night to go to bed early. Even if he had tried, Harry knew his brain would not have let him sleep without a fight. There was too much to try to understand. Lalo crying, like a man in love, not a revolutionary. Marisol dancing, like a frenzied teenager, not a widowed mother. Labels didn't work; labels were a joke. There was always something more to everybody. He wondered what more there was to Lewis. To Jean. To himself. The thing was, so much of it you *couldn't* know until a different situation forced it out of you. Life kept dealing you new cards, whether you wanted to play or not, and some of those hands were terrible.

Harry thought of his father, how great it would be to talk to him. Dad wasn't a big writer, but when letters did come they were always upbeat. "Chrome dome," he wrote, with *Daily News* clippings of the latest snowstorm. "I'm nearly as bald as Telly Savalas. When you get back you'll think you have Kojak for an old man."

"Whoa," Lewis said. "It's almost frigging curfew."

They headed back the eight or so blocks to Isabel's,

striding double-time. Harry hated the *toque de queda* —
the "touch of the stay" — which allowed no one out after one A.M., two on weekends. What burned Harry was
the symbolism of the curfew. Pinochet had grabbed
power more than four years ago; there was absolutely no
military reason for a curfew in 1978. But there it was, a
nightly nudge from the government to make sure you
remembered who was boss.

"This is absurd," Harry said. "What could they do
to you?"

"I don't want to find out," Lewis said, and broke into
a jog. Harry hesitated, thinking about slowing down to
make a point. But it was a pointless point. He sprinted
to catch up.

They reached Isabel's with five minutes to spare.
They sat on the bus-stop bench outside her wall and
worked on the last inch of wine. A Hyundai taxi blew
by, way too fast, driver hunched over the wheel after
squeezing out one last risky fare. An old Ford squealed
around the corner and sped up a side street. Then nothing. The city — the country — was officially under curfew until six A.M.

"It's past two," Lewis said. He offered the bottle.
"Kill it."

"We're outlaws, man," Harry said. There was a cer-
tain thrill about still being out. A small thrill, and a pitiful one, but it was there. He would be lying to say he
didn't feel it. He hated the soldiers and what they had
done to Lalo, to Marisol, and this tiny act of rebellion
meant *something* at least, a protest no matter how feeble
against the repression. It would change nothing, but
maybe like the curfew itself, his protest was symbolic.
He tilted the bottle high for the last swallow.

Headlights appeared up the road, creeping closer. With the lights still three blocks off, the rebels hid behind the gate in Isabel's yard. From his position of safety, Harry was ashamed at how hard his heart thumped as the *policía* car crawled by.

"Yeah, we're outlaws," Lewis said. "A regular Frank and Jesse-fucking-James."

"Want to go back out?" Harry asked.

"What do you think?" Lewis said, heading for the front door. Harry replaced Isabel's wine and crashed on the couch, wondering where real courage came from.

7

That Monday the American ambassador swore them in at five, followed by a reception for the new volunteers and their Chilean families. It was the first time he had seen Jean in a dress. "Do you like it?" she asked.

He hugged her from behind. "I like anything with you in it." She gave him a kiss on the cheek. It didn't seem possible she was taking the train south to her site tomorrow.

Harry wandered around, trying not to dwell on Jean's leaving, amazed that they had somehow already been in Chile two-and-a-half months. He drank wine with fruit in it and did his best to socialize, even shooting the bull with the ambassador about the Yankees' pennant chances next season. The guy seemed genuinely grateful when Harry rescued him from a conversation with Castle about embassy staffing.

When the party faded, Harry, Jean and Lewis went to La Cholita for dinner. Phil Dwyer tagged along. They celebrated with *lomo a lo pobre*, a protein overload of steak buried under two eggs, with potatoes and onions and *ensalada chilena*. A guitarist and harp player, dressed in Chilean *huaso* cowboy clothes, sang traditional songs and did it well. Everything would have been perfect if it didn't feel so final.

They paid for dinner and left with wine in their heads. The night had turned a lively cool, the air crisp, not humid.

"Great weather," Lewis said. "Somebody should bottle it."

"A lovely evening for a spot of genital shock treatment," Phil said.

"Taxi!" Harry called, and waved his arm. The cab pulled over and they piled in.

"*Al centro*," Lewis said.

Jean glared at Phil. "What's *with* you, anyway? You talk about torture like you enjoy it."

"Hey, it's perverse and I'm perverse," Phil said. "I can't help being fascinated that those pricks actually did that."

"Probably still do," Lewis said.

Harry held Jean's hand. "Fascination's one thing — joking about it is sick."

"Misfortune is not at all amusing."

They froze. The cabbie had spoken in English, without turning around. His eyes in the mirror were dark, sunken under eyebrows joined in a single thick bar across his forehead, like Brezhnev's. Jean gripped Harry's thigh.

The driver's mouth set in a grim line. Harry felt sheepish, a naive American. "You speak English," he said, feeling stupider than ever.

"Talk like that is dangerous," the driver said with a British accent. "You've obviously been drinking, but that's no excuse." He smirked. " 'The price of democracy is eternal vigilance.' Should I take Avenida Matta or Vicuña Mackenna?"

"Vicuña Mackenna," Harry said. That was the way the bus went.

"It's your money." He cut across a lane for a right turn.

"Is Matta faster?" Lewis asked.

"Yes, but maybe you rich Americans are out for a tour."

"Take the best route you know," Harry said.

"Best for you or best for me? A longer ride means more pesos for my poor thin wallet. Put it on your expense account."

Jean leaned toward him, her chin nearly resting on the back of the seat. "Expense account? We're Peace Corps volunteers, señor, not rich Americans."

"All Americans are rich. Add the dollars the CIA pays you for spying and your salaries are quite handsome, I'm sure. I'd drop you spies off here if I didn't need the money."

"We aren't spies," Harry said. "And even if the CIA might have been involved with the Peace Corps in the past, those days are gone."

"*Might* have been involved! You innocent *gringos*. My brother is exiled in Germany for being a Socialist who wanted a democratic country. I was fourteen years at the University of Chile, then fired for the crime of having him for a brother. Of *course* they still use electric shock torture. They would not give up one of their greatest pleasures, except maybe for Lent."

They rode in awkward silence. Lewis told the man to stop near the Universidad de Chile.

"Ninety pesos."

"The meter says sixty," Phil said.

"Fifty percent surcharge at night."

"What did you do at the university?" Jean asked.

He looked back over his shoulder. "English teacher," he said. His face puckered in a joyless smile, his uneven teeth dull as flints.

Harry passed him a hundred-peso bill and refused the change. "Thanks," the driver said, maybe sarcastically, but in a voice so flat Harry couldn't tell. He lit a cigarette with a wooden match as Harry shut the door. The ashtray was stuffed full of butts.

Even Phil was silent as they walked up the Ahumada, a wide commercial street open only to foot traffic. Bright lights spelled out in gaudy neon urged the world to buy. But most Chileans could only window-shop. Harry walked with an arm around Jean, thinking about that taxi driver. You could feel the frustration building in this country. A barefoot busker with one eye out for cops swallowed swords and fire for stray coins. Burger Inn peddled greasy assembly-line *hamburguesas* and *papas fritas* for double the U.S. price, and people lined up all day for the privilege. *Gringo*-style fast food had become a status symbol, a way to share the lifestyle seen on American TV shows, dubbed in Spanish and mistaken for reality.

The Ahumada ended in a few blocks at the Plaza

de Armas — Weapons Plaza — a square block of trees and concrete in the middle of the city. Across the street, an old blind man in a battered fedora played the same carnival tune over and over on a peeling red accordion with a tin cup attached to it. He'd shuffle, painfully slowly, halfway down one block, then back to the corner and up the other street till he hit the post office steps, where he turned around and did it again, and again, one shoulder always brushing the wall for guidance.

"Stevie Wonder he ain't," Phil said. "Why can't he just panhandle with a sign — I Am Blind and My Dog is Dead?"

Jean looked at him like he was a sidewalk worm after a rainstorm. "You've got *problems*," she said, and headed across the street.

Harry knew what she was going to do. "Is *everything* a joke to you?" he said.

"As a matter of fact, yes — but lots of jokes aren't funny."

They watched Jean drop coins in the accordion player's cup. She came back wearing an embarrassed smile. "Okay, so I did my good deed for the day."

Phil tapped her arm. "What'd you do, tell him to buy some sheet music?"

A skinny man with a golf ball-sized cyst on his neck and a tiny baby sleeping in a carriage was drawing caricatures under a streetlight. A small crowd gathered around his easel. Fifty pesos — about a buck and a quarter — for a five-by-seven inch colored chalk portrait.

"They're neat," Jean said.

"I can change that," Harry said, and volunteered

to go next. The artist's Adam's apple bobbed like a buoy as he worked, alongside that raw crimson cyst that seemed to pulse beneath the skin. The crowd tittered on the other side of the easel. Jean's eyes told Harry she was looking forward to being alone together; Phil pantomimed projectile vomiting. The drawing only took ten minutes: all head, with dark, wavy hair and a narrow face, green eyes and even Harry's cleft chin on a tiny body dressed in khaki pants and Izod shirt.

"I love it," Jean said.

He handed it to her. "It's yours."

Her face brightened. "Sweet," she said.

"I'd get mine done but toilet paper is cheaper," Phil said. "That'd wipe the shit-eating grin off your face."

"Let's go look for bullet holes at La Moneda," Lewis suggested. La Moneda, the presidential palace, was where Salvador Allende died during the *golpe*.

"Harry and I already checked one day," Jean said. "The *milicos* must have patched them all up."

"Do you think Allende really killed himself?" Lewis asked.

"Right," Harry said. "Five quick slugs to the back. It was easy."

They went to a nightclub, a downstairs joint with photos outside in a glass case of a dyed-blonde Latin bombshell stripper and an eight-piece band in gaudy sequined suits with pencil-thin mustaches and goofy smiles. But a bouncer with mountainous acne said there was no cover so they took a chance.

To Harry's surprise, the place was packed. The band was gleefully butchering salsa music, their singer gyrating like an auditioner for *Elvis: The Final Days* in girdle-tight white pants that pinched his butt like two loaves of bread in a diaper. "Dig Ricky Ricardo," Phil said.

They found a table in a dark corner, with damp stains on the tablecloth. Jean's foot rubbed Harry's calf. "Let's dance," she said.

"Let's you and me boogie, Jean," Lewis broke in. "That honky's got the rhythm of a sea slug."

"You look like you're worth a try, sailor," she said. Lewis tipped an imaginary hat at Harry and led her out to the dance floor. The singer wiggled grotesquely while the band played a melodramatic tango that Jean and Lewis massacred wholesale. Many customers, most of whom must have had the same tailor as the singer, glanced askance at the interracial couple, but Lewis and Jean didn't notice.

"Want to dance?" Phil said.

"With who?"

"With me, you heartless beast. You only want me for my body. Don't think I don't notice your eyes glued to the dance floor, scoping Lewis."

Harry supposed he *had* been staring. But who knew how long it would be until he saw Jean again? Tomorrow was almost here. Already.

Jean and Lewis came back laughing. "Our last night," he said. "Champagne?"

"Go for it," Harry said.

The waiter opened the bottle ineptly and wine foamed over the side. "*Mil* pesos," he said.

Phil grimaced. "A thousand pesos? Bend over and grab your ankles."

They pooled their cash to pay the bill, plus a hundred peso tip.

"Twenty-five bucks," Lewis said. "That's not so bad. What would it cost in the States?"

But this ain't the States, Harry thought. He scanned the dismal dance hall, remembering Jean's words on the hill in Valparaíso: *And most of all, we know it's not forever.* How many hours did the English teacher have to drive to make a thousand pesos? How many newspapers did Miguel have to sell?

And don't think the people in the shacks don't know it.

Jean held up her glass. "To us, I guess." She thought for a moment, then looked at her friends. "I hope we don't blow it."

They clinked glasses. The champagne was lukewarm and sweet. Harry watched Jean drink, he watched her smile, trying to memorize her for the long months ahead. A few songs later the band took a merciful break and out flounced the stripper, belly dancing to canned Middle Eastern music. She was so awful Harry pitied her.

"Shake that thang," Phil said. "Cellulite arouses me."

Harry drank the dregs of his glass. "Let's go," he said. "This place is the bottom."

"I don't know," Jean said. "It's kind of fun in an absolutely classless way."

Lewis turned the bottle over Harry's glass, but it was empty. Already. "Don't expect so much. Take it for what it is and enjoy it."

"Sorry. I just never figured we'd spend our last night together in a hole like this."

"You sound like some permanent change is coming

over us." Lewis clapped him on the back. "Cheer up, man, we're supposed to be celebrating."

"What's wrong?" Jean whispered in his ear.

Harry shrugged. "Can we just go somewhere else?"

"You buying?" Phil said. "If Harry's buying I might even *talk* to him, for chrissake."

Outside, with Jean on his arm, Harry felt better, though his moping had fizzled their energy. No one wanted to be the first to say good-bye. Phil told a few pitiful jokes that fell as flat as the sidewalk. They stopped in a cafe with chickens grilling on spits in the window.

"There's half of heaven for you, Lewis," Phil said. "Want to see if they have any watermelon?"

They ordered Escudos, malty beer with 5.6% alcohol. A bony kid came in lugging a wooden box, wearing scuffed black shoes without laces that were way too big for him. He pointed at their feet. "Shine," he demanded.

"We're wearing sandals," Harry told him.

"I'm the best."

"I'm sure you are, but we don't want shoe polish on our feet."

"I'll be careful." He looked up at them with big, round, pleading eyes, then locked them on Jean. He knew how to do it. *"Por favor,"* he wheedled, drawing out the words. Jean gave him five pesos and he moved on to another table without thanking her.

"Bleeding heart liberal conned again," Phil said, holding his beer bottle like a microphone. "That bum'll blow the dough on rotgut and a two-bit whore and wind up talking to God face-down in an alley."

"And what have *we* spent our money on tonight?"

she said. "You'd talk different if you'd grown up walking the streets at night, shining shoes for enough money to buy milk for the baby at home."

"I'd have given my eyeteeth," Phil said, "or my left nut for that matter, to walk the streets at night. I was lucky if my parents let me stay up to see the Beatles on Ed Sullivan. A typical deprived middle-class childhood."

"Milk for the baby?" Lewis said.

They followed his gaze out the window, where the shoeshine boy eyed the tray of a sidewalk candy vendor. He forked over a coin and took a handful of caramels, then stuffed one in his mouth. When the vendor was distracted for a second, he stole a few more.

"Maybe the starving baby likes caramels more than milk," Phil said.

"Take a hike," Jean said.

They did, soon. Lewis got up first. "I'm not even finished packing," he said. He tapped Jean's hand. "Meet you at the station at two?" She nodded.

Harry gave his friend a strong handshake. "Keep blowing that harp. And stay in shape because you're eating dust next time we run."

"Take care of yourself, *amigo*," Lewis said. Harry shook hands with Phil and they were gone.

"Well, lover," Harry said. "We're alone."

Jean surveyed the busy café. "You call this alone?"

"Got any suggestions?"

"In Santa Monica I'd say 'your place or mine', but here *I* live with a great family that I wouldn't offend for the world."

In a flash he understood. "You're not serious."

One look told him she was.

"You're evil, woman. You're evil and I love it."

"We're both moving out tomorrow — it's perfect." She called her family from a pay phone to say she was staying with a friend.

The front door squeaked when Harry pushed it open. He'd come to detest that squeak. Señora Cabezas always said her son would fix it when he visited but after ten weeks Harry was still waiting to meet him. Jean slipped in behind him and gently closed the door. She started to take off her shoes, till Harry stopped her.

"Don't bother," he said. They kissed beneath a broken cuckoo clock.

The garish blue light of the television seeped into the hall. "Is that you *mijito?*" Señora Cabezas called over the laugh track of the program.

"And the old bitch claims she's deaf," Harry whispered.

"What did you say, Harry?" He hated the way she trilled the double "r" in his name, though he didn't mind when other people did it. "Come kiss your *Mamá* goodnight."

Blood rushed to his face. "Listen to that crap! Stabs me in the back and calls herself my mother!"

He stepped into the doorway, pulling Jean with him. Smoke stung his eyes. Señora Cabezas lay propped up on two pillows, her hair in curlers, a half-smoked cigarette in one hand and a glass of red wine in the other. She jerked up straight, spilling wine on the pink bedspread.

"*Qué pasa?* What is *she* doing here at this hour?"

"We're tired and want to go to bed," he said. "So

please excuse us. *Buenas noches,* and thank you for the fine recommendation you gave about me to Señor Castle." He gestured toward the TV. "Tell me tomorrow how it ends." With his arm around Jean he walked out, nervous but laughing inside.

Jean was giggling. "She deserves it. Oh, does she deserve it."

"Harry come *back* here! I want to talk to you! I demand that —"

He shut and locked his door and took Jean in his arms, hugging her tight as they rolled onto the bed. He had never appreciated her more than at that moment, when leaving was so near. She stiffened once, when the Señora pounded on the door, but then they were together and with a gasp Señora Cabezas and Steve Castle and military *golpes* disappeared like rocks in quicksand.

Hours later Harry lay studying the shallow rise and fall of the sheet, loosely draped on Jean's chest leaving one breast exposed. He kissed her and got up, carefully so as not to wake her, and walked barefoot to the window. A streetlight bathed the room in a tired yellow. He leaned on the windowsill, flaking paint rough under his elbows. The buses had stopped running; the streets were deserted. Curfew was in effect. A *policía* car prowled by, slow and watchful. Behind it loomed the National Stadium, a dim outline in the night. On the sidewalk two dogs acted out a painful tug of war, joined at the groin and struggling to disengage themselves. He couldn't hear Señora Cabezas' TV. A floorboard creaked outside his door. Harry closed the curtains and sneaked to the door, gave one loud rap and heard a yelp. Jean laughed.

"You're awake," he said.

"Come hug me."

He went to her. They fit perfectly. "I miss you already," he said.

"Hold me tighter," she said. "Let's pretend nothing will ever change."

They made love in the darkness.

8

Jean was gone. Lewis was gone. A new group arrived and suddenly Harry didn't belong at the training center anymore. Of course he had prepared for it, but the change was drastic. Training and Spanish classes had smoothed the transition to Chile, but that routine and those friends disappeared overnight. He was living with Ray and working now; people depended on him.

And almost all of those people were kids. Harry spent time at practices around the city, helping any coach who asked. One day he'd show baseball films at a school in a slum, the next in a prosperous *barrio alto;* there was plenty of interest everywhere. Weeks passed; a month; then two. Harry did not cure any social problems. No child had a full belly because of his work; no one learned to read and no *desaparecido* returned home. But the smiles on his players' faces were justification enough.

Halfway through practice one afternoon outside the National Stadium, Harry heard music, marching-band music, Sousa or somebody, and it was getting closer. He turned from his umpire's position behind the pitcher's mound, and saw a squad of soldiers in green uniforms with white belts parading across center field. Some played instruments; others carried rifles. The ball thudded into the catcher's mitt.

"*Qúe fué?*" Barata the pitcher asked.

"*Bola!*" Harry guessed. The hitter, who had two strikes on him, grinned his relief and pounded the plate with his bat. Barata rolled his eyes and Harry knew it had been a strike.

"Stop!" Ray cried. He strode onto the field, pumping a bat up and down like a drum major's baton. His arms swung in exaggerated time to the music. "*Hijos de puta,*" he muttered as he marched past Harry, who watched the circus with mounting anger. The soldiers had trooped onto the field with no warning, and were trampling the grass within easy reach of a twelve-year-old's fly ball. They acted as if the boys didn't exist, as if it were self-evident that nothing took precedence over military parade practice. The outfielders scurried out of the way.

Ray quit his mock marching and stomped out to their leader. The music drowned his words, but he stood with arms akimbo, jawing at the soldier like a manager arguing with an umpire. Finally he spun around and stalked back to the infield, goose-stepping the last couple of yards with a cretinous expression on his face. Harry and the kids cracked up.

"Sorry, guys, that's it for today. The way Oscar stings the ball I'm afraid he'll smack a home run and brain one of them." The boys hooted and pounded Oscar on the back and on the batting helmet. He was the kid that Barata undoubtedly struck out on the pitch Harry had missed, the type that crouches in the box with trembling knees and prays for a walk. "Those who didn't hit today, remind me and you'll get extra swings next time. Okay, two quick laps and don't cut the corners." They groaned. "Or else," he said, waving the bat like a club. They laughed and took off.

Ray had held his temper in front of the boys, but he was fuming. "Peckerhead wouldn't even listen to me. Says he can use the field whenever he wants. I say don't you have your own parade grounds and the prick just smirks and says they don't want to wear out the grass. I could have slugged the fucker." Ray rubbed the slickness off a new baseball like he was trying to strangle it.

"There's five empty soccer fields," Harry said, slamming bats and shin guards into the duffel bag. "Why not use them?"

"Because those fields are dirt and they don't want to muddy their goddamn dress boots. He had the balls to tell me that. You think this is bad — last year they showed up with horses the day after a rain and left the outfield full of hoofprints. A kid stepped in one and tore up his ankle."

The soldiers marched in snappy formation, using the Nazi-style goose step. The commander's whistle screeched and they halted; their hands slapped weapons and leather as they performed precision rifle maneuvers.

"They never let you forget who's got the guns," Harry said.

Ray fired the ball into the duffel bag. "My dick's in the dirt," he said.

The sky was the same dull gray as the National Stadium. To the east, the snowcapped peaks of the *cordillera* barely rose above the smog. Two days earlier rain had washed the air clean and lowered the snow line on the mountains but soon the brown goop settled in again. The clouds spat raindrops. Ray and Harry helped the kids lug the equipment to the storage shed, then dressed in a hurry to beat the rain. It was hammering hard on the tin roof when they left. The soldiers ran for cover.

"Hope it rusts their goddamn tuba," Ray said.

They took a bus up Pedro de Valdivia Avenue. Rain bleared the grimy windows and sidewalk peddlers huddled under bus stop shelters. A small boy, even younger than Harry's players, hopped on in a threadbare blue student's uniform and squeezed through the crowded aisle with a sack of caramels. A safety pin held up his beltless pants. "*Caramelos un peso,*" he repeated in a bored monotone from front door to back. "*Rico los caramelos.*" No one bought any. After a final, spiritless look at the passengers, he jumped off at the next stop.

Ray shook his head. "How many candies would you have to sell to make that worth your while?"

Harry watched the kid climb on another bus. Though it was illegal, most drivers let vendors on free if no cop was around. "Twelve pesos buys a kilo of bread, and that at least fills your stomach for a while. I don't know what's worse — kids hawking stuff on buses, or adults so hurting *they* have to do it."

"Barata does it sometimes. He shines shoes, too."

Harry pressed his forehead to the damp glass. Their bus was so crowded that several boys rode outside the door, hanging from the handrail with one foot balanced on the bottom step. Last week *La Tercera* had splattered a photo across half its front page of a boy who'd slipped and rolled under a taxi.

They got off a block from the Peace Corps office

103

and went to check their mail. Monday was usually a good day for letters. Harry headed for the bathroom and almost collided with Steve Castle around a corner.

Castle manufactured a smile. "Workin' hard or hardly workin'?"

"Hi," Harry said, and kept walking.

Ray was chuckling in the mailroom, holding up a sheet of notebook paper like a Christmas present. "It's nookie time at the *hacienda*," he said. "Marta James is coming in from Talca and wants to know if our couch is open. Five'll get you twenty we'll be burying the salami in my bed instead."

Spare me, Harry thought. For a guy so aware of political repression, Ray's attitude toward women was neolithic.

"What makes you think she won't end up in *my* bed?"

Ray looked at him pityingly. "Because, Beaver Cleaver, you're a gentleman." He went to the door and made sure nobody was around. "Listen, Rookie," he whispered. "That's what's so great about Peace Corps girls. Bullshit like boyfriends, or worrying what their moron sorority sisters will think — what does that matter down here? No one gives a shit. It's like these two years don't count on your permanent record. Especially once winter starts, and down south they're stir-crazy from rain twenty-five days a month. Hey, I've been here a while. When the ladies come to Santiago, they come looking for action — whether they know it or not."

"Why not find some Chilean guy?"

"Some do, but use your head. You can't hide doodly-squat in those small towns. If a girl gets a reputation, the people don't respect her and her work goes down the tubes. Most don't risk it."

Harry thought of Jean. Eight weeks without her already. He had sent her five letters, and received six.

"What about Veronica?" he asked.

"I tell her a friend's in town; that's all she needs to know. She'll still be there Sunday night, tongue dragging on the floor after two days off." Ray sat back in a swivel chair, plopped his feet on a metal desk next to an old Royal portable, and opened the new *Time*.

"You're serious, aren't you?"

Ray looked up with half a smile. "Deadly," he said.

There was a letter from Harry's brother Dave, and one from Jean — number seven. Dave's was on top, so he opened it first; his letters were always full of energy and crazy wordplay that made them a hoot to read. Dave was an even better ballplayer than Harry. In one high school game he hit two homers and struck out sixteen, including Barry Hodges three times, and Hodges made it to Triple A ball before he got drafted and had a foot blown off in Vietnam. By Dave's junior year in college the big league scouts were watching, till he exploded his knee in a home plate collision — an injury so bad even the army didn't want him. He never pitched again and quickly got serious about his journalism major.

The letter was short and matter-of-fact, unusual for Dave. Manhattan was hot and muggy, Long Island a shade cooler when he went home last weekend. There would be a family cookout on Memorial Day, and Mom was already worrying about it and preparing a mountain of food. Dad wasn't working but he looked good, though he'd lost some weight and hair from the chemo. Dave had published two articles and a short story and been paid obscenely little. Guidry was 7–0, the only thing keeping the Yanks close. The Mets stunk. Write soon.

Rain pelted on the lawn. "Going to Marisol's tonight?" Ray asked.

"For dinner." It struck Harry how Ray went to see Veronica, yet still called it "going to Marisol's". Marisol did own the house, but more important her spirit dominated the place. She was a catalyst, a spark that recharged others without burning out, and her vitality attracted Harry. She was beautiful, but that wasn't all of it. She was more a special friend, the older sister he never had. Marisol fascinated him, and since Jean left, he found himself visiting her more and more often — without confessing that he had spied on her, and seen her dance.

He opened Jean's letter. She had washed her clothes two days ago and they still weren't dry. Rain had fallen for a week and everything in her room felt clammy. She tried to dry socks on the portable gas heater, but forgot about them until she smelled smoke and singed holes in the soles as big as the cockroaches in the bathroom.

She had little contact with anyone except *campo* women and the nurses in the tiny rural clinic, so understocked it sometimes ran out of aspirin. "All they talk about is their husbands and their babies, Harry. I'd go bonkers if I couldn't bus out of here and visit Lewis once in a while. My boots are slathered with mud, the sun might not come out again ever. I miss you so much. It's hard to believe it's summer back home. Someday we'll go bodysurfing in Santa Monica. Yours wetly, much love."

Ray rolled his magazine into a tube. "Taking off?"

"No, I'll see you home later. I have to get a gamma-globulin shot." Mainly, though, he wanted to be by himself.

"Bad *ass* news, pardner," Ray said, and left howling.

Harry fished a mimeographed paper out of the wastebasket and fed it into the Royal print-side down. "The rain in Chile," he typed. Four and a half months in this country. It didn't seem possible. He thought of Valparaíso, and hiking with Jean in the sun on the day they first made love. Her job was so much tougher than his, constantly dealing with illness and ignorance and gray, unrelenting rain. He imagined her boredom and frustration: could he live two years under those conditions? Her village had only two paved streets. When the dirt road to a remote medical *posta* in the mountains washed out, she and a doctor had to go on horseback. Jean was terrified on the rutted trail, hardly knowing how to ride, with nothing between her and the whitewater river below but a hundred yards of eroded cliff.

Lewis's letters told similar stories of downpours and difficulties. Still, Harry envied him for being near her. He missed Jean even more than he'd expected. Dad's hair is falling out. He couldn't imagine his father bald. Harry pecked out, "Falls mainly willy-nilly," and climbed upstairs to get injected.

The bus home was rush-hour jammed and Harry hung by the rail in a drizzle for five blocks before he managed to push into the crush of bodies. He transferred his wallet to his front pocket. Water slithered down the back of his neck. He had to stand the whole way, butt throbbing from the fat gamma-globulin needle. Not exactly a brutal hardship, he thought, compared to riding a horse over a dangerous mountain trail. What would I have done? I've never even been on a frigging horse.

"Who did this painting of Machu Picchu?" Harry asked that night. The watercolor hung in Marisol's living room, on the opposite wall from Lalo's Valparaíso and howling ghouls. Harry leaned closer. It showed the lost city of the Incas from above, nestled on a mountain plateau, the rock spire of Huayna Picchu jutting from the mist behind it, dark jungle surrounding everything.

Marisol smiled. "I'm flattered you recognize it. I did that when I was fourteen and my *papá* took me there on his way to Lima." She wore a bulky sweater she had knit, and sat working on another one in the rocking chair by the *estufa*, the portable gas heater. It was a damp, raw night, and like most Chilean houses hers had no central heating.

Harry thought about Jean, and going to Machu Picchu together. "For me Machu Picchu was like the Pyramids," he said. "Or Troy, or Atlantis. I'd read books and dream about exploring far-off places."

"Machu Picchu is like the last place on earth. You feel tiny in front of the mystery, yet it's wonderful because somehow you know that you fit into everything. You don't know how, but you're sure of it." Marisol stopped knitting and looked past him at her painting. "The best memory I have of my father is sitting with him above Machu Picchu. Sunset came. He put his hand on my shoulder. Neither of us spoke a word."

"Have you been back?"

"No. Doesn't life usually work that way?" Her knitting needles clicked again, steady as a clock. But faster.

A month later, toward the middle of June, Harry saw a jigsaw puzzle of Machu Picchu in a downtown store window and bought it for Marisol. The photograph was almost identical to the view in her painting.

"Let's do it now!" she said when he brought it over.

"We'll never finish, it's got a thousand pieces."

"You can't finish what you don't start." Marisol broke the tape and poured the pieces onto the coffee table. "First you have to get the border," she said.

Harry couldn't remember the last time he'd put together a jigsaw puzzle, but Marisol's enthusiasm was contagious. Panchy was asleep, Veronica was out with Ray, even manic Matador was curled in a contented ball on the couch. They sat side by side in the warmth of the *estufa*, sipping red wine, talking and occasionally matching puzzle pieces. A Violeta Parra record played softly, singing the haunting *"Gracias a la Vida."*

Harry chuckled. "Headbreaker," he said in English.

"Qué?"

"Rompecabezas. The Spanish word for puzzle means headbreaker. I thought of Humpty Dumpty falling off a wall — one big broken head. It's a funny word."

"I almost forgot to tell you! *'Rompecabezas'* — that's what Lalo calls his exhibit that opens tomorrow at the Portillo. I'm going with him, why not come with us?"

Suddenly the word wasn't funny any more. Harry

was back hiding behind the Citröen, crouched, holding his breath as Lalo muttered "Fucking headbreakers," then *"Rompefuckingcabezas"*. It made little sense to him then; now it was starting to.

"I have a Baseball Federation meeting." That was true, but more important Harry didn't want to tag along as a third wheel or some sort of groupie. He had run into Lalo a few times lately at Marisol's, and a coolness separated them. Maybe Lalo disliked Americans too much to open up; maybe he was embarrassed that Harry knew he had hit Marisol. Harry could only imagine Lalo's reaction if he knew Harry had seen him cry. Whatever the reasons, his only friendly gesture had happened one night on a dark street corner, without slowing down. But maybe that was enough. Harry still felt warm and liquid inside whenever he remembered Lalo's, "You're good. Don't let the bastards make you forget that."

"Why don't you like Lalo? Is it because of me?"

"He won't *let* me like him. I respect him. That's better." Harry locked together two pieces of cloud.

"Nothing would make me happier than for you to be friends. Please try." Her deep eyes penetrated his from a foot away. The record ended and the machine clicked off.

"Nothing would make *me* happier," he said.

"Nothing?"

Harry looked away. He would try anything she asked. He wondered if she knew that. Matador whined and she got up to let the dog out. Chin in hand, Harry admired her painting. She did that at fourteen? What luck to have a father who would take you on such a trip. But then he remembered eating peanuts with Dad and

Dave in the bleachers at the Polo Grounds, the year before they tore it down, cheering for the brand-new Mets as the Giants stomped them in a doubleheader. We're both lucky, he thought. I wouldn't trade. Machu Picchus are around a lot longer than Polo Grounds.

9

Harry stopped by the Portillo Gallery the day after Lalo's show opened. That morning he had given his weekly baseball clinic in Melipilla, a town halfway between Santiago and the coast that was rebuilding from a killer earthquake, but rain washed out the afternoon session and he bused home early. He hit Santiago just before rush hour and caught an uncrowded subway uptown.

The gallery was nearly empty. Harry carried a damp copy of *El Mercurio* that he'd used as an umbrella. The paper's tepid review called the exhibit "vital, but dense, abstrusely intellectual yet at times only marginally transcending the cartoonist's art." Yet, after an hour studying the art, Harry knew that *he* was impressed.

The exhibit filled three white-walled rooms. Most of the pieces were pen-and-ink drawings, some highlighted by watercolor, and a few watercolor paintings hung in one room. The political symbolism was lost on Harry in many of them, but he knew that if their messages were explicit Lalo could never have shown them in Chile. A desperate energy shone in the work, and as

Harry moved from frame to frame an unsettling feeling grew that they somehow fit into a larger puzzle that he could only begin to piece together.

Headbreaker, he thought. He stood in front of *Rompecabezas*, a vivid drawing a yard long by two-feet wide. A jumble of images orbited a man's head as it split jaggedly down across his forehead and between his eyes, one of which sparkled while the other cried. His open mouth contorted as if in agony, but musical notes danced out. A nightstick from a disembodied hand was crashing into his skull. A cubist guitar with broken strings flying was impaled by a hammer, blocking the rest of the English phrase "I remember you, Ama" with the coiled cord like a serpent's tail that plugged the hammer into an electrical outlet. A firing squad of rifles aimed at a blindfolded pen.

There was a lot more, but that's all Harry had absorbed when a voice at his ear asked, "Look familiar?"

Harry turned to see Lalo wearing a wool poncho Chileans call a *manta*. It didn't hide his loosely knotted tie. "Those are my eyes, you know, and Victor Jara's mouth, and Salvador Allende's nose, and Orlando Letelier's ears. Not that I'm in a category with those martyrs, but I'm still alive and my eyes were a convenient model. You *did* know they blew up Letelier with a car bomb in Washington, D.C.?"

"Of course I know. Who doesn't?"

"If I asked a group of oblivious Americans? The great and silent majority. If an American hadn't been killed, too? Nobody."

To Harry's surprise Lalo spoke resignedly, with no trace of bitterness. Harry sensed a sincere effort to reach out. Was this Lalo before the torture twisted him? He could easily be friends with this man. This man would never have struck Marisol.

"It's a great show, Lalo. I don't pretend to understand it all, but I like it."

"I can't ask for more. But what would you say if I weren't here?"

"I don't say what I don't mean."

Lalo searched for clues in Harry's face. His hands emerged from beneath the *manta*.

"Somehow I almost believe you."

They were alone in the room. In the adjoining one, two sets of footsteps creaked the hardwood floor. Lalo scanned the emptiness.

"Nothing like popularity," he said.

"The weather's lousy. You had a crowd for the opening, right?"

"Sure, because I invited all my friends." He realized what he had said. "Not that you're not my friend. It's just —"

"Hey, I wouldn't have invited me either. And don't worry about the show. When something's good, people eventually find out about it. And even if they don't, it's their loss because they missed something good. Same thing with my songs."

Lalo's face lit up. "You're an artist!" He kissed Harry full on the lips and pulled away to watch his reaction. Determined not to be flustered, Harry kissed him back. Lalo gripped Harry's shoulders, then swept an arm out with a flourish that billowed the *manta*.

"Any drawing you want in this gallery is yours."

Harry's heart beat faster. "Are you serious?"

"I don't say what I don't mean."

114

Harry hesitated, but only because scruples warned him not to be greedy. He knew which one he wanted, and Lalo could undoubtedly sell it for a hefty price.

"Maybe I could pay you something for it."

"Don't be such an American and insult me."

"*Rompecabezas*," he blurted.

Lalo looked sad and satisfied. "The only one in the whole show not for sale. I was going to keep it. But it's yours and I'm glad. If you'd picked any other I'd have considered it a failure." Hands pressed together at his mouth as praying, Lalo scrutinized the drawing. Harry felt simultaneously elated and guilty.

"But swear you'll never sell it."

"I'd never dream of selling it."

"I don't trust dreams. I have no room for them." Lalo checked his watch. "Time to go if we want to get a good table. Ready?"

"Ready for what?"

"Ready for anything. Or don't you trust me?"

The two pairs of feet entered the room: a skinny soldier and a dumpy girl about sixteen, who clung to him for balance on her high cork heels. He looked bored, she looked determined not to be.

"Pieces of the fucking puzzle," Lalo muttered.

"Ready," Harry said.

They took a cab to El Parrón on Providencia, by far the most expensive restaurant Harry had set foot in. They ordered a *parrillada*, meats grilled on a brazier set up next to their table, and the bottle of Cousiño Macul was the best wine Harry had ever tasted. The meat sizzled. Lalo talked. He was thinking of quitting his job and returning to New York to devote himself to his art and working with Chilean refugees and anti-junta groups. He was hopeful, excited about tomorrow, eager to make a difference. Harry marveled at the change.

The waiter set down two snifters of cognac for dessert. Lalo lit a cigarette. He crumpled the cellophane of the pack and watched it expand again. Harry felt the wine glowing inside.

"A toast," Lalo said, and held up his glass. "To Ron Guidry and his 11–0 start. May he never lose."

"What?"

"You're not a Yankee fan?"

"Those bums? No way, I'm from Met territory." The bizarreness sunk in. "Wait a minute. What do *you* know about baseball?"

Lalo took a long drag, eyes gleaming. "Boston leads the AL East, Nettles got off to his usual fast start. The Yanks are way back but you wait, Reggie Jackson will get hot and they'll take it all. A friend sends me *Daily News* clippings every Sunday. Why're you looking at me like that? Never seen a baseball fan before?"

Harry was floored. His original, pigeonholed impression of Lalo had been so skewed. The more he got to know him, the more of a mystery this guy became.

"You like to surprise people, don't you?"

"I like to get them thinking. If that takes a surprise, so be it."

"If you like baseball, why'd you jump on me that first day at Marisol's?"

"To see how you'd take it. Do you think Peace Corps dollars should be spent on baseball coaches in Chile?"

"Truthfully, no."

"But it was a good opportunity so you grabbed it. Situational ethics. I'd have done the same in your place. Sometimes I'm full of shit. Put your wallet away."

"Lalo, this is a big bill."

"Call me a typical Chilean. I'm like the copper mines in the north — I enjoy being exploited by gringos. Anyway, advertising earned this money. It's whore's wages." Lalo smoothed out some bills and laid them in the waiter's tray over the check. "Let's go. I have something to show you."

The rain had stopped but the gusting wind had teeth as they waited for a taxi. Lalo looked snug in his long *manta*, arms hidden inside. His hands emerged to light another cigarette. Harry's breath condensed like smoke.

"Where're we going?"

"Are you really a Mets fan? When's the last time those jokers went to the Series?"

"1973."

A cab pulled over. Harry reached for the door. Lalo peered up at the blank city sky.

"I had other things on my mind that fall," he said.

They rode in silence deep into south Santiago, a part of the city Harry had never seen. Lalo chewed off one fingernail after another, spitting the slivers onto the floor. "Here," he said finally. They got out at an unlit streetcorner. Lalo waited until the taxi was out of sight, then led the way down one block and halfway across another. Twice he glanced back over his shoulder. Harry did the same.

"Who would be following us?" he whispered. The wet street was empty. Dubious small businesses —

cafeterias, a bakery, a greasy-windowed used-auto-parts shop — hid behind locked metal grates.

Lalo lit another cigarette, and dropped the burning match in a puddle. "Fuck up and your friends can get hurt too," he said. "Come on, you don't have to whisper in here."

He turned into a shadowy alley and stopped at a door between two garbage cans. It was one of those scummy dark corners of a city that usually stink, but somehow this place didn't. Lalo knocked once, paused, then gave three quick raps. The door opened a crack, then swung wide.

"Lalito!"

"Jorge!" Lalo stooped to embrace a jockey-sized man in a black beret, who peered at Harry over Lalo's shoulder. He had a noticeable glass eye that showed far too much white. He winked it and burst out laughing.

"Introduce me, Lalo! I can tell the gringo and I see eye to eye!"

"Harry Bayliss, Jorge Alacrán, my old friend and owner of this *peña*."

The little man pumped Harry's hand. "George Scorpion, that's me," he said. "Lalo and I used to verbally save the world several times a week at the university. But that was a long time ago and I'm sure he's told you."

"He hasn't told me anything. I don't even know where we are or what we're doing here." Harry stopped short at the sound of an acoustic guitar, filtering through a second door in front of them.

"The gringo needs some wine, then the explanations fall into place." Jorge used the word "gringo" endearingly, not as a sneering epithet. "How long have you worked for the CIA?" he asked in Spanish, but before

118

Harry could respond Jorge clapped him on the back and swung open the inner door.

They entered a cramped, dimly lighted room crowded with mismatched tables and chairs. There was a bar directly across from them and a low stage to their right, where a brawny man with a thick moustache sat on a stool, playing a nylon-string guitar and singing to an audience that filled most of the fifty or so seats. Spurs, old *mantas*, *sombreros* and other artifacts of Chilean country life decorated the walls, along with posters of the twelve regions of Chile, from the Atacama desert in the north to Tierra del Fuego in the south. Harry immediately loved the place.

"First carafe on the house to honor the *gringo*," Jorge said. "*Tinto o blanco?*"

Lalo grinned wide. "*Gringo* gets us free wine, *gringo* chooses the color."

"*Tinto*," Harry said. The crowd had joined in the chorus of a traditional drinking song, and everyone was clapping. Harry and Lalo found seats and Jorge brought them the red wine, then moved on to other tables. "I have to keep an eye on things," he said, and went away chuckling.

"Why does Jorge keep calling attention to his eye?"

Lalo filled their glasses. "To try to convince himself that he's not self-conscious about it. Jorge was unlucky enough to be downtown the day of the *golpe*. He got caught in a crossfire and flying glass sliced his eye open. A few months later they arrested him. Never charged him with a crime, never brought him to trial, just locked him up for over a year, then told him to report the next day for his old high school teaching job as if nothing had happened. No explanation. *Nada*."

"Why'd they arrest him?"

"For the same crime as me — some of our friends belonged to the Communist party."

"And those friends?"

"Dead or exiled. Every one." Lalo took a long gulp of wine and turned to the stage. "Lucho Godoy is a damn good singer," he said. Hands shaking, he lit a fresh cigarette with the butt of his old one.

Harry listened to one song, a satire about President Pinocchio and how his nose grew with every lie until it stretched all the way from Santiago to Washington, D.C. Godoy was an excellent musician, and Harry applauded like crazy with everyone else. But he had something on his mind.

"Lalo?"

"Yeah?" Lalo refilled his glass. Harry had hardly touched his.

"Did Marisol ever get in any trouble?"

"Not as far as I know. If she did it wasn't *my* baby."

"You know what I mean. Trouble with the *milicos.*"

Slowly Lalo faced him. "Marisol? They left her alone. Having a famous old man helped, and she never had anything to do with politics. What informer would be pig enough to turn her in? All she ever wanted was conciliation."

"And you didn't?"

"I did with her." Lalo's glass was empty. "But by then she was married with Panchy on the way."

"Marisol said her husband died of a brain hemorrhage when Panchy was a baby. Did you try to get back after that?"

Lalo stared Harry in the face. "*Gringo,* put two and two together. Silvio Huerta didn't just 'die'. They

120

dragged him out of his house at three in the morning and Marisol never saw him alive again. *You* decide if that hemorrhage was coincidence. Me, I think she's lying to herself."

Harry froze. Only his balls moved, retracting tight to his body.

"Get 'back' with Marisol?" Lalo said. "How, when it was four years before I could even get 'back' to this country?"

Jorge breezed up, making the rounds. "Lucho's great tonight, isn't he? Sometimes when he drinks too much too early. . . ." He shook his head. "More power to him, but it's best this way."

"You want someone to play?" Lalo's words were sharp, not slurred at all. "Put the gringo up there. I've heard him, he's good."

"You're a musician, Harry?"

"I play; I'm no musician."

"He's good, Jorge."

Jorge leaned closer. "If Lalo says you're good, you're good. I'm always looking for new talent I can trust and obviously I can't advertise. You could do a few songs when Lucho takes a break. He'd lend you his guitar."

Harry's stomach flopped. The soldiers killed Marisol's husband. They took him away and she never saw him again. Gone, like that. The thought of singing now made him sick.

"Thanks, Jorge, I appreciate it. Maybe some other time."

"The offer stands," Jorge said, and moved on to another table.

Harry reached for his wine but his hand was shaking. He put the glass down without drinking. "Jesus

Christ, Lalo, you tell me that story about Silvio and expect me to get up and sing?"

Lalo aimed smoke rings at the ceiling. "Ever hear of Victor Jara?" he said.

A few songs later Godoy took a break. The carafe was almost gone, and brown-stained butts piled up in Lalo's ashtray. Neither of them had spoken since Lalo's Victor Jara remark. Harry was thinking about the past, the past of his new friends, the horrors they'd endured. Lalo sat motionless, so still he made Harry sweat.

"Lalo," he said. "How does Marisol keep going? How does she stay happy?"

Lalo stood up. "Come with me." He threaded a path between tables. Harry followed him into the bathroom marked CABALLEROS.

"Lock the door," he said. Harry threw the bolt.

Lalo methodically removed his tie, eyes fixed on Harry. The urinal was a hole with grubby treaded footprints to stand on.

"Three days after the *milicos* took over, they arrested me." He handed Harry the tie and began unbuttoning his shirt. "For a week they played with me in the National Stadium, then took me to a lunatic asylum. Genital shock, cigarette burns, nightsticks to the kidneys, punches in the gut. Then they let me go, with twenty-four hours to get out of the country, and wouldn't let me back in till eight months ago. Four years in exile, mostly in New York." He opened his shirt.

"Jesus." Lalo's belly was branded with a sloppy red "C" of scar tissue around his navel, like a horseshoe on its side, an angry, awful red that still looked as painful as a new wound.

"*Comunista*," Lalo said, his voice measured but quavering. " 'C' for Communist. They used my own ciga-rettes to do it. I wanted to pass out but I couldn't." His fingers fumbled as he buttoned his shirt.

The door rattled. *"Ya, vámos.* Hurry up in there!"

Harry tried to imagine the agony of having a letter burned into his skin. It was like Nazi concentration camp inmates, tattooed for life with an identification number. How could you not hate whoever did that to you?

"Lalo, I don't know what to say."

"Don't say anything. It's what you do that counts."

Lalo spat in the hole in the floor. "Marisol's got scars, too. But they're all on the inside." He slid open the bolt.

"You tell *me* how she stays happy, gringo. I have no fucking idea."

10

C must have become sea in Harry's unconscious: for days he dreamed of the ocean. But the world was burning. The water never put out any fire, never cooled anything. Cigarettes glowed everywhere, with the music to the old Marlboro Man TV ads; a screaming Vietnamese girl, naked except for a coat of napalm, ran forever down a dirt road. Hamilton Berger, the prosecutor who always lost to Perry Mason, came on television to tell the nation smoking had rotted his lungs, had given him cancer and he would die lickety-split. "I beat 'Big C'," John Wayne said with his finger on the trigger.

"Dad!" Harry shot up in bed, his heart pounding.

Ray thumped on his bedroom wall. "Yo, Beaver Cleaver. If you're gonna spank your monkey, at least keep it quiet."

Marta James giggled. "You goofball," Harry heard her say. Marta was en route to Peru, a vacation from the cold rains at her site in the south — with a stop in Ray's bed, just as he had predicted. Ray had introduced her to Harry on the fly, on their way to his bedroom at midnight.

Harry turned on the light and checked the

clock — that was hardly an hour ago. He was drenched in sweat. Since winter started he'd been wearing T-shirts to bed instead of nothing, and this one felt like he'd just played nine innings in August — August in the northern hemisphere. August was only five weeks away. Trembling from chill and the dream, he peeled off the shirt and got a new one. Hanging eye-high above his bed, *Rompecabezas* watched him.

"Oh," he heard behind the wall. "Oh, oh. Oh, yes."

Harry thought he heard a knock on the front door. It had to be nothing. Thinking of Marisol's husband Silvio, he pulled the covers to his chin and tried to sleep. But a ring of fire scorched his stomach. A soldier spat in Harry's face and lit a fresh cigarette with the butt of the old. The slimy hawker oozed down Harry's cheek toward his mouth. He was helpless to stop it; the ropes bit hard into his arms. Unopened cartons of cancer stretched wall to wall and high as the ceiling — Merit, Kool, Lucky Strike. The soldier would never run out.

That was what you had to understand: they would never run out.

"Oh, oh," said the other room. "Oh, yes."

Do you ask a friend to tell you about her dead husband, who was probably murdered though she refuses to believe it? Do you ask her to relive the worst time of her life, just to help you understand? Harry had no answers. He turned twenty-three and told no one. A card from his parents had fifty dollars and a note from Mom that ended "Much love". "Ditto, Dad" slanted beneath it in another handwriting and different ink color. It was Dad's writing, but different, as if he did it without looking. And his father never did anything without looking.

"Go see Jean," Marisol told him a few nights later. "You know you want to."

"But my work," Harry said.

She didn't pause from braiding little Panchy's hair. "*Mijito*, sometimes you're still very much a gringo. Don't talk to me of work. Live while you're alive."

There was nothing but sincerity in her voice, no reproach; Harry provided that for himself. She has to be thinking of Silvio, he thought. She has to. But to ask now would be pure selfishness, all for me, especially with Panchy here.

Panchy looked up smiling from her picture book. "Will you read to me, Harry?"

"Sure, *mijita*," he said. But the warmth froze at the thought of Silvio — what the soldiers stole from him, and from this child who would never sit in her father's lap and sound out the words.

Lalo had advised Harry to catch the night train to Corolhue, but Harry wanted to see the countryside. After half a year in Chile he'd hardly traveled south at all, only north to the warm, desert towns where baseball was popular, and he felt citified and remote from the experience of most Peace Corps volunteers. Jean's last letter had described the honor of getting the first taste of a freshly slaughtered pig's blood. To keep the people on her side, she couldn't refuse. Harry remembered laughing with her at that vegetarian restaurant in Miami. It already seemed an impossibly long time ago.

Marisol had errands to run downtown, so Harry

caught a lift in her battered 2CV Citröen to the subway station on Providencia. They rode the escalator underground, and Harry bought two tickets. Marisol took his arm as they walked to the tracks. It felt great to be with her, like having a sister and a friend at his side as he set off to see his lover. The best of both worlds. Harry had thought about sex with Marisol and couldn't help but be tempted, but he worried about destroying the relationship if he pushed things — and the image of Jean, toughing out winter in an isolated *campo* health clinic, put a guilty damper on the plan. He remained a reluctant monk while Ray cruised to Veronica's when he wanted her, and kept Harry awake too many nights with various Peace Corps women "passing through".

The Metro wasn't crowded. They sat in the orange plastic seats, the same as on the Paris Metro, people said. Marisol tapped his guitar case. "Will you leave the bed long enough to play this?"

Harry felt himself blush but he enjoyed her teasing. "I really want to get together with Lewis and play. It's been a long time. Don't you think it's worth the effort to do something with an old friend?"

A strange look came over her face. "Lewis an old friend? You only met him this summer."

"Actually I met him in Miami, in winter, before we came here. But you're right."

"So I must be an old friend in more ways than one. I'm old enough to be your mother."

He grinned. "Not unless you had me when you were eight."

Two soldiers got on at the Santa Lucía stop, kids about eighteen with cloned military haircuts. New draftees, Harry thought. Putting in their two years. He had nothing against them, felt sorry for them, actually. They'd probably rather be wearing most anything but those uniforms.

Stiffly Marisol watched them pass, duffel bags in hand. "Old friends are wonderful, Harry, but if they're far away, then new friends are more important. Most of my old friends scattered after the *golpe*. Times change and old friends change with them. Are you the same now as when you came here?"

"You know better than that."

"It's easy to forget."

"And other things are impossible to forget." Harry paused, undecided, then added, "Like losing someone you love."

If he expected answers he got none; she only nodded, nibbling her lip. The train swayed and picked up speed. Marisol got off downtown at the Universidad de Chile stop. She kissed him and said to send a postcard, then started up the stairs, not the escalator. She waved once. Harry waved back, thinking about the last time Silvio had said good-bye to her, the night the soldiers arrested him. The train surged into the black tunnel and Marisol was gone.

Lights in the countryside flickered, yellow specks refracted by wriggling rainwater on the train windows. Darkness had fallen hours before, after a murky twilight when streetlights didn't reach the ground and Harry's overhead lamp made his eyes burn when he tried to read. A gray roof of clouds had covered the sky all day. The central valley was lush in the winter dampness, and *campesinos* worked muddy fields on either side of the tracks, hunched over plows or stooped to pull weeds. Barefoot boys tended cows.

The train was an hour late, and Harry worried about Jean. He hoped she wasn't too cold or uncomfortable, stuck there on his account. He put down his book, switched off the light and watched the black landscape shoot by. Silhouetted hills looked like female curves. He wanted Jean badly; it had been a long time. He was ravenous too, and first looked forward to buying them a great dinner at her favorite restaurant.

Rain spat on the open platform at Corolhue. Harry stepped onto the rough, soaked concrete, adjusting his stride to miss a puddle. Jean was nowhere in sight. Locals in wide-brim hats and thick wool *mantas* went about their business, oblivious to the weather as if anesthetized. A burro waited patiently at one end of the platform, a statue but for the steam jetting from its nostrils. The train chugged off into the night. Harry cut through the rundown station house and checked both directions on the narrow, sleepy street, then paced inside, his mind racing through the gamut of conceivable disasters.

"Taxi?" asked a young man with rotting teeth, but Harry had no address to give him. Jean lived twenty miles from this town. He shook his head.

Jean burst through the swinging doors, as if she'd been running to stay dry and couldn't stop in time. She wore a gray *manta* with red, white and black stripes on each side. She had no hat, and her wet hair, cut much shorter than he'd last seen it, clung against her neck. Her hiking boots were plastered with mud.

"Sorry," she said. "When I found out your train was late, I went to make a phone call. How are you, Harry?"

"Is that all the greeting I get after twelve hours on

a train? Come here, you." He took a step forward and pulled her to him. She hugged him back as he kissed the rain on top of her head. "I'm great," he said. "Now that I'm with you again."

Jean held him close, her face in his chest. "Who'd you call?" he asked.

"Lewis," she said into his coat.

"Lewis?"

"I let him know we wouldn't be back tonight. The last bus to San Tomás and San Isidro left fifteen minutes ago."

"Shades of Valparaíso. Remember?"

"Hey, you brought your guitar! Great."

"I figured that on the off chance I could pry myself away from you, my main man and I could play some tunes. Why'd you call him, anyway? Did you guys have something planned for tonight?"

"No. Not really."

"You can't risk sneaking me into your room at the *pensión*, right? So I figure we should rent a hotel room and spend the nights here in Corolhue. Good plan?"

"We could stay with Lewis in San Isidro."

"We *could*, but then we'd either have to abstain at night or be as classless as my roommate and keep him awake. You know what Ray calls his bedroom? The Fornicatorium."

"I have some work I should do tomorrow at the clinic."

"Let's worry about tomorrow when it gets here. Tonight we're in Corolhue and I couldn't be happier." He squeezed her shoulders. "Lead me to a hotel and we'll drop this stuff off and get us some dinner. I'm starving."

"Get *you* some dinner. I ate in San Isidro."

"That's okay. How about some wine for dessert?"

"I guess so. But I'm pretty beat. I had a hard week."

Dirty water ran gurgling in the gutters, and the taxi driver Harry had refused splashed them when he sped off. Jean walked quickly, head down, damp *manta* flopping past her knees. His mind raced over what he might have done to put her in this somber mood, but nothing fit. Her job must be depressing her. Her recent letters had complained about lackluster support, even sabotage, from lazy hospital administrators who didn't like outsiders coming in and making them look bad by working hard.

He hooked a finger in the neck hole of her *manta*. "Jean, what's wrong? Is there anything I can do? You know you can tell me."

"I'm tired of rain, Harry. I'm tired of goddamn rain." She touched her hand to her temple. Her skin was pale now, the summer tan faded. Her bottom lip trembled. "Yesterday I helped a doctor deliver a baby out in the *campo*, but he came out all blue and deformed and never started breathing. They wrapped him up and put him in a basket." Jean's shoulders shook under the *manta*. She took a deep breath that was more like a long sniffle. "Then the mother started crying, Harry, and looking at me. She just kept staring at me and moving her lips without saying anything, like the old ladies with their rosaries. The doctor tried to comfort her but she wouldn't take her eyes off me, like somehow it was my fault."

Harry set down his guitar between two puddles. Pack still on his back, he wrapped her in his arms. She rested almost inert against his body. "Don't take it so hard," he said. "You did your best. There was nothing you could do."

"Don't you see? That's exactly it. We all try our best, but in the end there's nothing we can do. It's hopeless."

"Come on, Jean, the bad times will fade. Everything does."

"That's what I'm saying." She wiped her eyes with the back of her hand. "That girl was only fifteen, and they think the baby was her father's." She pulled out of his arms. "Let's get you a room."

Get *me* a room? Harry thought. They checked into a decrepit, pink stucco hotel. Jean had no luggage, and the baggy-faced old lady at the desk glared at them until Harry paid in advance for a double room. Moral outrage was no match for three hundred pesos.

They went out for a sandwich. Inside a bar a pack of men bellowed Chilean folk songs to the tune of a single guitar, played by a guy who looked like a Latino Buddha. Dozens of beer bottles littered the plastic tables, as if some primitive rite decreed that no one could leave until not one more bottle could fit.

"Beer for a change," Jean said.

"What do you mean?"

"Out in the *campo* they mostly drink wine. It's cheap, it's pretty good, and once you finish work there ain't much else to do. *If* you have a job — with so much unemployment the drinking's even worse. I see tons of alcoholics."

While I see lots of kids playing baseball, Harry thought. *Campesinos* don't care about politics. Only one question matters: Which government steps on me the least?

"In their place, I might do the same," Harry said. Jean said nothing. She walked straight ahead, not interrupting her stride for puddles and mud that Harry tried to avoid. He remarked on it.

"*Campo* habit," she said. "I wasted a lot of steps and the people laughed at me for being a wimp and my boots ended up muddy anyway. So now I don't worry about it."

Harry ordered two cheese-and-avocado sandwiches at Fuente de Soda Frank Sinatra, which was getting ready to close. They sat on stools and asked for two cold beers. The counterman shook his head.

"No cold beer. Only *natural*."

"But you have a refrigerator." Harry pointed to an old clunker Frigidaire.

"We have cold soda," the guy said. He ran a grimy rag over the counter.

"Why not keep some beer in there too?"

"I don't know." His tone said he thought it was a stupid question. "Most people drink *cerveza natural*."

That hadn't been Harry's experience in Chile. "What about people who like cold beer?"

"I don't know."

"Wouldn't it be good for business?"

The man scratched his head. He reminded Harry of the sandwich shop owner in Santiago who closed every noon for a lunch break.

"Be cool, will you?" Jean said. "Arguing will only make him stubborn and you never get anything done then. Some things you just have to accept."

"I try, but this is absurd."

"Get used to it."

"*Qué?*" asked the counterman, obviously resenting the English.

133

"Two warm beers," Harry said. They tasted pretty good in the chill dampness. Harry drank two with the sandwiches. Jean fiddled with the bottle cap and didn't finish hers. When they left the counterman was stocking the refrigerator with soft drinks.

Harry couldn't help but compare the hotel room to the one in Valparaíso where they'd first made love, five months ago. He bounced on the bed. In some ways those long months felt like days, but as he watched Jean pull the *manta* over her head and drape it on a chair, then smooth back her hair, he felt a heavy sense of change separate them like a border checkpoint.

"At least it doesn't smell like mothballs," he said.

"Like in Valpo?"

"You remember." As he rose to go to her, she turned the doorhandle.

"I have to go to the bathroom. Can I use your toothbrush and towel?"

She was back soon, her face rosy from washing. "The toilet only semi-flushes and there's a dying cockroach in the wastebasket, but the water's hot. I was freezing."

"It's toasty in bed." He picked up the toothbrush. "Meet you there in two minutes."

The bathroom cockroach was on its back in a gruesome pile of toilet paper, legs twitching. The toilet had no seat. Harry brushed his teeth in record time. When he returned Jean was in bed, covers pulled up to her chin. Her clothes were piled neatly on the floor. Weak light filtered from a lamp with burn marks on its shade. Harry stripped naked and slipped between the sheets. He cuddled against her, then stopped in surprise. She still wore her thermal undershirt and her panties. He slid his hand beneath the worn elastic waistband.

"What gives, honey?"

"I'm cold," she said, looking at the ceiling.

"I know a great way to warm up."

"Don't you at least want to talk first?"

He kissed her hand. "We've been talking since I got here. What do you want to talk about?"

"I don't know. About us. Anything." She turned her head toward him. Her eyes glistened, but her voice was calm. "I suppose you'd just rather have sex. You're a man, after all."

"What's that supposed to mean?" He smiled, hoping she was kidding.

"That for you sex is fun, like any other game, and doesn't mean much more than that. You don't need time to switch modes."

"Switch what?"

She flopped on her side, facing him. "To adjust emotionally, Harry. Of course if there's no emotional involvement, it's easy."

He pulled her close. The hair on her legs was long and soft, well past the bristly stage. "You're not being fair," he said. "I haven't had sex since our last time in Santiago and I haven't tried. I don't have to switch modes because I never left the last one."

"Don't worry about staying faithful, Harry. It's not like we're married. You don't owe me anything."

"I guess I'm just a romantic. Or dumb."

Jean didn't laugh. "I wish life could be as simple as you think it is." She laid her head on his chest. "I really do. I don't want to see you get hurt."

"What do you mean, get hurt? You've been talking in riddles all night. Here, at this moment, in bed with you, life *is* simple. We've been apart for months. I missed you. I rode on a train all day to see you, and now I want to make love to you. What could be simpler than that?" He massaged her back, kneading hard to loosen tense muscles. Her lips were pursed, her eyes closed. He started to take off her shirt. Her hand caught his wrist.

"Harry, please. I'm still cold." She wriggled out of her panties. "Would you bum totally if I left the shirt on?"

Confusion must have shown on his face. "I'm sorry," she said. Then she brightened and tried to humor him, the way Dave used to when he'd beat up on Harry and had to get him laughing so he wouldn't squeal to Dad.

"Come on, pretend I'm an Eskimo. You're screwing an Eskimo in this freezing igloo, and everything smells like seal blubber and polar-bear hide."

He laughed in spite of himself, just like with Dave. "Only if we do more than rub noses," he said.

Twice he looked at Jean's face as they made love. Both times her eyes were open but she immediately shut them. Her hands rested inertly on his shoulder blades. He stayed with it a long time, trying to inspire the enthusiasm he remembered from her, but nothing was happening. He gave up and finished; her hands dropped to the mattress. She squirmed as if uncomfortable, so he kissed her and rolled off.

"How miserable was it?"

"It was fine." Her index finger traced a curving line down his throat. He kissed her again, on the mouth, on the neck, even on the breasts through the shirt.

Jean closed her eyes with a sigh. She covered them with one arm. "That light hurts my eyes."

"It's about a five-watt bulb, for God's sake."

"I can't help it, my eyes burn."

"Hard day at the office?"

"Harry, I'm super tired. I'm sorry."

He pulled away his hand, got up and turned off the light.

"This isn't easy for me, Harry. I've got so much on my mind right now."

Her voice was almost pleading. Rain drummed on the roof, harder than before, and Harry tried to picture unbroken weeks of this weather, and fighting to do a tough job in it. Give her a break, he thought. He answered slowly. "I'm sure you do."

Without warning she began to cry. "Oh Harry, I like you so much. I can't stand to hurt you, I just can't stand it."

Harry could see nothing in the black room. Jean sobbed on his shoulder, her tears rolling down his side like sweat. He couldn't tell if she wanted to be held or left alone.

"You wouldn't hurt me, honey. Why would you hurt me?"

Her tears ran faster. He held her, trying to comfort her like a brother, like the way he had held Marisol after Lalo hit her, keeping any hint of sex out of his embrace.

"I wish I could have stayed the same for you," she said. "But nothing is the same anymore. I'm sorry."

"What's not the same?"

She whispered so softly he had to struggle not to ask her to repeat it. Because he knew he had heard right.

"Lewis and I are lovers."

"You are?" The question sounded so ludicrous, like when he was fourteen, heart jumping as his father stood in the doorway telling him Grandma had died in the hospital. "She did?" he'd asked.

Jean's head nodded on his chest. "I'm sorry."

"Stop saying you're sorry. Sorry means you regret what happened, and you obviously don't." His stomach constricted and fluttered at the same time, a flock of hummingbirds pecking at his guts.

"I never planned it," she said. "You have to believe me. It just happened. After a while here, I needed somebody so bad, and Lewis and I helped each other."

Lewis's face taunted Harry from the front page of his memory, licking his lips, repeating, "Jean is one fine lady. One fine lady. . . ."

"*He* planned it, that's for sure. He's wanted you since training."

The rain pounded on the roof.

"Don't blame Lewis, it's nobody's fault."

Of course she was right, but that only made it worse. "Why didn't you write and let me know?"

"I didn't want to lose you as a friend. I figured as long as we were far apart there was no sense telling you. You didn't have to know."

"But you let me come down here anyway."

Jean's face distorted, as it had when the soldier broke her camera, back during training. The difference was that this time she cried. "I wanted to see you, Harry, I really did. And I hoped you'd still want me for a friend because I meant more to you than an easy lay."

Neatly reverse the guilt, he thought. "You know

that's not what I meant. But you could have at least told me, instead of setting me up for this."

"I chickened out on the phone. Can you forgive me?"

Minutes passed; no one spoke. Harry's eyes stung and he needed sleep, but his brain wouldn't quit. His heart beat harder than the rain. Jean lay motionless a foot away.

"Harry, are you asleep?"

"Yes."

"Look, I can't help what I am. I can't give to one, then turn that part of me off like a faucet and give to another. I feel divided and everyone gets cheated. No one wins."

"No one wins. I'll remember that."

Eventually Jean's breathing grew shallow. Harry tossed and turned but no position could tranquilize his mind. Finally he left the bed and stretched out naked on the rug. He shivered. An eerie sensation crept over him that his father was in the room, watching. He sat up, temples throbbing, and peered into the darkness. He was ashamed for Dad to see him like this, feeling sorry for himself. He climbed back into bed and pulled the blankets over his head. Finally, the rain drowned out his thoughts.

A crowing rooster rousted him at dawn. Jean didn't stir, immune to roosters from living in the *campo*. He dressed silently and crept to the door in stocking feet, hoping to leave without waking her. But then he saw her muddy boots on the floor. One stood upright, laces dangling; the other lay flopped on its side. He went back to the bed and woke her with a kiss, which she returned before she was fully conscious.

"Write soon," he said.

"You're leaving?"

"Three's a crowd, and you've got work to do. Give my best to Lewis." The forced cheerfulness felt thick on his tongue.

He kissed her cheek and walked out, waiting until he reached the street to set down his guitar and wipe his eyes with his flannel shirtcuff.

The rain had let up. He played the guitar on the station platform, but couldn't stop thinking how it would have sounded better with Lewis's harmonica. Suddenly he remembered his promise and hauled his gear to the post office to send Marisol a postcard. He would be home two or three days before it arrived — maybe longer with the shaky mail system. In the time it took to buy a stamp, the rain started again. You fucking fool, he thought, and hurried back to the hotel, but he was too late. The room was empty. He asked directions and ran to the bus terminal, lugging his pack and heavy guitar; a toothless beggar smiled at his question and pointed to the first bus to San Isidro receding in the rain.

Harry was soaked. He bought a paper and read it over three cups of coffee, fighting not to feel sorry for himself, thinking of Marisol, thinking of Lalo buttoning his shirt over the red letter that scarred him forever: "You tell *me* how she stays happy."

The train left forty minutes late. Rainwater on the window gave the countryside a steamy, hazy look. Like a dream, he thought. A very wet dream. The cool glass jiggled against his forehead. Peasants plowed the mud. He wondered if Jean was with Lewis yet.

It was a long, gray ride home.

11

In Santiago, rain fell every day for two weeks.

Beautiful fresh snow blanketed the mountaintops, but smudgy clouds and smog usually obscured the view. Harry spent hours in his room, reading and playing his guitar, writing songs that sounded decent one day and abysmal the next. Rain slapped on the roof and splashed down the drainpipe outside his window. Most days he couldn't practice baseball. Even when the clouds broke for a while, the field was sopped and unplayable. Only the grass thrived. Baked brown in the summer, it drank in the winter rains and grew lush and green.

Ray flew north to Arica on the Peruvian border, in the Atacama Desert where rain never falls, to give a course in baseball coaching to local schoolteachers. Harry had the apartment to himself, but often he'd catch a bus to the Peace Corps office to see if anybody was around to talk to. One drizzly afternoon he rode random buses across Santiago till the sun went down, killing time as he watched the city change from rich to poor and back again. Twice he decided to quit and return to the States; twice he changed his mind. He started a letter home asking for advice, but ripped it up after a paragraph. This was his problem, not theirs — and even more than he wanted to see them, he feared disappointing his father. How many times had Dad said that the one thing he couldn't stand was a quitter?

Harry visited Marisol nearly every night. He'd wait for the bus up the block at the Polla Gol parlor on the Plaza Egaña, where people filled out their cards for the weekly soccer pool. He could tell what day it was by the size of the crowd; Monday the place was deserted, but by Friday dozens clumped around the door to bet before the deadline.

One Friday in August, Harry finished a song he'd written for Marisol. The rain had let up, but he zipped his jacket to the throat against the chill. Bodies jammed the Polla Gol and crowded the bus stop, teenagers to grandmothers and all ages in between marking cards and reading newspaper predictions and player injury reports by streetlight. Tired of being jostled, Harry edged back toward a less hectic spot near the wall. A man bumped him from behind and grabbed his shoulder.

"Perdón," Harry said. "Are you all right?"

The man smiled and hurried past. Harry's bus pulled up. The instant he sat down he realized his rear pocket was empty. He jumped off at the next stop and sprinted back, but of course the thief was as gone as Harry's wallet. Sweating from the run and furious at his stupidity, Harry leaned against a lamppost and watched the world trying to hit it rich. He fell half a peso short of the fare in his change, and had to go back and scrounge the apartment for coins. He stewed with frustration on the next bus, standing because all the seats were taken; as always, the worst part was knowing he couldn't do a thing about it. Losing some money was no catastrophe, but the photo of him and Dave in Little League uniforms, of his grandfather teaching him guitar chords, of the family together at Christmas just before he left for Chile? He stomped his foot and passengers pretended not to stare at him.

He found Marisol and Lalo sitting quietly in her living room, drinking gourds of *mate*, an herb tea with a kick far stronger than caffeine, through metal straws. The Machu Picchu puzzle, far from finished, gathered dust on a cardtable in the corner.

"Why the long face?" she asked.

"I just got ripped off." He told them the story.

"The bastard," Lalo said. "But he probably needed it a lot more than you do." He lit a cigarette. Half a dozen butts were already crushed in the ashtray.

"It's not the money, Lalo. I lost photos that mean a lot to me, that I'm not sure I can replace."

Lalo's glare froze Harry in his chair. "You want photos? Here. Here's a nice one." He picked up a newspaper folded to a middle page and tossed it in Harry's lap.

"Eighteen Bodies Found in Mass Grave", read the *El Mercurio* headline. In the photo, lumpy bags were lined up near a ditch. Harry skimmed the article but Lalo filled him in faster than he could read.

"Unidentified," he sneered. "Everyone knows they're *desaparecidos* the butchers say left the country with false passports when the shit flew. But it's out now, those fuckers. Even this rag had to print it, and they won't be able to keep it off TV. They can't cover up this one."

Marisol emerged from the kitchen with a steaming mug and a sugar bowl. *Mate* was too bitter for all but the terminally macho to drink without sugar. "Some justice might come out of this, but I don't expect much anymore." She looked somberly at the photograph, then at Harry. "Careful, *mijito*," she said. "It's hot."

"You might have known some of them," Harry said, thinking of Silvio. He watched her as he dumped a teaspoon of sugar in his cup. "Maybe they were even your friends."

Her face told him nothing. "More likely they were *campesinos* shot during the *golpe*," she said.

"Gunned down in cold blood," Lalo said. "After the animals got their rocks off torturing them first." He sat hunched on the edge of the couch, knees jiggling up and down, smoke trailing from both nostrils and wisping around him like fog. Above him hung his drawing from 1974, elongated insect men howling in the vortex. His eyes blazed. *"Bastardos,"* he hissed, and sucked on his *mate*.

Harry was zinging from *mate* and adrenalin. He didn't know what to say to Lalo, who stared at Marisol as if in a trance. I'm an outsider, he thought, trying to understand a complicated situation — political, social and personal — after the fact. But the situation is mine now, too. Lalo slumped back on the couch, legs splayed. Marisol knitted a sweater. Harry sipped his *mate*. How many more shallow graves were scattered around the country? As horrible as Silvio's fate was, the *desaparecidos* were even worse — only in nightmares would their families ever know what happened to them. Rumor had it that some were thrown alive from airplanes over the Andes and the Pacific.

Marisol shifted her eyes from one man to the other. *"Por qué el silencio?* Quiet houses make me nervous." She knit too far and had to unravel a few stitches. "It's cold in here," she said.

Harry got up, grateful for something to do. "I'll get the *estufa.*"

"It's in my bedroom," Marisol said.

He found it next to her double bed. A Spanish translation of Capote's *Other Voices, Other Rooms* lay on her pillow. He spied on himself in a large mirror over her dresser, then wheeled the heater almost to the hall before succumbing to temptation. He returned to the bed and stretched out cruciform on the homemade coverlet. The bed squeaked and he sprang up, embarrassed. But there were no footsteps in the hall.

Sharp whispers from the living room stopped when he rolled in the *estufa.* Lalo mumbled something under his breath. Harry felt like an intruder. "How do you fire up this thing?" he asked, though he knew perfectly well.

"Turn on the gas and light a match," Marisol said. "*Fosforos?*"

Lalo tossed him his box, and Harry knelt to strike one. "What if it explodes?" he said. "When I was a kid that happened to a guy in the next town trying to tap a beer keg."

"Scattered hunks of meat like poor Orlando Letelier." Lalo chain-lit another cigarette and scowled at the dark front window. Harry blew out the match.

Marisol's knitting needles ticked off the seconds. "Can't you talk about anything happy any more, Lalo?" Her tone was even, not querulous, not weepy. Harry loved the way her fingers worked, nimbly creating row after row.

Lalo eyed her, cigarette hanging from his lips.

Harry felt invisible, as if they had forgotten he was there.

"I'm just facing facts," Lalo said.

"You're facing *some* of them." She turned to Harry. "Need more hot water?"

"Please."

Lalo's eyes followed her into the kitchen. His fingers drummed on his knees. "Someone has to do something," he said quietly. "Who will do it if we don't? But she's right, I'm no good to anybody dead. And neither are you."

A cold knot tightened in Harry's belly. "What are you saying?"

"Strange accidents happen in this country. Don't trust the wrong people." He dragged hard on his cigarette. "Hell, don't trust me," he said through the smoke.

The teakettle whistled. Marisol brought in the water. She put her hand on Harry's shoulder as she poured, gave it a gentle squeeze. Lalo didn't react when she motioned toward his gourd. She set the kettle down on the newspaper and grasped his hands.

"They can't lie their way out of a mass grave. Something has to come of it. It's got to."

Lalo smirked. "Sure, and some low-level pissant *milicos* will take the rap. Never anyone who gave the orders."

"Maybe not," Harry said. "Watergate finally got to Nixon."

Lalo stood up and put on his coat. He wrapped a scarf loosely around his throat. "This ain't the States, gringo," he said. "They don't have to be subtle here. Speaking of subtlety, I'm tired, and Marisol wants me to go. See you later." He kissed Marisol's cheek, nodded at Harry and walked out whistling.

Marisol blushed, a slight crimson flush that could have come from sitting too close to the *estufa*.

"Will he be all right?" Harry asked.

"Lalo's stronger than you think," she said, as if trying to convince herself. "He won't snap, unless it's for some creative madness. You've heard him say the best artists live on the edge. Before the *golpe* it was a game with him, but now he deliberately pushes himself too far. He's frustrated, Harry — Lalo lives for art and politics, and both are blocked and censored here."

"Then why did he return to Chile?"

"Because this is his country." She stared at Harry as if amazed that he had to ask. Looking at Lalo's tortured drawing she added, "And to ask me to marry him."

"Do you love him?" Marisol's hair, lustrously dark and curly, fell past her shoulders. Harry ached to touch it.

"As much as I've loved any man, even Silvio. But Lalo and me living together? *Qué desastre!* I'd lose my oldest and dearest friend, and gain a husband who made me miserable — and vice versa."

Harry remembered eavesdropping with Lewis that night, and Lalo's mournful "So it's over between us." He moved his chair next to hers. "Do you remember what you told me, that new friends can be more important than old ones, especially if the old ones are far away?"

She leaned forward. "*Sí*," she said, drawing out the word like a question.

"Well, I want you to know you're my best new friend." To do something he drank from the lukewarm dregs of the *mate*. He grimaced at the bitterness and Marisol laughed, a ringing laugh that dissolved into a smile Harry wished he could keep forever.

"You're special for me too, Harry. You're different, and I like you. You're also one of the few men who've known me as long as you have without trying to get me into bed."

That caught him off guard. Did she take it as an insult or a compliment? He stammered something about being involved with Jean.

"But you're not now."

He shrugged. "No."

"Then why not stay here tonight?"

He grinned to hide his nervousness, which only made it more obvious. "Okay," he said.

"I'm glad that's over." Marisol lifted his hand to her lips and kissed his fingers, then gently sucked his thumb, all the while watching his face. Harry smiled idiotically, embarrassed, confused, never wanting her to stop. She touched his eyelids, closing them, and he felt her breath warm and soft in his ear.

"I've been hoping this would happen for a long time," she whispered. Marisol took his face in her hands, and for the first time they exchanged a kiss that was far more than friendly. She looked into his eyes from inches away.

"Play something, Harry. Something of yours." She tucked up her knees and rested her chin on them to watch, a position Harry found amazingly sensual. What impressed him most was that she didn't have to work at being sexy.

Veronica's guitar leaned in a corner. Harry fetched it and sat on the couch. He had sung in front of Marisol many times, but suddenly butterflies attacked, monster ones. He tried to mask his nerves by stalling, fiddling with the pegs of strings already in tune. He so much wanted her to like his song for her, really like it and not just say so to be polite.

"I wrote you a song. Finished it today."

"*Fantástico!* Let's hear it."

The question escaped before he knew it. "What did you and Lalo talk about when I went for the *estufa?*"

"I told him that it was Friday night and I didn't care how important or horrible it was, I wanted to talk about something besides a massacre. Is it so wrong to concentrate on happy times?"

"No, just harder to find them sometimes." Harry fretted silent chords, his right hand damping the strings. "Funny," he said. His grip tightened on the guitar neck. "I had a weird feeling you were talking about me."

"I asked him to leave early so we could be alone."

"Did that hurt his feelings?"

"You must understand something. Lalo and I were lovers for over six years, off and on. He was the first boy I ever slept with."

The news shocked Harry. "There's plenty that people don't even tell their friends, isn't there?" he said.

Marisol caressed his thigh, and jealousy and torture swept away like twigs in a flood. Their eyes met. Harry started to put down the guitar.

"Sing my song, Harry."

Harry unfolded the paper in his pocket and spread it out on the couch. After a deep breath it was easy.

> *She's a path in the forest,*
> *She is leaves on the trees,*

She is birds singing in chorus,
She's the lady who's holding the key. . . .

Harry looked at the floor. Blood flooded his cheeks. When he raised his eyes Marisol was watching him, chin resting on her fist.

"Beautiful," she said.

"Did you understand all the English?"

"I didn't have to. Let's go to bed before someone comes." She turned off the lamp, and Harry remembered the night he saw her dancing. Marisol stood and tugged at his wrist. One finger looped in his belt and the other to her lips, she led him silently past Panchy's door to her bedroom. Swollen by humidity, the door scraped the floor and caught six inches from the jamb.

"We can't close the door?"

"Harry, come here." She patted a spot next to her on the bed. After a last glance at the door, he sat down. Marisol massaged the back of his neck. "Relax," she said. After a minute she got up and slowly removed her clothes in front of the dresser mirror. Her reflection smiled at him.

"It works better skin-to-skin," she said.

Harry tried not to fumble. With Marisol he felt like a beginner, but completely comfortable because learning was so much fun. He hugged her so tight she gasped.

He was scum if he didn't ask. *"Protección,"* he whispered. "I can't let you take the risk. But I have a —" His heart sank. No, he didn't. The condom was stolen with his wallet.

She nibbled his earlobe. "It's sweet of you to worry. But I have an IUD inside." Her tongue flicked in his ear. "Everything's okay."

They started slowly. As they sank back, Harry noticed Brueghel's *The Fall of Icarus* and something by Dali on the wall behind her bed, but soon his eyes were clamped tight, shutting out the world. This is too good, he thought. This can't be happening to me.

"*Mamá? Mamacita?*"

They froze. A small shoulder shoved at the stuck door. It began to give.

"Are you all right, *Mamá?* I hear noises."

"Panchita!" Marisol said.

"I don't believe it," Harry said. He rolled off and tried to yank the covers over them, tangling with Marisol as she fought to get out of bed. She rushed naked to the door as Panchy's face peeked around the corner. The little girl rubbed her eyes with her fist; from the other hand hung the tail of a furry stuffed monkey, grinning head dragging on the floor. Marisol hustled her away.

"Do you want a drink of water, honey?"

"Why is Harry in your bed?"

"Because he's tired."

"Oh."

Harry pulled the covers to his chin. Marisol came back smiling like the sun.

"What's going to happen?"

"What do you mean?"

"Panchy! Your daughter just saw us doing it!"

"Harry, calm down." She cuddled up beside him. "She was half-asleep and probably won't remember a thing in the morning."

"I feel like a child molester."

Marisol licked his nipple. "Stick to Mother," she said.

He did, though at first he kept alert for a little voice at the door. But concern melted as the night grew sweeter. Once they saw headlights through the shutters, but it was just Veronica getting a ride home. Harry thought of the massacre photo, on the table under a cold kettle. The news story was terrible, painful, but right now it was far away. For the first time in weeks, Harry looked forward to tomorrow.

12

The rains broke that weekend. By noon on Saturday the sun shone summer-bright, and Sunday Harry practiced with the boys on a jungle-green field that looked posed for a postcard. Rain had washed away the smog, and the sun sparkled on the clean snow of the mountains standing tall beyond right field. Harry felt strong and alive cracking balls to the infielders. The kids were high-spirited, glad to be playing and getting dirty again, and everyone hustled and looked good, especially Barata. The little pitcher threw hard and kept the ball low, and few of the hitters could touch him. He loved to play so much it was a joy to watch him.

Harry returned to his apartment in a buoyant mood, jacket slung over his shoulder, smelling spring in the air. He unlocked the door and was halfway through the tiny kitchen when a toaster popped out from around the corner.

Ray was attached to it, tanned like a lifeguard. "Want to take a bath with me, big boy?" He wagged the toaster in Harry's face, laughing dementedly. "I bought this for dirt in the free port in Arica. You'd have preferred

153

maybe a *televisor a color?* They're actually selling color TV: up there, first ones in Chile."

Harry edged by and threw his jacket over a chair. "I expected you three days ago."

"Some things are worth waiting for. Rookie, Arica kicks ass. Sunshine in the middle of winter. I went to the beach every day. Swimming in August! And it's a tourist city, tons of backpackers and sweet foreign poontang passing through all the time. Plenty of outstanding local beaver too. Leaving was hell. Sheer hell."

"You look good, you bum," Harry said. Ray's jock style and macho attitude got on his nerves, but Harry had to admit he livened up the apartment. Besides, there had been a string of burglaries in the area, and with Harry at Marisol's, the apartment was fair game at night.

"How'd you get in from the airport?"

"Bus station, baby. Right downtown. I decided to see some of this great country from the ground."

"You took the bus when the Peace Corps was springing for the plane?"

Ray grinned and draped an arm around Harry's shoulders. "Here's a deal for you, Rook. Turn me on to some beer, and I'll tell you a story of the master at work."

Harry took out a sparkling cold 600 milliliter bottle of Pilsener Cristal, then pried off the cap with his Swiss army knife and poured half of it into a glass. He kept the bottle. "OK, Casanova, let's hear it," he said.

"Ready? Take good notes. I decided to fly only as far as Antofagasta, where jolly Polly Morris — talk about a world-class set of kazangas — just happens to reside."

"Good decision?"

"I hope the neighbors had earplugs." He held up his

empty glass, foam clinging to the sides. "Got any more of this swill?"

"Why didn't you fly home from there?"

"Because I thought Ice Queen Anne Peters might be worth a ten-hour bus ride through the desert."

While Veronica worried because you were days late, Harry thought. He poured the rest of the bottle into Ray's glass. "Well?" he said.

"Can the preacher-man tone, okay Mom? Or I'll tell some warped jokes I heard from this dipshit Phil Dwyer in Arica."

"He was in my training group."

"My condolences. Anyway, Peters stayed frozen so I split on an early bus to Santiago and here I am, studly as ever. How's Vero?"

"Concerned as hell about you."

"Good, she'll be psyched for a big dose of Uncle Ray's sausage therapy. And Marisol?"

"Couldn't be better. We've gotten real close lately."

"You horny skunk — did you finally poke her? It's about time, everybody could see she's been wanting you for months." Ray chugged his beer and stood up. "Gotta crash. I need some Zs."

Months? Harry thought. She's wanted me for months?

"Why didn't you tell me?"

"You weren't listening, preacher," Ray said over his shoulder.

Harry's gut tightened when he saw the note. It sat alone in his mailbox, folded once and stapled shut. "H. Bayliss" was scrawled on the outside, in Steve Castle's handwriting. Harry tore it open: "See me ASAP. Castle." He crumpled the page and slam-dunked it into the wastebasket. Something was wrong. Something definitely was wrong. Dad, he thought — but no, that would be an emergency, they'd have called. But what if I wasn't home? Harry's hands were trembling, something he'd thought only happened in bad movies.

"Hey, Harry."

The voice was so tentative it was almost a whisper, but it startled him. He hadn't heard footsteps. Harry turned, sheepish at being so jittery. Lewis stood in the doorway.

He was holding a pumpkin, a big, bulbous, deep-orange pumpkin with a thick green stem. For a long moment neither of them moved. Harry leaned against the row of mailboxes.

"Long time no see," he said.

"I don't blame you for hating my guts."

"Who says I do?"

"Admit it."

"It's over. I hope you and Jean get married and have a dozen little brown kids in the suburbs."

"You've got the wrong idea."

"I don't have any idea. I'm doing fine. Save your sympathy for someone who needs it — unless it makes you feel better to say it."

The pain in Lewis's face cut Harry. Lewis started to reply, but pursed his lips and swallowed. He carried the pumpkin with his arms hanging down, fully extended; it had to be getting heavy.

"What's with the gourd?" Harry said.

Lewis seemed relieved. "The kids in my school gardens program grew it. Their first big pumpkin. They wanted to give it to the Peace Corps office after I told them about Halloween. It's a beauty, ain't it?"

"You learn how to grow pumpkins in Minneapolis or at Yale?" Harry took it from him and hefted it. It *was* heavy.

"Any hoser can grow pumpkins." Lewis stuffed his hands in his pockets and traced an arc on the floor with his right toe, like a nervous infielder smoothing the dirt. Harry noticed he'd drawn a face on one side of the pumpkin, with silly features more like a Smile button than a fierce jack-o'-lantern.

"I felt like a prime freak carrying that sucker on the train. I get enough stares just being black without hauling around Mister Pumpkinhead."

"There *are* hardly any blacks in Chile."

Harry set the pumpkin down. He wondered what Lewis would do in his position. Buy him a beer? Say good-bye? Tell him to shove it and walk away without a second glance? The meeting with Castle shot back in his mind, and worms squirmed in his stomach.

"So how is she?" he asked.

"All right, I guess. She got tight with a young doctor who moved to her hospital. I don't see her much."

"Already?"

Lewis nodded.

"Bummer," Harry said, but part of him celebrated.

"Things can change real quick, Harry."

"Don't I know it."

"I need your sarcasm, right? Look, man, I'll tell you what — you would have done the same thing I did."

"Is that a fact?"

"You weren't married to her, Harry. You were together for a few weeks during training. Well, great, but

157

training's not reality. The job's the reality, and the loneliness, and the goddamn rain."

"Nice speech. Sounds like you rehearsed it."

"I did. In my head, a million times. And Jean did, too. We didn't just jump on each other. It took a long time. But then winter set in, and day after day the rain. . . ."

"I know about the rain."

"No, you don't. Nobody does until they've lived in it. No offense, but you just can't know what it's like out in the *campo*. You're coaching baseball in Santiago."

"So you're saving the world and I'm on Easy Street?"

"I'm not saying that. I just want you to understand, that's all. Because if you do maybe you won't be so pissed off at me."

Harry didn't want to hurt Lewis. A few months ago he gladly would have, but now his world was different. He had Marisol.

"You and Jean," he said. "You still friends?"

"Yeah. I mean, I damn well hope so."

Harry rocked the pumpkin with his foot. Lewis rocked on his heels.

"Listen, I gotta go talk to Castle."

"I got shit to do, too." Lewis picked up the pumpkin. "See that technique? I learned that down here. Never lift without bending your knees. Terrible for your back. And you don't want a hernia."

Lewis stood there holding the pumpkin. "Well, see you around," Harry said. He stuck out his hand. Lewis tried to balance the pumpkin in his left arm, and when it almost fell Harry lunged out to steady it. They shook hands over the top.

Bill Umbdenstock walked in. He was the biggest

douche bag Harry had met in the Peace Corps, to the extent of bragging he had only joined to learn Spanish so he could quit and "land a fat job with a multi-national". He took some envelopes with corporate logos out of his box. "What are you fart-faces up to?"

Lewis drew closer. "It be a voodoo rite, Massa Bill. Goan bring de rain and mean Massa Castle he be moanin' when I sticks de needles in dis heah head. I'ze gwine to git you too, Massa Bill, lessen you gits down on yo knees and repents!" He bugged out his eyes like a frog.

"For Christ's sake," Umbdenstock said, and stalked off.

"IBM didn't think your résumé was long enough?" Lewis called after him.

"Lie to them," Harry said, just as loud. "They never check. They let you in the Peace Corps, didn't they?"

"Ignore the ignorant," they heard faintly.

When their laughter stopped, they had nothing to replace it. Lewis tried.

"When you get out, can I buy you a beer?"

"I might need one," Harry said.

Harry hadn't set foot in Steve Castle's office since the time he nearly got the Braniff Award. Castle was cleaning his fingernails with a Bic pen cap. His glasses lay on top of a very official-looking and undoubtedly deadly dull report. They didn't shake hands. Harry sat down without waiting for an invitation.

"I got your note."

"Good, good." Castle leaned back in his chair, the corners of his mouth twitching. "Harry, I don't want to give you the impression we're not satisfied with your work as a volunteer."

Harry cleared his throat. "I do my best."

"In fact, we're *quite* satisfied." His head wagged, and the twitching cracked into a thin smile. "I've had some long talks with the directors of the Baseball Federation, and with Ray Clark too, and no one has anything but praise for the work you've done."

Get to the point! Harry screamed in his head. His palms were clammy on his knees.

"We're very aware of everything you do and try to act accordingly." Castle lit his pipe, blew out the wooden match and watched the smoke curl away from the burnt-black head. "Mind if I smoke?"

"No." Harry could have slugged him.

"You're not just being polite? I can't stand cigarette smoke, for example."

"No."

"You're probably wondering why you're here."

"The thought has crossed my mind. But take your time, I don't have to be anywhere till 8:30."

Castle let out a horse laugh, pipe still clenched in his teeth. "You're not afraid to call a spade a spade, are you Bayliss?"

"What are you getting at?"

Castle chuckled. "You've played the game by the rules for some time now. If you hadn't I'd never have considered this move."

"*What* move?"

"As you're aware, I'm sure, the baseball training course that Ray taught in Arica was a big success. So much so that the schools up there have requested someone to help them initiate a program of their own. The

Baseball Federation proposed sending a volunteer to do the job and you're the logical choice."

"Arica?" Harry's first instinct flew toward the adventure. But then he remembered. Marisol.

"Arica is a beautiful city. I'm sure it'll be a welcome change, just what you've been waiting for." Castle leaned toward Harry confidentially, and winked. "And just between you and I, with both Phil Dwyer *and* you up there, it'll give me a better excuse to visit your site. I've heard those beaches are nothing to sneeze at." He grinned and sat back again, hands folded over his belly. "Well, what do you think?"

Harry remembered kissing Marisol good-bye after breakfast, how she felt under the flannel bathrobe, how she watched him till he closed the gate and waved before walking away, and in an indelible instant he knew he didn't want to leave her.

"I'll have to think it over. I mean, I want to do what's best for the program and everything but this is really sudden."

"Harry, you're a Peace Corps volunteer and you'll go where you're needed or go home. Now get the hell out of here and go talk it over with Ray."

The secretaries gave Harry strange looks when he left the office, as if they knew something he didn't or wished they did. *Desaparecidos* and mass graves, he thought, and I'm whining about getting transferred to a place called "The City of Eternal Spring".

But I don't want to lose her.

Outside, Harry sat on the stoop and stared blankly at orange trees. His eyes closed. A rap on the door at three A.M., then rough hands wrenched him out of bed and machine-gun slugs ripped his chest. "The pretty

American", Lalo taunted as they crumpled together onto other bloody bodies, still warm in the pit.

A finger tapped his shoulder; Harry jerked around and bumped his nose on a grinning pumpkin. Lewis stood above him like a conqueror.

"Did the bogey-pumpkin scare your pink ass?"

Harry laughed, but his heart was pumping hard, even minutes later in the café. He kept seeing mutilated bodies tumbled in a ditch, and across the way, no farther than the pitcher's mound from home plate, a firing squad of soldiers in dress uniform taking dead aim. They wouldn't get you, he told himself. You're innocent. You're an American.

And Marisol? And Lalo?

Maybe to be innocent in the eyes of the men with guns is to be truly guilty.

13

Three days later Harry and Marisol were walking in La Reina. He still hadn't told her about Arica. There was no such thing as the right time to do it. They turned a corner and saw the armed *carabineros* they knew would be there. Harry started across the street.

The two *pacos* eyed him as he approached, camera dangling from his neck. They stood guard in front of a padlocked metal gate, painted green. A whitewashed wall topped with broken glass surrounded the yard. Over the jagged shards Harry could see the red tile roof and second floor of the house where Manuel Contreras, the former head of the DINA, the Chilean secret police, was under house arrest for ordering the assassination of Orlando Letelier in Washington, D.C. Strong pressure from the U.S. had forced the move — an American had also died from the car bomb.

"Could I please take your picture?" he asked in his most naive tourist's voice, as if the two *carabineros* were hairy-hatted guards at Buckingham Palace. He hoped his smile looked more convincing than it felt. He remembered Jean's smashed, unhinged camera, silent tongue of film trailing on the pavement.

"Prohibido," growled the beefy *paco* to the left. His stubby fingers, fat like bumblebees, gripped the stock of his machine gun. "Maybe we should confiscate that camera to see if you've already taken photos."

"No, *señor,* that's why I asked permission first. I know the rules."

The other officer had a face like a bad boxer but he spoke kindly. "If you want pictures, go to the changing of the guard at La Moneda. Much prettier than us."

Harry returned his smile. "Just one quick photo?"

"Go!" said the first cop. "If your government minded its own fucking business we wouldn't be here now. Go!"

He went, forcing himself to saunter, to not seem afraid or intimidated, but his back felt like there was a target painted on it. Then he noticed Marisol was half a block ahead, walking head down, hands in her pockets. He jogged to catch up.

She refused to look at him. "What did that accomplish? Nothing — except now two more of them know your face."

"I just wanted a photo."

"To prove what? That you can get arrested and beat up for pressing a shutter?"

"To document the barbarity."

She rolled her eyes. "Oh, please. Don't be an idiot!"

Marisol had never talked to him like that before, or in that tone of voice. He had tried to impress her — Harry the *gringo* revolutionary, rebel with a cause. But instead of a hero, she thought he was a fool. A young fool. And he still hadn't told her about Arica.

They took a bus downtown to Santa Lucía hill, where Pedro de Valdivia founded Santiago in 1541. A few artists had set up easels to paint the fountains at the foot of the hill, snowcapped *cordillera* in the background. Flying spray twinkled like stars in the sunlight. A subway train rumbled underfoot and cars sped along Avenida Bernardo O'Higgins. A brief rain had cleared the air, but already exhaust fumes were building up.

Marisol took his hand. "Let's climb to the top. Let's find out how far we can see."

She led the way up the wide, stone stairway, worn slick from countless footsteps. The gardens were in full bloom, luxuriant with multi-colored flowers beneath lazily fanning palm trees. Harry thought of Arica, where the cold rain never falls and most days are as clear and sunny as this one. Maybe there aren't as many soldiers, either. And a person can relax at the beach after work instead of dealing with jam-packed rush-hour buses. And the women are out for a good time and don't care if you know it. Marisol had pulled ahead, dark curls bobbing with each step, and now stood leaning against the balustrade, smiling and motioning for him to catch up.

"*Flojo!*" she cried. "Lazy! Don't you have to be in shape to play baseball?"

He took the last steps two at a time and swooped her up in a bear hug. Her fingers kneaded beneath his shoulder blades, which she knew he loved. Marisol kissed him so hard his lips pressed against his teeth. Then she drew back. She fished a coin out of her pocket and tossed it into a shallow pool. It clinked off the green metal statue of Ganymede whose cup continually fed the fountain, and plopped into the water. The coin flashed like minnow fins as it wobbled to the bottom, half sinking into a clump of algae.

"I made a wish," she said, shielding her eyes from

the sun with one hand as she gazed at the statue. The boy wore a garland around his head and a fig leaf for pants.

"What did you wish?"

"If I tell you it won't come true." She smiled again, but sadly. In a strange way he couldn't explain, Harry loved her sad smiles even more than her happy ones. Anyone could smile happy. But he'd never seen a sad smile like Marisol's, damp eyes and a subtle cloud passing over her face, gone before most people would notice.

Their shoulders touched. Their elbows rested on the warm, hard stone. "Can I make one, too?" he asked.

"Only if you tell me what it is."

"But then it won't come true."

"You don't *believe* that crap, do you?" She tickled his side and tried to slip away but he grabbed her and held her tight from behind. Her hair smelled like clover and he buried his face in it. He shut his eyes and hugged her even closer. There was a mysterious pleasure in the pain of needing her so much, an uncontrollable sensation of surrender that made him almost giddy. He knew beyond all doubt he didn't want to leave her. And he knew that today he had to tell her about Arica.

Marisol gently rocked him back and forth. "Peso for your thoughts," she said.

"It must be a great view from the top." He let her go. What he had to tell her refused to come out. Ganymede balanced effortlessly on one leg, water flowing from his cup like something forever.

They climbed switchback pathways, past creeping vines clinging to granite terraces. The hill was tiered like a Maya pyramid, and at each level they saw more of San-

166

tiago sprawling in the distance. When they reached the peak they were over two hundred feet above the street.

Marisol stretched her arms high over her head, reaching up on tiptoe as far as she could. The sun cast her thin shadow down the steps; she closed her eyes and basked in its warmth. Harry chewed off a slice of fingernail. A dried earthworm shriveled in the sun and he wondered how the hell it got up there.

"I wish I had brought my camera," Marisol said, looking out across the rooftops to the mountains. Her hands clenched the iron railing.

"What's the problem? I've got mine. And you already have photos from Santa Lucía." Harry cleared his throat and spat on the rocks, furious with himself for stalling.

She turned to face him, her back pressed to the railing. The wind toyed with her hair, blowing a few strands over one eye. She brushed them back. "But none with you in them. They'd be nice souvenirs after you move to Arica."

Marisol stood with one heel on the lower rail, hair breeze-blown across her face again. Harry felt as ridiculous as he did relieved, as nervous as he was surprised. She'd done his job for him but that didn't make it any easier.

"You know," he said.

"Ray told me. Four days ago. He was excited and wanted to tell somebody, and he knew Vero would blab and spoil the surprise for you. So he told me."

Harry tried to smile but his bottom lip trembled. His throat felt knotted, stuffed with old cotton. "You didn't say anything," he said.

"*I* didn't say anything?"

Neither of them moved. In that frozen instant, poised on top of the city in front of shining white mountains, sun swimming in her hair, Marisol represented every reason Harry had for staying in Chile. Nine months ago he would have jumped on the first bus to Arica, but *that* Harry still thought donkey carts were quaint and had not seen marching soldiers destroy a kids' baseball practice, or malnourished children selling caramels on buses. *That* Harry had not met Marisol.

They stood together, not quite touching, staring at the horizon. The words "I love you" fought on his tongue, but he couldn't bring himself to say them. Somehow it seemed selfish, as if all that mattered were *his* feelings.

"Someday you'd have to leave anyway," Marisol said. "You'll return to your country and I'll never see you again. That's the way it works."

"Don't say that."

"Maybe it's easier this way." She sounded like a mourner searching for consolation.

"I don't want to lose you," he whispered. A tear spilled onto his cheek.

She slipped her arm in his. "*Te quiero mucho,* Harry."

"I love you, too."

She kissed his cheek. "I'm glad you said that. I've known it for a while, Harry. Now you do, too — before it's too late."

14

You've got to be shitting me." Ray looked up from his month-old *Sports Illustrated*. He took off his glasses, which he hated but needed for reading. "Are you *serious*?"

"Completely." The maid called them to lunch. They paid Señora Maria five dollars a day plus meals, a relatively high wage, to wash, cook and clean for them twice a week. Harry never got used to the feeling of having "help", but she was working there when he moved in and there was no point in taking her job away. Most middle class Chilean families had maids.

"I want to stay in Santiago."

They sat down to *cazuela de ave*, chicken soup with potatoes and a two-inch chunk of corn on the cob. The soup was steaming but Ray blew on a spoonful and tried to eat it, scalding his lips. "Damn. Listen, Rookie. How can you pass this up? Great beaches, gorgeous beavers out struttin' their stuff in *tangas* — I've wiped my *ass* on stuff bigger than those bikinis."

"I don't know how to break this to you, but I'd rather have a better reason than bathing suits to move over two thousand kilometers away."

"How about year-round sunshine? The kids can

play ball all year." Ray put down his spoon, and counted on his fingers as he made each point. "The people are enthusiastic and really want you there. You'll be a big fish in a small pond. Not to mention being fifteen kilometers from the Peruvian border, so it'd be cake to bolt to Peru and Bolivia. You're the one who's always barking about Machu Picchu. There's even some Peace Corps company — Dwyer's a rusty dildo but he's halfway funny."

"I know all that."

"So what the hell else do you *want?*"

"I want you to go instead."

Ray froze. A spoonful of *cazuela* hovered a foot from his mouth. His expression was like a dam breaking.

"Well, aren't you ecstatic?" Harry said. "Your dream come true. I stay here with Marisol and you blow off to Arica to chase Annette Funicello or the perfect wave. And we don't shortchange the baseball program because we still cover all the bases. Pun intended."

"What about Veronica?"

Harry had thought of that. She would cry, but she'd be better off without him. "You've never let her get in the way of your life before."

Ray scratched his chin. "All right, you made your point. I'm tempted. Who knows if they'd approve it? And I'd have to extend in the Peace Corps for another year."

"You were going to do that anyway." Harry dipped a hunk of bread in *ají* and popped it in his mouth. Chewing he said, "If you want to play, you have to pay."

Ray's fingers drummed on the table. A fly buzzed frantically, snared in a spider's web in the corner. Sunlight streamed through the window. Ray got up to draw the curtains, and stood watching the doomed fly struggle as the spider trussed it with silk rope.

"Damn well could be," he said.

Ray left for Arica on August twenty-third. Harry drove him to the bus station in Marisol's car. A cab cut him off to pick up a fare; Harry swerved into traffic, heard a tremendous screech of brakes and the blast of an air horn, and saw a truck's grille and license plate filling his rearview mirror.

Ray white-knuckled the dashboard. "Jesus Christ, let me at least get out of the city alive!" Last night at the going-away party Veronica had started to sob, and Harry felt horrible, responsible. Ray told her to stop depressing everyone. It was selfish, he said.

"Sorry," Harry said. He was shivering from the close call. A second, that's all it took; one moment of not paying attention could change everything forever. He drove slower, past the huge outdoor Mapocho food market where ragged vendors scrambled through traffic, peddling whatever: newspapers, dishcloths, long-stemmed roses.

Ray sighed. "I'm going to miss this place. But maybe I'll meet some eager gash on the bus." Minutes later they shook hands and Ray's high white Converse sneakers with green laces walked up the steps of a sleek new Flota Barrios double-decker. Ray waved and Harry waved back, still shaking inside. He bought a paper from a boy wearing scuffed shoes tied with string, and left without waiting for the bus to pull away.

He had big shoes to fill on the baseball field. The boys idolized Ray. He was their hero. Barata cried when

Ray broke the news. Harry nearly did, too, as brawny, bearded Ray walked off beyond the backstop with the scrawny, brown-skinned kid, his hand resting on the boy's heaving shoulders.

In a way, though, the boys' reactions reassured Harry. Baseball and their coaches obviously meant a lot to them, maybe gave them something they couldn't find anywhere else in their lives. He thought of the kids whenever he looked over at the National Stadium and asked himself for the thousandth time how he could justify his cooperation with the military government, even to his minimal, tacit extent. The players always gave him unspoken answers. One day it was Esteban Fuentes, grinning and waving a clenched fist to Harry after beating out a drag bunt they'd been practicing for weeks; another time, the hugs the whole team gave Pedro Morales and Esteban's twin brother Enrique after they turned a 6–4–3 double play. He couldn't ignore the kids to soothe his conscience. They needed heroes and examples, needed them as much as Lalo and Marisol needed Victor Jara.

One afternoon in early September, Harry was supposed to show a film on the '75 World Series and give a baseball demonstration at an elementary school in Las Rejas, a poor barrio. But when he arrived after a long bus ride, he found only incredulous looks and a succession of teachers and administrators who shifted the blame to anyone who wasn't standing there at the moment.

"Besides," a teacher said eventually. "The projector's broken."

"It is?" said the principal, a greasy lizard. "I thought I told you to get it fixed."

The teacher shrugged. "Must have been Jaime."

When no one protested Harry knew Jaime was elsewhere, undoubtedly armed with his own quota of alibis if they found him. Deal with it, he thought. So today's a washout; we'll set it up again.

"How about if we reschedule for this time next week?" he asked.

"*Bueno,*" said the teacher, but the principal shook his head grimly.

"*Imposible,*" he said. "*Es el once de septiembre.*" And he walked off.

September eleventh was the fifth anniversary of the military *golpe.* The teacher watched the principal enter his office and shut the door. His nose wrinkled.

"Of course that prick wants to celebrate what got him his job."

"What happened?" Harry asked.

He could almost see the teacher's brain working. Unknown gringo: CIA agent? Government contact? Pinochet sympathizer?

"Two weeks," the guy said. "We'll do it in two weeks. *Gracias. Hasta luego.*"

He shook Harry's hand and left in a hurry. The elbows of his shirt were threadbare and shiny. Outside, Harry waited for the bus and studied the miserable wooden shanties of the *callampa.* He doubted he would get a call back from the school, and when he tried to reschedule it would be a coin flip whether he'd have any luck. A woman with swollen ankles was sweeping the dirt in front of her house with a homemade broom so short she had to hunch over. A muttering man in a

"University of Yale" T-shirt stumbled by with a jug of wine; he stank from five feet away. He stuck his toothless face near Harry's and offered him a swig. Harry waved him off with a smile.

The guy squinted a cloudy eye. "My wine ain't good enough for you?"

"No, friend, I'm just not thirsty." Harry took a step back and lucked out, as a small green *liebre* pulled into view. He got on and headed for Marisol's. PLES D'ONT SMOKIN read a carefully lettered sign above the driver.

It took Harry over an hour to get across town, and then Marisol wasn't home. When he rang the bell, he was surprised not to see Matador the manic dachshund leaping on the back of the couch, yipping and pawing the picture window. Harry tore off a piece of the folded paper he always carried for song ideas, slipped a note under the door, and wandered off.

"Hey, buddy," cried a voice from the street in English, "want a fourteen-year-old virgin? She knows how to do everything and isn't shy."

Harry whirled around. Then he grinned at the driver of the silver Mercedes. "Lalo!"

Lalo pulled over and opened the passenger door. Harry got in. "I've been trailing you for two blocks. Don't you ever look up from the sidewalk? That could have been the meanest father raper of them all at the wheel."

Harry recognized the line from *Alice's Restaurant*. "I'm no father. And this neighborhood's no threat."

"There's father rapers everywhere. And worse."

Looking at the trim, well-kept houses of La Reina, Harry wondered.

"Did you hear?" Lalo said. "Matador's *desaparecido*."

"What?"

"Someone must have swiped him. Marisol's heart-broken. She doesn't even like dogs that much, but . . . Matador, he was Silvio's dog."

Harry grimaced. Losing the dog was one thing, but losing him in a way that would make Marisol doubly remember Silvio's death was truly cruel.

"So, gringo, what are you doing out here?"

Harry told his story of the wasted trip to Las Rejas.

"Nothing's wasted," Lalo said. "Not if you don't let it."

That sounded like unusual idealism, coming from Lalo. "For instance, now you realize how so many people in positions of power — not just in schools, but all over — got their jobs." Lalo stubbed out a cigarette in the full ashtray. "Where you headed?"

"I don't know. Home, I guess. How come you're not at work?"

"Big deadline tomorrow. They always let their 'creative genius' stay home those days. I tell them I need to be alone in my studio and they're gullible enough to believe it."

"If your ads keep winning prizes they're smart to believe it."

"I'm a whore — we both know it. How about those Yankees? Thirteen games back a month ago and now they're chasing Boston, with a big series in Fenway this week."

"You're not a whore, Lalo."

Lalo slid into first gear at a stoplight. He sighed, fingers tapping on the wheel.

"I don't care what you say, gringo, I think the Yankees can do it." The light changed. "You've never seen my place, have you?" he said, and hung a quick left without waiting for an answer.

The house was a few miles north and east toward the mountains, not far from the Peace Corps training center and the army base. Harry couldn't help remembering that midsummer January day — Jean flanked by scowling soldiers, her camera crunched on the road.

"I have an orange tree," Lalo said. He pulled into a driveway. "Get the gate, will you?"

Harry lifted the latch and swung the gate open, then closed it behind the Mercedes. "Nice wheels," he said.

"It was my father's." If Lalo was embarrassed driving such a capitalist automobile, he didn't show it. He led the way across the grass to the white stucco bungalow. "My mother doesn't drive, so when he died she kept it for me — for almost two years, till I could come back."

"Your dad died while you were in exile? Then you couldn't —"

"Couldn't even be at my old man's funeral?" Lalo shrugged, but the nonchalance seemed forced. "I wasn't the only one."

"Had he been sick a long time?"

"Cancer. It gets everybody these days."

"My Dad has it, too."

Lalo paused for a second, then swung open the heavy wooden door. "I'm very sorry to hear that." He went into the kitchen and came back with two bottles of Escudo. "Live for today, right?" He handed Harry a beer, and they clinked bottles. "To today," he said. "The first fucking day of the rest of your fucking life."

"Cheers," Harry said. The beer was fresh and stinging cold. Lalo's house was small, but uncluttered: just a little furniture, a cheap stereo and a lot of books, mostly paperbacks, many in English. And a few of Lalo's paintings on the white walls; Harry recognized the style immediately. Anyone who saw *Rompecabezas* on Harry's bedroom wall would know it was the same artist.

"Where's your studio?"

"You mean my capitalist headquarters?" Lalo glumly set down his bottle on a two-week-old *New York Post* and started back through the kitchen. "Today the artist prostitute spreads his scrawny legs to convince the booboisie to buy a new television they don't need. Did you know color TV was coming to Chile?"

"Ray told me they're selling them in Arica."

"The last campaign was for dandruff shampoo. I got a plaque and a raise for that contribution to society."

Drawings, layout plans, photographs, X-acto knives — all kinds of paraphernalia was piled on his drawing board by the window. Three easels were lined up with paintings in various stages of completion, and a workbench was littered with pencil sketches and pen-and-ink drawings. A huge painting in the style of *Guernica* filled almost an entire wall. Harry moved closer.

"Lalo, this is amazing."

Lalo looked pleased despite himself. "It's not too bad. But totally derivative." He stared at Harry. "An artist has to find his own style."

Harry touched the drawing board. In one picture Pegasus was standing on a magic carpet, watching a console TV in a sky full of stars.

"How's it coming?"

"It's not worth caring about."

"Then why don't you quit?"

Lalo looked down at the flying horse. "Soon. But first I must save all the money I can, to take to the U.S. to help the movement there. Outside pressure is our only chance, *amigo*."

"You're really leaving again?" Harry's heart beat faster. Lalo had called him his friend.

"Would you rather I stay and sell more TVs? Or maybe it'll be laundry soap next time. Or those disposable douches you have in the States — it's only a matter of time before *they* make it down here."

Harry had no answer. "I hope it works out," he said.

"Have another beer," Lalo said.

"After I hit your bathroom to make some room."

Tacked above the toilet was an autographed poster of Reggie Jackson in a Yankee uniform, coiled after a tremendous swing, grinning at the horizon as the ball disappeared in the distance. As Harry zipped up he remembered a quote from Reggie that he still believed, and probably always would: "There's no better feeling in the universe than hitting a baseball right on the nose, as hard as you can."

Lalo was back in the studio, staring at the jumble on his drawing board. He held out a new beer without looking up. Harry took it. Lalo had substituted a blonde woman in a bikini for Pegasus.

"Maybe she could be on *top* of the horse," Harry said.

Lalo lit a cigarette, eyes still hard on the board. "Or under it. That'll get their attention."

Harry wandered around the studio. In a corner, on the floor next to some wrinkled, clay-stained tennis shoes, leaned a couple of old Dunlop Fort wood racquets in their wing-nut presses. Harry had bought a Wilson

T-2000 the summer before, the new aluminum racquet Jimmy Connors used. Wood was on the way out.

"You play tennis, gringo?"

Harry glanced over; Lalo still stared at the paper. "Sure. You?"

"I used to."

"What happened?"

"It wasn't fun so I quit."

"What's not fun about tennis?"

Lalo finally looked up. "Want to bat some seeds now?" he asked.

Harry gestured at his clothes, wondering where Lalo had ever heard that slang. Lalo waved him off. "I'll lend you a pair of shorts. And I've never seen you wearing anything but sneakers. I gotta get out of here while I still have some mind left to lose."

Harry passed the drawing board as they left. A new sketch had the bikini woman side-saddle on Pegasus, smiling beatifically at the television and fondling a remote control like a magic wand.

They drove down tree-lined Principe de Gales, back toward the city, and stopped at La Reina park. "This place didn't used to have courts," Lalo said. "But I haven't been here for ages so we might as well check. It's not like the States, you know. There are hardly any public courts in Chile, and at those you have to pay."

"So only rich people can play?"

"Basically. And that's basically why I stopped." Lalo locked the Mercedes. He made a sour face. "So here we are, an ugly American and a Chilean socialist in a luxury sedan, searching for a court."

They were friends now, Harry thought, despite Marisol, despite all of Lalo's other demons. They walked through the park, racquets on their shoulders, not saying a word, and that was fine — it was the comfortable quiet, not the edgy, elevator kind people fight to fill before it gets worse.

Harry was the one who noticed the boxing ring, set up beyond a pair of soccer fields where kids were playing. Except on TV, he had never seen one before. He pointed. "Is that what I think it is?"

They headed over. The ring was empty. It was a good three feet from the ground to the floor, and four or so more to the top rope; when those pro wrestlers heaved each other around it had to hurt.

Lalo tugged on the middle rope. "Why do they call it a ring?" he said. "It's square." Without waiting for an answer he climbed up and in.

The goalie at the nearest field was watching them instead of the game. Harry ducked between the ropes. It was harder than it looked, hard to do smoothly.

Suddenly smiling, Lalo began unbuttoning his shirt. "This is our chance, *amigo*." He flipped the shirt backhanded onto the top rope.

"Chance for what?" Harry asked, trying not to stare at the scar-tissue C on Lalo's belly.

Lalo slowly raised his fists. "To find out."

"You mean find out how a boxer feels?"

Lalo feinted and jabbed, quick feet dancing. "What do you think I mean?" he said, and the smile grew.

Harry draped his shirt on a corner post, trying to imagine, trying to feel the real thing, face to face with a man whose job is to punish you, to hurt you before you can hurt him. The ring shrinks, and shrinks fast: Lalo and his smile bore in and Harry retreated, bobbing and weaving. Your own fists get in the way, obstruct the view; thick gloves must only make it worse. The rough ropes chafe your spine. You raise your arms, protect your face in an improvised rope-a-dope, hoping those thousands of situps, those interminable hours of stopping a medicine ball with your gut have cemented the muscles, toughened them to take the pounding until the opponent, arm-weary, drops his guard. The two of you fall into a sweaty clinch, so close it's hard to know where one stops and the other starts. The referee forces you apart. Somewhere, very far away, the crowd roars for blood.

At least twenty people, mostly kids, had gathered around the ring, cheering and yelling instructions. "Smash him!" Harry heard. "*Vamos!*" Lalo's smile was tight-lipped, then not a smile at all. What's going on here? Had Lalo planned this fight? Why is he leading with his right? Harry read the left hand, saw the fat punch coming from back by Lalo's ear and ducked slick and smooth to evade it, jaw-first into Lalo's right jab.

Blood flooded his mouth; pain filled his brain. The spectators howled.

"What're you trying to do, break my hand?" Lalo held his wrist and sucked his cut knuckles.

Harry tried to talk but blood and saliva spilled down his chin. He leaned over the ropes and spit three, four, half a dozen times, scattering the crowd. Bright blood speckled the fresh grass.

The pain faded, leaving a ragged throb behind. Harry spit again. Already they were old news. Only two kids around six years old were left, edging as close as they dared to the red-stained grass.

"That was a pulled punch if you didn't walk into it."

"If you didn't lead with your right," Harry said, "you wouldn't have messed me up."

Lalo wiped some blood on his leg. "What the hell do you expect me to do? I'm left-handed."

Harry knew that; he'd seen Lalo draw. Why did his brain cramp when it counted?

Leaving the ring was even more awkward than climbing in. The last kids ran off toward the soccer goal. No one noticed them put their shirts back on and walk away. Harry pushed a loose tooth with his tongue. They returned to the car, faster now, not looking for anything. Going back always felt quicker, even as a kid, dead tired in the back seat with Dave, Dad driving the family home after a day at Montauk or a trip to Connecticut to see Harry's grandparents.

Still tasting blood, Harry said, "Good thing I don't box for a living."

"I guess you're a lover, not a fighter," Lalo said, without taking his eyes off the road.

15

Infeliz hijo de puta!"

Lalo perched on the edge of the couch, glaring at the small black-and-white screen of Marisol's TV.

"Take it easy, Lalo," Harry said. "Your ulcer."

"*Silencio!* By the whore mother, listen!"

"*Por Dios,*" Marisol said. "We've heard it all before and we know what's coming." She went on knitting a sweater in the spring warmth of October, a skein of red yarn in her lap. She did such fine work that people ordered things from her all year.

"Bah!" Lalo lunged forward to turn up the volume. His knee bumped the coffee table and a full glass of milk teetered, sending a small white tear slithering down the side.

President Pinochet's reedy, cartoonish voice blared from the set. He read from a prepared speech, seldom lifting his eyes from the pages. He looked hot and miserable in his tight uniform; his face sweated. Behind him sat the other three members of the ruling junta, rigid in the tailored uniforms of the navy, the air force and the police.

"Law, order and decency are returning to our

beloved *patria*." His fist banged the podium. "There are no quick answers. Economic recovery will be slow at first —"

"At first!" Lalo said. "You've had five years."

"But we must stay the course which we know is just, unmoved by demagogues and traitors, Communists who would return to the days of breadlines and chaos to regain power."

Marisol's knitting needles stopped clicking; her chin nuzzled Harry's shoulder as she watched the screen. When she kissed his ear, her warm breath set his blood racing. Still, he wished she wouldn't do it with Lalo right there.

"Chile needs strong leadership! The people have given us a mandate to do a job, and we will not swerve until that task is finished and we have totally erased the mistakes of the past!"

Lalo smacked one palm with his fist. "How many 'mistakes' have you already killed off? And the army gets blanket amnesty for the murders!" He was nearly off the couch, sitting on the very edge of the cushion. Marisol ringed her arms around Harry's neck, and hugged reassuringly. Her breast nestled against his back.

"And put this country on a bright path to tomorrow, to make us proud to be Chileans again."

"*Qué horror*," Marisol said in disgust, and hugged a little harder. Harry squeezed her wrists to show he was with her, that he was appalled, too.

"What does a butcher of his countrymen know about pride?" Lalo sneered at the television, at the image of the gray-haired general with the Stalinesque mustache waving to the crowd, the other military men on the dais applauding like robots. Lalo turned with upraised finger to make a point, but swallowed his sentence when he saw Harry and Marisol. His mouth formed a cockeyed circle, then he snapped it shut and grimaced, as if trying to dispel a bitter taste. Three wrinkles creased his forehead.

"You're like two horny teenagers in a goddamn drive-in!"

"What's a drive-in?" Marisol asked.

"Ask him to take you to the States and show you." Lalo's face was flushed, and a thick purple vein bulged in his neck.

"I just might." Marisol unwrapped her arms. Her jaw set tight in a way Harry had never seen before. "And I won't need your opinion to do it." She picked up her knitting, but after a few stitches tossed it down with a sigh and went to Lalo.

"I hate them too, *amigo mío*," she said. "I hate them with all my heart. But I won't let it poison my life."

Lalo stared at the screen, a commercial of pudgy Don Francisco plugging his muscular dystrophy telethon. Harry sat tense and motionless, thinking of Miguel at El Oasis restaurant, and newspaper headlines, and a little mummy boy in a museum who couldn't care less.

Lalo shut off the TV, then winced and grabbed his belly. Marisol handed him the glass of milk, but after a tiny sip he put it back on the table.

"See how stubborn you are?" she said. "The doctor tells you to drink milk, but do you listen? I think you like to suffer."

"Milk is for the unweaned," he said, and took a gulp of wine.

Marisol settled back next to Harry. "You know

what you're like, Lalo? One of those heroes in our epics who end up sacrificing themselves for some 'glorious' cause. You try to live up to an image you've created, instead of being yourself."

Lalo drank more wine. "What you refuse to understand is that *I* don't matter. *I'm* not important; the revolution is important."

Harry couldn't keep still any longer. "But what good is a revolution if it's not for each individual? Why die for others if you don't believe each of them means something? And if you believe that, then you're just as important as anyone else."

"And just as unimportant." With a long swig he emptied the glass, and held it bottoms-up over the milk. Two violet drops broke the surface and sat there like bruises.

"Death is never glorious," Marisol said. "Old men invented that idea to get young men to fight, and young men are foolish enough to believe it."

"*Some* of them are," Harry said, instantly aware of how smug that sounded.

Lalo whirled toward him. "Where were you during Vietnam?"

Harry had taken French his senior year in high school to prepare for Canada if he got drafted, and even researched the entrance requirements of McGill University in Montreal. But he couldn't know for sure what he'd do until he had to face it — and he never did.

"I was seventeen and a half when the draft stopped. I got lucky."

Lalo snuffed and swallowed, his Adam's apple bobbing. He scratched his beard and smiled. "You're lucky to be so lucky," he said. The smile didn't fade. "Saved by governmental decree, just like the *milicos* who massacred the eighteen people at Pilquén. Nixon says you don't have to put on a uniform; Pinochet says any military atrocity during the 'national emergency' can't be prosecuted. Your fingers must be crossed all day to be so lucky."

"I don't appreciate being compared to murderers."

Lalo stared at him a long time. "That's too bad," he finally said.

"Yeah. And so was Pinochet's pardon. But what the hell does that have to do with your ulcer?" Harry thought of his father, living with pain he couldn't control. "It's not brave to live in pain if you don't have to, it's stupid. What good are you to anybody if you're dead?"

Marisol's needles ticked steady as a metronome, as if totally divorced from the tense, expectant body that sat touching Harry's, alert to every word. Lalo watched them both, his tongue playing with the corner of his moustache. He spoke softly, almost pleadingly.

"Maybe I would live longer if I took care of myself. Maybe seventy years instead of fifty, is that what you're thinking? Well, they're bound to get me before that anyway, so I'll be damned if I waste my time drinking milk."

"Who's 'they'?" Harry asked.

Marisol closed her eyes. "Lalo, please don't be a martyr in my house."

" 'They' is whatever might do me in before any ulcer could. Might be a *milico* bullet. Might be Marisol drives off a cliff with me in the front seat."

Marisol dropped her knitting in her lap. "I can't believe how much you've changed. Sometimes you act so sick of this world that you'd actually *want* them to get you, just so you could leave it."

"At least I'd go out with better vision than when I came in." He got up. "Speaking of leaving, I only came by to watch Mussolini's speech. I'll leave you two alone at the drive-in."

"Where are you going?" Marisol said. "Stay for supper."

He waved his hand. "I'm eating with Jaime Flores. He got a letter from Aldo in Germany that I want to read."

Marisol perked up. "Aldo Quiroz?"

"Yes, Aldo Quiroz — old sexy legs himself."

"You'll never let me forget that, will you?"

"What are you talking about?" Harry asked.

"How is Aldo?"

"I won't know until I read the letter, now will I?"

"Sarcástico!" Marisol swiped at Lalo but he jumped back in time and wagged a finger at her.

"Por la puta madre, you've slowed down, woman!" He made a sweeping bow like a ringmaster and backed out the front door, then paused outside the living room window. "In case you haven't heard, gringo, the Yankees beat the Dodgers in the World Series. Six games." Whistling "Take Me Out to the Ball Game", he sauntered down the driveway like a man without a care. He didn't look back.

Harry pulled Marisol close. "Who's Aldo?"

"A friend. Exiled since 1973." She still stared out the window, though Lalo had rounded the corner and was out of sight. "Aldo is very important to Lalo and his friends."

"Sounds like to you too. 'Sexy legs'?"

"That was a long time ago. I said it to make Lalo jealous, and for him it's been a joke ever since."

"It makes *me* jealous."

"Aldo is one of the leaders of the anti-junta movement in Germany. He writes to us of things we'd never find out in the press here and asks if his efforts are doing any good."

"Are they?"

"Only international pressure keeps the *milicos* from being worse than they are. It's the only influence we've got anymore." Marisol reached for Lalo's milk glass and drank from it. She licked away the white mustache. "Harry, I'm worried about Lalo going to the States."

"Why? Sad is one thing, but why worry? Even after the Letelier bombing, he's probably safer there than here."

"Because I'm afraid they won't let him come back."

It was never clear whose idea it was. Hours before dawn they lay naked in Marisol's bed, a damp, tangled sheet barely covering their thighs. They rubbed noses.

"Like Eskimos," she said.

"This igloo needs air-conditioning." Harry kicked off the sheet. "I love you," he said. She laughed. They kissed.

Harry studied their bodies, glorying in the wonderful differences. Reggie Jackson was wrong: this was even better than hitting a baseball right on the nose. He wondered if Reggie had ever been in love.

"Do you realize this is the first time we've spent the whole night together? Panchy should stay at your mom's house more often."

"I'm glad you say 'spend the night' and not 'sleep', because maybe we'll never go to sleep!" She rested her head on his chest. The shutters were thrown wide open, and a full moon lit the room. The air smelled of dew and fresh-cut grass.

"If we could only do this every night," he said.

A spark jumped between them. Their eyes met, and Harry knew she had felt it, too.

"You know how tight money is around here. I've been thinking of getting a boarder for months. I don't do much painting these days, so I could easily make my studio into a bedroom."

Marisol kissed his chest, his belly — then stopped and peered up at him.

"Got anyone in mind?" she asked.

In early November, cool spring raindrops pattered their faces as Harry and Marisol unloaded the Citröen and carried his stuff to his new room. Marisol had cleared out everything but a bed, a chest of drawers, and a long table he could use as a desk. As he unpacked, Panchy and Veronica appeared in the doorway. Veronica held up a big spoonful of steaming beans, cupping one hand underneath in case of spills.

"Taste, Harry. Tell me if it needs more *ají*."

He blew on the spoon and tasted, and immediately started fanning his mouth as if his tongue had been blowtorched. He hopped from one foot to the other and gasped for water. He panted and swooned. Then he gave back the spoon.

"Too bland. Add more *ají*."

"You were fooling, but I knew!" Panchy held up her arms. Harry hoisted her over his head and swung her until she giggled.

Veronica lingered at the door. "Any word from Ray?" she asked with badly faked nonchalance.

"Not yet," he lied. He'd gotten two letters, both extolling the high life in Arica. "I guess he's not much of a writer."

"I guess not." Veronica turned away.

Marisol reached on tiptoe to dust the shelf in the closet. Harry rubbed her shoulders.

"Nothing?" he said.

"*Nada.* She's written four times that I know of."

"What a scummer." Harry rationalized again that he'd done the right thing by convincing Ray to go to Arica. The guy was already keeping a tab of his conquests: two college girls from Arica, one Peace Corps volunteer on her way to Cuzco, one hairy-armpitted German tourist who traveled with a box of condoms and insisted on using her self-timer to take photos of them together in bed. Veronica was better off without Ray in the long run. But still he felt lousy.

"Will you forget about me so quickly?" The gleam in her eye told him she didn't really expect an answer. Her tone reassured him that moving in was the right decision. Marisol was the only woman he had ever been able to talk to about love — their love — without feeling self-conscious. She had introduced him to a softer part of himself, a part that he was starting to like.

Harry took the rag and leaned over her to clean the back of the shelf. "Besides, we'll stay so close together we won't be able to forget about each other if we tried."

"Till death do us part," Marisol said. "See? I'm already practicing wedding vows. Getting nervous?"

"I do."

She snatched the rag from him, snapped it once

and draped it over her head like a bridal veil. She fluttered her eyelids.

"You'll get dust in your hair." Harry reached for the cloth but she hopped back.

"Ashes to ashes. It'll wash off. Let's go eat beans."

"Let them eat beans!" he cried, and arm in arm they marched to the kitchen.

The rain stopped during lunch and they decided to take a walk with Panchy. Veronica stayed home to watch soap operas and be depressed. Iron-gray clouds still hung low, but patches of blue sky steadily widened. The sun peeked out, then hid again. They strolled aimlessly toward the *cordillera*.

"*Caballo!*" Panchy pointed down the street. A massive, sway-backed horse slowly approached, hooves clip-clopping the pavement as it pulled a rickety wooden cart. The driver lazily flicked its haunches with a long switch, more out of habit than purpose because it didn't affect the animal's pace at all. Harry stood hip-to-hip with Marisol on the sidewalk.

"Not many horse carts in this part of Santiago," he said.

"Come now, we're too sophisticated. Horses pollute the road; cars only pollute the air." She took Panchy's hand as the horse drew near. Across the street, in the park where Harry and Lewis had seen street kids sleeping under a bush, a worker swept the walks with a broom of lashed-together palm fronds. He had to stoop to reach the ground.

That guy makes thirty-two bucks a month on the government Minimum Employment Plan, Harry thought. I get two hundred fifty as a Peace Corps Volunteer.

"My first impression of Chile came on the ride in from the airport. A boy was driving a two-wheeled donkey cart in front of a Coca-Cola billboard. I didn't expect to see that just outside a city of four million people."

The driver passed with a lecherous, toothless grin. He doffed his ratty cloth cap. "Pretty young to have a kid that big, ain't you sonny?" he yelled, and rolled off cackling and stomping his feet.

"Get some dentures, you old fart!" Harry shouted in English. He wouldn't swear in Spanish with Panchy listening. The driver, quaking with laughter, shook an upraised fist without turning around.

"You're not really angry, are you?" Marisol said as they crossed the street. "He was only making fun."

"I'd better get used to it, I guess."

"That's what happens when your lover's an old lady."

Harry slipped a hand in her back pocket. "In American slang a lover *is* an old lady. And I'm your old man."

"I'm a package deal, Harry." The smaller half of the package skipped on ahead, avoiding the cracks in the sidewalk. "What's a fart?" Marisol asked.

"A *peo*."

She made a face. "Does that mean the man smells or that he is nothing but wind?"

Her question made Harry want to hug her, so he did. "Neither. It means that he's better than shit because the smell goes away in a few minutes, and you can't step in it."

"Fart," she said. "Old fart."

Their tennis shoes squished on the damp sidewalk. They passed under a palm tree and Harry slapped a low-hanging frond, showering them with droplets. He kissed a bead that shimmered on her forehead.

"*Mira,*" she said.

Ghostly words barely seeped through coats of whitewash: *VIVA ALLENDE/UNIDAD POPULAR,* a piece of the past spray-painted in foot-high letters on an adobe wall where Panchy stood, staring up at a chattering squirrel. When Marisol and Harry got close it scurried off, bushy tail in the air.

"You scared him! You came too fast and made him run away!" Panchy leaned against the wall and started whimpering, and when Marisol went to comfort her she slumped below her grasp. An ancient Ford pickup bucked by and backfired loud as a shot. Harry jumped; Marisol's head whipped around, her face disfigured with fear. They exchanged sheepish smiles as the truck dawdled past, gears grinding.

The explosion made Panchy forget what she was crying about. She saw another squirrel on the grass and chased after it. Marisol watched her daughter. "You felt it, too," she said.

Harry nodded. "Once in college I was with a Lebanese friend and a car backfired," he said. "I almost had a heart attack but he didn't flinch. When I mentioned it, he just laughed and said he was so used to shots and bombs in Beirut that they were like Muzak. Background noise he hardly even noticed."

"*I* never got used to them," Marisol said. They wandered hand in hand, fingers intertwined. The sun broke through the western sky and glistened on puddles. Panchy climbed a black iron fence that looked like jail bars, but hopped down in a hurry when a German shepherd bounded snarling toward her from the lawn.

Harry squinted into the sun. "I don't want to leave you."

"Let's not worry about the future. So much can happen —"

"No, I mean my vacation with Lewis. I feel bad about moving in, then leaving you so soon."

Marisol took a giant step to avoid a sidewalk line. Harry caught her off balance, tugged at the right moment, and she dropped back into his arms like a tango dancer. Her upside-down face said, "When you get to be my age, you learn not to call off a vacation for anything. The chance might not come again."

"I miss you already."

She spun herself upright. "I'll miss you too, but the real shame would be missing the beauty down south. You've worked hard. You've earned a break from Santiago, *mijito*."

Harry knew she was right, but already it was hard to imagine a month without her. His thirst for travel was as strong as ever, but now he wanted to drink it with Marisol. He had never been so happy nor wanted so much at once.

"Next vacation we'll travel together," he said. "We'll go while Panchy's in school so she can stay at your mother's. We'll go to Peru and Machu Picchu and climb Huayna Picchu up into the sky. You're smiling — I guess I sound ridiculous."

"If you're ridiculous, Harry, then the world should *be* more ridiculous."

Random raindrops sprinkled through sunbeams. A rainbow arced across the sky. Panchy giggled and reached for it on her tiptoes, making sure that they noticed her efforts.

"Almost, *mijita*," Marisol said. "You're almost there."

"You can do it," Harry said, and boosted her as high as his arms could stretch.

"I touched it!" she cried. "Just with one finger but I did!"

"I told you so," Harry and Marisol said together.

16

A week later Panchy was at a friend's house and Harry had no afternoon practice, so he and Marisol went on a picnic to Cajón de Maipo, a lush valley running east to the Andes. It was only an hour's drive, and the late spring weather was perfect. Harry uncorked a liter of wine and they sipped from a plastic cup as the city receded behind them. He felt as warm as the day and as cool as the wine; Marisol laughed and talked of a brand new year just around the corner.

Thirty kilometers outside of Santiago, among small farms and vineyards, Harry was surprised to suddenly see a long brick wall close to ten feet high, topped by broken glass. Both the bricks and the glass had seen better days, though if somehow you made it to the top of the wall your hands — at least — would still be sliced to shreds. Vines climbed on a tottering sign: *HOSPITAL PSIQUIATRICO SAN JUAN DE DIOS.* The heavy metal gate was swung open, and a dust cloud hovered over the dirt driveway from the truck that had just entered.

"Marisol, stop. Turn around."

"What?" She almost imperceptibly accelerated, as if the reaction were out of her control.

"Did you see that sign?"

"What are you talking about?"

Her voice told him he was right. "That's the place," he said. "That's where Lalo was tortured."

"You don't want to go there, *mi amor*. Really, you don't."

He corked the wine. "Go back," he said. "I mean it."

Marisol pulled off the road. She gripped the wheel with both hands. "Why? *Por Dios*, why?"

"I have to." He touched her arm. "Please."

Shaking her head, she wrenched the gearshift into first and made a U-turn. They crawled through the rusted gate and bounced uphill for a hundred yards on the pitted gravel driveway. Marisol stopped in the shadow of an L-shaped two-story building that needed paint as badly as the sign out front. Harry put his camera in his daypack.

"Wait for me. I'll probably be right back."

The white tips of her teeth bit her bottom lip. "Are you kidding? I'm not staying here by myself."

The compound was dead quiet. Harry got out first, dust puffing from his sandals on the parched ground. Marisol walked with him toward the building, but a stride apart, and ignored his hand when he held it out to her.

The heavy wooden door was locked.

"This is a mental asylum," Marisol said. "Of course it's locked."

Part of Harry was relieved. Now he could go on their picnic, conscience clear. He had not run from this chance to try to understand the horror Lalo went through. But most of him was ashamed of that relief, and more excited than scared when they heard locks click and the door swung open. A bulky man in a white lab coat stood on the threshold. He peered at them, and jotted something on a clipboard, then smiled without showing his teeth.

"*Bienvenidos.* Welcome, Christmas visitors."

It was the second week of November.

"Come in," he said. "Please."

Two steps inside the entrance the stench hit them, rank like the cow barn on Harry's grandparents' old farm, without the sweet smell of hay mixed in. The doctor slammed the door shut and locked it loudly. He crooked a finger. "Come, visitors," he said, and led the way into a cavernous room. Filthy plaster chipped off the walls. Shuffling patients stared with empty eyes. The bedclothes were dingy white, the patients wore white smocks, even the bed frames were painted a drab, institutional white. Fingers clutched at Harry's elbow. He jumped away, fists clenched and ready. But it was only a boy, a thin barefoot kid no older than twelve, lost inside an adult-size smock that dragged on the floor. He reached toward them, palms cupped upward, pleading silently with dark eyes half hidden under unkempt bangs. This kid could be playing ball for me, he thought, like Barata. Desperate to do something, he handed the boy a peso.

"*Por favor!*" A pretty brunette nurse rushed up and pried the coin out of the kid's fist. He began to wail and pound his heel on the floor with sickening thumps. Still crying, he clutched at the nurse's leg.

She returned Harry's peso. "He would only eat it."

The nurse dislodged the boy and he slumped to the floor. "Doctor, who are these people? Who authorized their visit?"

"Nurse Chacón, what's my title?"

"I'm sorry, Doctor, I just thought —"

"Please don't think. You're not good at it. If I want Christmas visitors, we shall have Christmas visitors." He gestured forward. *"Adelante."*

"But Doctor, what about regulations?"

He didn't deign to look at her. "Regulations are for little people."

He led them down a dismal hall. Bedpans were stacked on a cart next to a water pitcher. Harry was repelled but grimly fascinated. Where did the horror happen to Lalo?

In a large, high-ceilinged room an orderly was teaching four men to shave at what was once a watering trough for cattle. They shared two cracked mirrors missing chunks of glass. They used old-fashioned shaving cream with a brush, the way Harry's father did, and in a flash Harry was back at the bathroom sink, eye level with the waist of his dad's pajamas as he lathered his face and scraped the foam away. Now he saw a grizzled, emaciated old man with a permanent grin shaving one cheek over and over in slow motion, letting the soap dry like scabs on the other. The man continually looked to Marisol for approval, the way a child makes sure his mother watches when he leaps off a diving board. He sliced himself and blood spilled down his cheek; Harry and Marisol flinched but he didn't react. Grinning dreamily, he cut himself again.

The doctor smiled too. "Progress," he said with great satisfaction. His index finger tenderly smeared blood across the man's face. He pointed the stained finger toward a narrow door.

"Come, gentle visitors," he said, wiping the blood

on his lab coat. "Feel the cool sun on your face today, for tomorrow we die."

They followed him, exchanging anxious glances behind his back. The doctor fumbled through half a cluttered ring's worth of keys before finding the right one, then flung open the heavy door and walked out into the light. Marisol stiffened in the doorway. She gasped.

Ten feet away, sitting splaylegged on the ground against a fence post, was a man with no face.

He had a lower jaw, and a gruesome attempt at a mouth — slack lips around a toothless cavity that puckered and sucked on themselves. But there were gummy red sockets where his eyes and nose should have been. Flies swarmed and settled in the holes. Tufts of brown beard sprouted near his ears and under his chin. The flies were the worst, the ultimate indignity. The man yawned and stretched, reaching out his gnarled hands as if inviting Harry into his arms. The decayed pit of his mouth seemed to be laughing. Harry imagined the man's breath, a sour rotten swamp. The hands fell back to earth and clawed at the dust.

The knot in Harry's throat was too thick to swallow. "This is what you wanted to see?" Marisol said. "Are you happy now? Is the world a better place?" She grabbed his hand and pulled him away. He followed willingly. Outrage and curiosity had brought him to the asylum, but he needed more than that to deal with people without faces. His chest was so tight he could hardly breathe.

"This is the exercise yard," the doctor said. "Many of the patients have made astounding progress." Sweat beaded at his temples as he scrawled on the clipboard.

"Regulations! Little people!" he sneered and marched ahead, still scribbling.

They passed grotesque men in various stages of disconnection, fenced in like livestock. Some stared straight ahead, expressions blank as boards; others timidly approached, wearing crooked smiles, and tried to touch them — especially Marisol. A skeletal, balding man stood ramrod straight against the fence, eyes clamped shut and arms rigid at his sides, so tense that he trembled. "No blindfold," he muttered, over and over. "No blindfold, no blindfold."

Five yards away a guy no older than Harry lay prone in the dust, aiming an imaginary rifle at the man's heart. His index finger curved around a trigger that wasn't there. "Fire!" he screamed, but made no shooting motion. The gaunt man collapsed in a heap.

"Coward! Swine! I never pulled the trigger! I wouldn't waste a bullet on your miserable carcass!" The executioner sprang to his feet while the condemned man sobbed in the dirt. Contemptuously he flung the gun to the ground and spun away, then hunkered low when he saw the intruders. His head jerked from side to side, searching for an escape route.

"Marisol!" he hissed. "Are you crazy, too?"

She froze. "How do you know me? Who *are* you?"

The executioner's lip quivered. He seemed about to weep. "Of course little Tito never got any attention. Aldo and Lalo — Tito just got in the way. My legs are as sexy as Aldo's! And younger, and stronger!"

"No . . ." Marisol's face twisted horribly. "Tito Quiroz?"

Tito thrust a fist in the air. "*Viva la revolución!* She remembers me! Marisol remembers Aldo's little brother!"

He exulted and tried to raise the condemned man to his feet, but the body's limbs were jelly. Tito tweaked its sunken cheeks. "She remembers me!" He sprinted to the man with no face and shook his hand, then let it drop slack again. "Marisol remembers little Tito!"

The doctor took furious notes on his clipboard.

"Tito disappeared during the *golpe*," Marisol whispered.

Tito crouched toad-like, squinting up at them. "Talking behind my back? Who are you?" He jabbed a finger at Harry.

Harry ached to help this man, but he was even more afraid of him. "*Un amigo*," he said.

Tito's eyes widened. He licked his lips. "Then I will tell my friend a secret that is not a secret because everyone knows it except my friend. Your doctor is insane. He is a schizophrenic loony, although a decent doctor for a madman." He broke into tears and clamped his hands over his ears. "Shit oh goddamn shit, when will I stop being *observed*?"

The doctor rushed over and placed a hand on Tito's neck. Tito groaned and shoved the doctor back, knocking him off balance, and the clipboard dropped in the dirt. The paper was covered edge-to-edge with the single word ASYLUM repeated over and over, in dozens of shapes and sizes. The doctor snatched it up.

"It is strictly forbidden to fraternize with the patients, and this man is a compulsive liar and not to be trusted. His progress is extremely slow. Unfortunate."

Two attendants flanked Tito and pinned his arms. "No more exercise for this troublemaker," said the doctor.

"No!" Tito yelled. The attendants dragged him,

thrashing and cursing, toward the asylum. *"Viva Allende, viva Allende y la Unidad Popular!"* The condemned man calmly waved good-bye. As the attendants carried him inside, cries of *"Viva Allende!"* echoed in the asylum. Then stopped.

The exercise yard fell cemetery-still. Patients and doctor and visitors stared at each other in the heat. "No blindfold," mumbled the condemned man, flat on his back, arms spread as if crucified. "No blindfold, I tell you."

Harry was stunned. His pilgrimage for Lalo had decayed into something more terrible than he could ever have expected. He had come to bear witness to the atrocities of the past, not to find that past still alive.

"How long has that man been here?" Marisol said.

The doctor shrugged. "I don't keep records. That's a job for the little people."

"His name is Tito Quiroz and he's been missing since 1973!"

"You're quite mistaken. That fellow's name is Vaca, and he attempted to spill his mother's brains with a shovel. He has a fertile imagination and an ingrained persecution complex that resists all treatment. A deranged chameleon, not to be trusted. I apologize for the inconvenience."

The man with no face whimpered and pawed the air. "No blindfold," moaned the condemned man, louder than ever.

They passed a doorless, reeking bathroom. A long, coiled turd slouched in a urinal. The boy they had seen earlier, the only child among the men, ran up to Harry and hugged his waist. Small fingers gripped his spine with desperate strength; tears wet the front of his shirt.

Harry fought off his impulse to escape. He embraced the narrow shoulders, trying to squeeze some love into the frail body.

"It's all right," he lied. "Everything will be all right."

The child held out his cupped hand. Harry imagined him choking on a dirty metal coin with the bust of a Chilean war hero on it, and shook his head. The kid howled and sank to the grubby floor, beating his forehead against the concrete. The doctor kept moving as if nothing were wrong. Neither he nor Marisol looked back, but the boy's wailing and the thud of his head followed them down the corridor.

The doctor stood in the military at-ease position, clipboard behind him. "Perhaps it is time for Christmas visitors to depart."

He had an orderly unlock the door. Harry saw what they had passed under without noticing on the way in: an arc of paper streamers high on the wall, spelling *FELIZ NAVIDAD* in pastel letters. "Meddy Creesmas, no?" said the doctor. He extended his hand. "A contribution to the hospital would be in order, I believe."

Harry put a hundred-peso bill in his palm, and they hurried to the car. His voice caught in his throat; it sounded like someone else's. "The boy is still in there," he said.

"Which one?" Marisol wiped her eyes and started the engine.

They drove to Cajón de Maipo. Harry cooled the now-warm wine in a gurgling stream. They dangled their bare feet in the water.

"Tito's family is all in Germany," Marisol said. "We have to let them know. And we have to try to get him out."

Harry's feet looked white and dead underwater. Fish-belly white. Frog-belly white. White as a lab coat.

"I'm sorry for making you go in there."

"So am I. But at least we found Tito."

"I'll be missing you in a few days. This is no memory to leave you with."

She touched his lips. "Get out of this madhouse city for a while, *mijito*. I mean it."

He forced himself to smile for her. Asylum, he thought. Could there be a stranger word? Vacation coming up: asylum in the beautiful south. Political asylum. Insane asylum. Suddenly they were both crying, holding each other. The past was not dead, and the past was full of pain. Is she thinking of Silvio, he wondered, and all that she has lost? You tell *me* how Marisol stays happy, Lalo had said that night in the *peña*. Well, to begin with she stays out of mental institutions.

Harry kissed her tear-streaked face, without wiping his own. "My dad says that what doesn't kill you makes you stronger."

"But what if it —" Marisol bit her lip, and looked down into the clear stream. "We can't give up, Harry. We *can't* let what we saw make us give up."

"I won't give up," he said. "I love you."

She smiled one of her sad smiles. Later there was another, when Harry snapped a photo of her standing in the stream, jeans rolled to her knees. In the asylum he had not removed the camera from his pack. It had seemed terribly wrong, like photographing Peruvian Indians who believe each picture steals a piece of their soul.

17

A month with Lewis in southern Chile was a perfect refuge, the kind of asylum Harry needed. Camping on a bend in a sapphire stream, a boy on horseback crossing the water with a gift of delicious fresh boiled milk; four days on a boat from Puerto Montt to Punta Arenas with a stop at Puerto Edén, the people rowing out to them in dinghies loaded with clams, oysters, king crabs like creatures from another world; fishing the Río Serrano in Torres del Paine National Park, where the sun set at midnight, llamas eyed them from the mountains, and a dentist from Santiago horsed in a seven-kilo trout; hitching a ten-hour ride in a coal train caboose from Chile to the vast emptiness of Patagonia in Argentina. His father would have loved it all; Harry sent frequent postcards home and to Marisol.

Their Argentina visas would expire in three days, so they hitchhiked hard through the desolate *pampa* for seventy hours, traveling one night with a gypsy caravan, the last two in a Chilean eighteen-wheeler. Pedro the truck driver changed Lewis's Chilean money so they could buy food, and at the ski resort of Bariloche in the Andes they had a lakeside picnic just a couple of miles from the border. They rode up to the checkpoint on the last day of their visas, grubby and beat yet elated with their trip — and were told they couldn't pass.

"Not our fault," intoned a uniformed flunky. "Road-work on the Chilean side."

"We'll chance it," Pedro said, and gunned through to customs.

Until Argentina, Harry had never heard of a country that searched baggage on the way *out*. Soldiers snapped questions at them as they probed every corner of their packs. Harry kept his temper; he remembered the father of the Oasis restaurant family. *Desaparecido*. There had been even more *desaparecidos* in Argentina than in Chile.

A jeering private found a condom in Lewis's can of Band-Aids. He dangled it between thumb and forefinger, as disgusted as if it had just been used.

Lewis tried to smile. "Just in case," he said.

The soldier curled his lip. "Our women don't need your kind, darky."

Another guard sprinkled Harry's foot powder on his wrist, sniffed it and tasted it. The urge to laugh welled up in Harry like a sneeze, but he knew the thugs were itching for an excuse to work them over. Without closing the top, the soldier tossed the can upside down on Harry's clothes. The guards eventually let them pass, with the warning that the Chileans would force them to spend the night at the border.

The Chilean police waved them through with a verbal declaration and no inspection. One of them even smiled. Harry and Lewis traded surprised looks: they had expected major hassles.

"How extensive is the roadwork up ahead?" Pedro asked.

The guard looked puzzled. "What roadwork?"

Pedro let them off in Valdivia at dusk. They walked to the bus station and bought tickets to San Isidro.

"You know something?" Lewis said. "I'd do it all again, even with you. Anything to be so far away Castle can't get on your case, no matter how hard he tries."

"That does make life worthwhile." Harry was thinking of Marisol, and how he'd be with her the next day.

It was a forty-five minute ride to San Isidro. During a quick stop in San Tomás, Harry remembered the time he visited Jean, that fiasco in the rain in Corolhue. He had never even made it here to her town. He wondered what she was doing now.

"I doubt you'll see her," Lewis said.

"See who?"

Lewis sniffed. "Man, you are one transparent motherfucker. Your eyes are all over that window."

"I don't *care* if I see her. But if she happens to walk by. . . ."

"Would you say anything if she did?"

Harry thought for a second. "I talked to you, didn't I? Life's too short to lose friends."

No *gringa* in muddy boots appeared. The bus pulled away.

Lewis lived in a crumbling building rented to him by the director of his hospital. They ducked through a low wooden door in the fence and followed a path under a grape arbor. Chickens clucked moronically at their arrival and Harry knew a rooster would blast him from sleep at dawn.

It was blissful to drop their packs in a real room. "Take the first shower," Lewis said. "I want to say hi to the doc and get my mail."

The water was freezing but it transformed Harry into a human being again. A cold shower to survive one last celibate night, he thought with a smile. He rubbed himself dry.

Lewis sat at his desk, reading mail. "Hey, something for you."

Harry stood naked in his rubber sandals, vigorously toweling his hair. Lewis handed him a telegram. It was in English, though it cost twice as much to send one in a language other than Spanish:

YOUR FATHER DECEASED 11 DECEMBER STOP FUNERAL 14 DECEMBER STOP CONTACT IMMEDIATELY STOP CONDOLENCES STOP

CASTLE

Harry crumpled the telegram. It fell to the floor. Lewis half-rose from his chair.

"Harry, what's wrong? What's wrong, man?"

Harry leaned against the wall, between a map of South America and posters of Malcolm X and John Lennon. He wanted to answer but knew he'd cry if he opened his mouth. He tried to settle himself as Lewis picked up the message and touched his shoulder, but words choked him and thinking made him dizzy.

It was December 17th.

The sky was low and gray, clouds fat with snow and ready to let loose. Dirty remnants of the last storm clung to the roadsides as Harry drove his mother's car to the cemetery. Some kids were playing hockey on a pond, so he figured school was out for the day. He was disoriented from the hectic trip home, from remote San Isidro to New York City as quickly as possible. English had swirled around him when he stepped from the debarking tunnel at JFK, a confusion of accents and dialects that struck in his ears like a record played too fast. A woman wheeling a suitcase bumped him and gave him a nasty look. "*Perdón*. I mean excuse me," he said, figuring that four gin and tonics on the flight might have made him clumsy. They certainly hadn't helped him to sleep.

The cemetery was on a side road, but visible from the highway that roared behind. Harry hadn't been there since his grandmother's funeral. John the Baptist was verdigris-green and spattered by pagan pigeon shit, but continued to smile benignly at the indignity and the tidy rows of flat tombstones. Harry marveled at the neatness of the place, its austere but peaceful symmetry. There are worse places to be, he thought, though he didn't formulate any alternatives.

"Christ," he said, and shut his eyes as he stepped on the brake. His hands trembled as he put the car in park. The defroster blasted suffocating hot air, yet he didn't shut it off. He clenched the wheel, conjuring up images of Marisol. He saw her waving good-bye at Pudahuel Airport, tasted her toothpastey tongue at bedtime, smelled the fresh jasmine in her hair. John the Baptist's back was framed in the side-view mirror. Rock salt crunched beneath his tires as Harry backed up to make the turn he had missed.

It had to be that one, the one there with the newest

flowers. A squirrel found an acorn and scampered up a nearby oak, bare but for a few withered leaves, precariously hanging. The ground was frozen solid. Harry hacked at the turf with the heel of his hiking boot, as if to make a tee for the kickoff of a sandlot football game, but he might as well have attacked a sidewalk. Someone would have to hold the ball if they played today. He remembered the solid thwack of his Dad's kickoffs, the ball arcing end over end, high into the autumn sky.

Harry thought back a few hours, to meeting his brother at the airport. "Dad got so sick these past months you'd hardly have known him," Dave said. There were dark circles like bruises under his eyes.

"But his letters always said he felt great! Why didn't anyone tell me?"

"He made us promise not to." Dave put his arm around Harry's shoulders, something he'd never done before except in light moments. Harry was glad for his brother's touch, but nearly cried because of it. People rushed by on the way to the baggage claim.

Dave dropped his arm. "He didn't want you to see him the way he was."

Harry stared at his brother.

"With you he could pretend that nothing had changed. You were therapy for him. The disease . . . he was embarrassed by it. He'd apologize to us, like it was his fault. But you still had the old Dad in your mind and he could be his old self, his real self, because he knew that's what he was to you. You did him a favor not being here."

"I'm not stupid. I saw only what I wanted to see, and Dad deserved better."

"You saw what *he* wanted you to see. That's what counts."

It was a simple stone of polished marble, set flush to the ground: R. DAVID BAYLISS, JR. 1927–1978. His father had hated the name Reginald which, to avoid confusion with Harry's grandfather, his family had luckily never used. On rare occasions Harry's mother would tease his father, calling "Reggie!" in a high-pitched voice when painting the house or some other chore kept him from dinner and she wanted to get his attention. He'd ignore her, but never long enough for her to have to call again. And though he called it poetic justice when the Yankee Stadium crowds started chanting "Reg-gie! Reg-gie!" to celebrate Reggie Jackson's home runs, he named his first child David Robert. Harry hunched his shoulders and shivered in the bitter north wind. His eyes watered. Branches swayed like skeletons' fingers. The squirrel had disappeared. Harry wondered where squirrels go.

It's hard to break the stillness of a cemetery. The sky was so low he felt trapped. He knelt to touch the cold stone, smooth as glass, and slide his fingertips over each intaglioed letter. The flowers, withering, threatened to blow away like fallen leaves.

Suddenly, Harry saw himself as he imagined his father must be seeing him. A burst of energy propelled him to his feet. He looked at the sky with his eyes closed and breathed in the arctic air. Possibilities were limitless. Time was the only boundary. He overflowed with love for his father, the man who had insisted that he go to Chile and therefore the man who had led him to

Marisol. He and Marisol would climb Machu Picchu, climb to the top. He would never hold back again.

He blew warmth onto his palms and rubbed his hands together, then stretched out on the hard ground and gazed at the huge unbroken cloud of sky, his father's headstone only inches behind him. He rolled over and did forty pushups, slow ones with no cheating, the way his dad had taught him. The dead grass advanced and receded from his face.

Dad would appreciate pushups more than tears at a funeral, Harry told himself. He jogged a lonely lap of the grounds, hugging the wrought iron fence, not cutting corners, alive and grateful, determined not to despair. The wind stung his eyes; tears spilled over.

Harry picked up his pace and started a second lap. He hoped his dad was watching.

18

He flew back to Chile three days after Christmas. It was a miserable, bumpy ride, and in the sleepless night hours Harry couldn't help but recall the smooth flight south nearly a year ago, Jean's head soft on his shoulder. Their relationship had been intense for a moment, but crumbled the second it was tested. Had his relationship with Marisol been tested? To calm his mind he thought about how her smile would be waiting for him at the airport, and managed to bury any questions for a while. But he knew his optimism was a shallow grave. The plane lurched again and Harry gripped the armrest, eyes shut tight.

Marisol *was* waiting when the flight touched down. Her black curls bounced as she ran to meet him. She didn't seem eight years older than him, or at least, she didn't make him feel eight years younger. Lalo had quit his advertising job and flown off to the U.S. while Harry was traveling with Lewis. He'd written only once, Marisol said, a cryptic note on a postcard of the Statue of Liberty, mailed inside an envelope for privacy: "Things are moving. *Viva la revolución.*"

As the months slid by, Harry did his job, the way

his father would have wanted, visiting schools all over Santiago to start and nurture baseball programs, give promotional talks and demonstrations, show instructional films. Four times a week he practiced with the 12-year-old all-stars, preparing them for the upcoming national championship in Arica.

Then he saw his pitcher fall off the bus.

Tuesday afternoon practice was over. Harry could never get the entire all-star team together except on weekends, because some kids had morning classes and others went in the afternoon. Poorly paid teachers had to work longer hours to cover both sessions, yet students still overcrowded the schools. That morning's *El Mercurio* had trumpeted Pinochet's announcement that the Air Force had bought four new Mirage fighter planes from France. Chile's future was at stake, said the president. Priorities, Harry thought, as at the bus stop little Barata adjusted the safety pin that held up his threadbare blue jeans, and wound up to hurl an imaginary baseball. Harry ruffled the kid's cowlick. The runt of the team had pitched well again today. He grinned and followed through on his pitch.

Classes must have just let out, because the bus rolled up to the stop jammed with blue-uniformed school kids. Younger ones rode municipal buses free when school was in session; older kids only had to pay half a peso. Even the steps were crowded, but any Santiago bus rider knew that if you kept pushing somehow you'd fit into the crush of bodies. A few people squeezed off and Harry moved aside to let a wheezing old lady, totteringly fat and carrying a mesh bag of groceries, climb the steps first. Children pulled at her arms to get her up, but Harry didn't have a socially acceptable way to help — he couldn't very well shove her from behind. He waited until she'd reached the second step before muscling in, after transferring his wallet to his front pocket. The woman only had a bill and the driver had to waste time making change. Harry twisted his neck and saw Barata clinging to the handrail, his entire upper body outside the bus as it pulled away.

A *paco* sat in the front seat, a policeman wearing the familiar military green uniform with cracked white leather belt and holster. Like elementary school children, *pacos* didn't pay to ride. The old woman stood panting, ankles nearly as thick as her knees, with no room to even set down her bag. Give her your seat, you prick, Harry thought. The cop finally registered her presence, and checked the nearby seats to see if there was a student or other man who might be expected to give up his seat.

"Take my seat, *señora*," said the disgusted voice of the woman sitting next to him. She began to rise.

Shamed, the *paco* stood up quickly. The driver hit the brakes and the old woman slammed backwards into Harry, who knocked a gum-chewing girl into the metal dashboard. Barata gave a surprised yelp. The woman next to the *paco* looked out the window and screamed.

Harry shoved people aside. Barata lay crumpled against the front tire of a parked black Mercedes, blood oozing from his mouth. A chunk of his scalp hung from the silver spokes of the wheel. His lips quivered but no words emerged; the rest of him was as inert as a neglected doll. Harry picked up a bloody tooth, then another. He gagged and acid vomit burned his throat.

"Hand over the teeth," the *paco* demanded. "I saw you take them."

"I only —" Harry's rage cut him off. "*Do* something!" he said.

The *paco* buttoned the teeth in his shirt pocket. "Back!" he barked at the growing crowd. "Stay back!"

Harry ran for an ambulance. A man at the third gate down answered and promised to call, though he wouldn't let Harry inside. Sprinting back he heard sirens wailing. A police car beat the ambulance by five minutes.

"Is he dead?" a boy asked. He stared open-mouthed at the broken body.

Harry felt his eyelids twitching.

"I think he's dead," the boy said.

Barata was motionless when he was loaded into the ambulance. The maid of the Mercedes owner pulled a garden hose out to the sidewalk and rinsed off the wheel, a can of chrome polish at her feet.

"Damn it, Marisol, it's true! *Paco* stands up, driver slams on the brakes. Why? Because he saw the *paco* and panicked, because he thought he'd get a ticket for unsafe driving with people hanging off. It was an instinctive reaction." Harry was ripping a wine cork to shreds with his fingernails, dropping the pieces in the ashtray where a cone of Marisol's incense burned.

Marisol stirred a pot of steaming beans. "But Harry, try to be fair. It was a tragedy, but how can the *paco* be faulted for giving up his seat to an old lady?"

"Because he waited, that's why! If he'd stood up when she first got on, before the bus moved, nothing would have happened! My boy would still be alive!"

He glared at the wispy ribbon of incense smoke. Jasmine hovered in the air. Marisol rubbed his neck from behind, thumbs kneading the hairline, then worked down to his shoulders. Having her near was warm comfort, even when they didn't share a word. But comfort was not forgetfulness. It could not defuse his hate.

Marisol rested her chin on top of his head. "It's terrible, Harry. Terrible. But blaming people won't bring the boy back. I'm sure the *paco* didn't want him to die."

"Of course he didn't! *He* didn't kill Barata, his attitude did. But don't you see? You can't separate the man from the uniform with these guys, and the uniforms infect everything. This country has to stand up to the uniforms while there's still spirit left." He felt smothered by guns and crewcuts, by polished buttons and marching boots.

"Yes, *querido*, but foolish chances lead to disappointments — or worse. If you're not happy, what good is anything?"

"I suppose Tito is happy? He's having a fine time, right? 'No record of any Quiroz or Vaca at this institution.' God knows what they did to him."

"Who wants to play coloring?"

Panchy stood in the doorway, coloring books in one hand and a box of nubby crayons in the other. "You can have *El Ratón Mickey*, Harry. It's newer, see?" She set down the crayons and flipped the mostly uncolored pages, her face eager and hopeful.

Harry smiled at her. "Sure, *mijita*, let's play coloring," and Panchy skipped off to the living room.

"She is why I have to be careful," Marisol whispered.

"I know." Harry remembered the night of Marisol's argument with Lalo, the night of her desperate dance. "But she's also why we need to fight to change things."

He kissed her, and she returned the kiss urgently. It was time to tell her.

"I've decided to sing at Jorge Alacrán's *peña*," he said.

"*Maravilloso!*" Marisol hooked her fingers in his belt. Then her expression darkened. "But what if Castle finds out?"

"Hurry, Harry! I already have the grass all colored in green and I'm starting on the sky!"

He gripped Marisol's wrists. "I'm sick of being afraid," he said, and went out to fill in empty pages.

The *peña* was packed, all tables full and people standing two-deep against the walls and the bar. Although she had promised not to, he knew that Marisol had advertised his performance. And why not? If more people came, more would know his solidarity with them. You're not afraid, he told himself again. You're nervous; that's normal. But you're not afraid.

"Lalo was on *gringo* TV," Mauricio said, jabbing out his cigarette in a clamshell ashtray. Smoke streamed from his nose and mouth. "My cousin Aurelio in Washington saw him on the news, at a rally protesting Letelier's murder."

"Waving his fist and yelling?" Veronica asked.

"Probably. It was Lalo, after all. Aurelio said he looked thinner than usual, and the *gringos* walking by barely paid any attention."

"You hear that, *gringo?*" Jorge said laughing. He clapped Harry on the back. "Maybe the *chilenos* will not listen to you either!" Everybody laughed and drank. Harry was thinking of Lalo, who gave up a high-paying job for his beliefs. He wished Lalo could be at the *peña*, seeing Harry take a stand. He decided to play the song he'd just finished for Lalo.

Smoke thickened in the room. Harry could never get used to how many Chileans smoked, and how much. He thought of Barata's funeral, sitting in church with Barata's solemn teammates. He couldn't imagine any of those kids dragging on cigarettes. Death comes too quickly to need help. He remembered the maid hosing off the Mercedes tire. He remembered rolling Barata's teeth like dice into the *paco's* beefy palm. Harry's hands were tight fists under the table. He unclenched them and tried to relax.

"Have some more *chicha,* it smooths out your voice," Jorge said. The carafe clinked on the glass as he gave Harry a refill without waiting for an answer. Harry felt the potent wine exaggerating his senses, heightening the hot, smoky closeness of the room. He sucked the tart taste off his tongue and sipped again.

Veronica touched his forearm. "Careful, Harry, *chicha* can kick you in the *culo.*"

"Ai, Vero, you're worse than *Mamá,*" Marisol said. "Harry's an artist, and artists are always alcoholics and drug addicts. He can't help it."

"A toast to the gringo!" Jorge cried. "An artist!" Glasses clinked over the middle of the table and tilted into purple-dyed mouths.

Harry was the second of three acts. A five-person *conjunto* opened, playing traditional *altiplano* instruments and singing folkloric ballads and Andean tunes. Many of the songs dealt with the historic oppression of peasants and laborers. Harry silently applauded the group for not doing *El Condor Pasa,* a good song, but as overexposed as "My Way." Claps and whistles brought them back for an encore, then the stage was empty except for two guitar cases off to one side.

The calm Harry had cultivated all day began to break down. Sweat trickled like ants down his flanks. Marisol's reassuring hand rested on his knee, but his mind was a scary blank, suddenly devoid of lyrics. At least he had taped a list of songs on his guitar. The calluses on his fingertips drummed the rough wooden table. They were sore from a week of hard practicing. Jorge pointed to him and approached the stage.

"Turn around," Marisol said.

A grinning rock of a man with a mustache like a woolly bear caterpillar extended his hand. Harry immediately recognized Lucho Godoy, the singer he had heard that first night he had come with Lalo. Harry shook; the guy had a grip like a linebacker. Godoy was the best songwriter Harry had heard in Chile, but his anti-establishment songs would never get recorded.

"Warm them up for me," Godoy said.

"*You're* next?" Harry said. A bolt of panic shot through him. No wonder the place was packed.

Godoy raised his glass. "Knock 'em dead, *amigo*."

Jorge was announcing Harry's name. Marisol was the first to begin clapping. He maneuvered his way to the stage with dreamy detachment, as if his every movement belonged to someone else. He needed a deep breath and took it when he knelt to pick up his grandfather's old Martin, blond and polished and nestled in the snug brown plush of the case, new strings gleaming. Harry raked them with his thumbnail, and to his relief heard them ring out in tune.

After a wavering smile, he made grammar mistakes in the first two sentences he spoke. Spanish felt clumsy in his mouth. Nervousness didn't transform the audience into a faceless mass; in fact, he tended to pick out individuals. An obese man in a black beret poked a finger at a page in a slim book and looked up triumphantly at his companion, an overly made-up woman with a wine glass to her lips who did her best to ignore him. Mauricio the poet scribbled furiously on a paper napkin. Marisol sat with legs crossed at the knees. She held her glass high and pointed to it, adding a questioning arch of her eyebrows, and Harry nodded yes. She brought him a full glass and everyone applauded, then laughed when she kissed him on the cheek. As easy as stepping through thin ice, she had broken his tension and headed back to her seat. He toasted the crowd, drank, and let the music talk.

He played mostly his own tunes, set off by an occasional Bob Dylan or Neil Young that most people recognized. Harry's confidence grew with every song; each one seemed easier, more natural than the last. He didn't need to refer to his list, his voice felt true and strong, the notes sparkled off the steel strings. The Martin played like a helpful partner, eager to make him sound his best.

"I wrote this song for my friend Lalo Garcia," he said near the end of his set. Expectant faces watched him, and it struck Harry how so many people knew about Lalo in one context or another — artist or expatriate, torture victim or friend, anti-junta campaigner or well-paid advertising designer. He represented so many Chileans and the ambivalence permeating their lives. Harry hoped many of them understood when he sang:

He never rescued his people
though to some he was a symbol.

And he was true to his art
though never quite true to himself.

He swallowed the dregs of his *chicha*, smiled his thanks and lovingly replaced the guitar in its case. The applause astounded him. Shouts for an encore brought him back to the stage, where he played Victor Jara's *"Te Recuerdo Amanda,"* about a factory worker who is killed in a labor rebellion, leaving Amanda to live on alone. The song was banned in Chile. A power welled up in Harry as he sang the final words, a feeling that he was doing something more than complaining about the system, something unequivocally worthwhile. You *can* throw off the straitjacket, he thought. We're starting right here. Harry was so exhilarated he lifted Marisol out of her chair and kissed her full on the lips.

"Hey *gringo,*" Godoy called over, his nose red from drinking. "After you, I'm afraid to go on! Why don't you just play some more?"

"No way." Harry hugged Marisol with one arm. "Would you leave a woman this beautiful twice in one night?"

"Don't worry, I'll take good care of her!" Godoy shook with laughter.

Jorge gave Harry the thumbs-up and brought another carafe of wine, on the house. But Harry hardly noticed.

"*Gracias,*" he whispered to Marisol as they sat down.

"For what?"

"For bringing me the wine, for being here — for everything."

"Let's drink wine tonight and love each other and not worry about tomorrow. Promise?"

"I love you because you're so sensible," he said.

They hadn't gotten drunk for a long time, but tonight they were working on it. Marisol even accepted a cigarette from Mauricio. Harry was enjoying that ideal state of intoxication when the interior glow and the exterior situation mesh perfectly, a warm sensation of well-being, an energetic contentment. The friends at his table, and Godoy and Jorge — they were the hope for this country and would not forget what freedom meant. The cool *chicha* soothed his throat. Mauricio winked and held up the verses he'd jotted on the napkin. Godoy was belting out a ditty about the joys of Chilean wine, as Marisol's fingers traced gentle patterns on the back of Harry's hand. He decided to come to the *peña* often, where people were not afraid.

At first, no one knew it was a raid.

Applause for Godoy drowned out the original commotion. Harry saw the four *pacos*, nightsticks drawn, before he heard anything unusual. Some people tried to escape but police blocked the exits. Jorge was talking to a monkeyish little cop, gesturing with his hands and pointing toward the stage. Godoy grimaced in disgust and started another song, but everyone's attention was backward. He stopped and took a drink. Harry's high disappeared in an instant, his palms sweating at the prospect of Castle giving him the Braniff award. Don't be afraid, he told himself.

"Damn them," Marisol said. "Damn them forever."

"What right have you to disturb a peaceful gathering, people listening to music?" Jorge's voice easily carried throughout the room; dead silence had fallen.

"Subversive propaganda has no place in this country!"

225

"But —"

"*Silencio!*"

"You can't —"

A *paco* rammed his billy club into Jorge's kidneys and he snapped back with a groan. The cop grabbed him in a headlock and dragged him, moaning and clutching his side, out the door. They shoved Godoy face-first against the wall and cuffed his hands behind him.

"*Mi guitarra,*" he pleaded, but the cop flung it aside. Harry heard the wood crack and a string popped loose. Godoy's expression of misery fused into fear as he was led away, the broken string still bobbing.

"*Documentos,*" demanded another *paco*. By law, Chileans must carry a green government identification card. The cops were checking every person in the *peña*. Harry handed over his red card, which identified him as a foreigner, to a baby-faced cop with a greasy nose.

He stared at the card, comparing Harry to it. His hair was much longer than in the photograph, taken when he first arrived, and his face was thinner. The cop held out the card and Harry reached for it. The *paco*'s hand slapped to his pistol.

"Hands down!"

"Harry!" Marisol cried.

"Shut up," said the cop. He peered at Harry. "*Americano?*"

Congratulations, Harry thought, you can read. "*Sí,*" he said.

"*Pasaporte.*"

"I'm a Chilean resident."

"You are a foreigner. Your passport."

"The law says that a resident only needs to carry a card."

Baby features twisted into an ugly sneer. "I need *you* to tell me the law?"

Harry remained silent.

"*Do I?*"

"No."

"No, what?"

"No, sir."

"I bet you're as red as this card," he said, jabbing it at Harry like a knife. "*Comunista.*"

"No!" Marisol said.

The cop dropped the card. "Pick it up."

Harry hesitated. The *paco's* hand closed around his nightstick.

"Are you *deaf*, communist?"

Fearing a knee in the mouth or a hardwood club crunching his skull, Harry genuflected to retrieve the government's proof that he existed. His heart slammed against his chest, but he forced himself to straighten slowly, passively, making no motion that could possibly be construed as aggressive.

"Move it, faggot!" The *paco* shoved Harry's forehead with rough knuckles and forced him upright, then moved on to Marisol. Harry thought of Jackie Robinson and restraint. The *paco* thrust Marisol's card at her as if disappointed that it was in order, and strode to the next table, black boots clomping.

The cops kept them waiting. Harry imagined what it must have been like in the National Stadium, trapped, terrified, but not too scared to be bored, your life in the hands of men with guns who don't need a reason to hurt you. They weren't allowed to speak, and their hands had to stay above the table. No smoking; Mauricio was frantic within minutes. Veronica gnawed on her fingernails

227

till blood seeped from her thumb. Marisol hunched forward with her chin in one hand. Harry rubbed the inside of her calf with his foot.

Over an hour passed. Two new *pacos* marched in and headed for the stage. One unplugged the microphone and hauled it away, along with Godoy's wounded guitar. The other grabbed Harry's Martin.

Harry hadn't latched the case, and when the *paco* jerked up the handle the top flopped open like a trap door. His grandfather's guitar tumbled out and crashed on its face with a horrible splintering twang. Everyone in the place jumped. Marisol grabbed Harry's wrist to restrain him. Jaw clamped shut, he glared at the *paco* who stuffed the guitar back in its case and hurried off, shoulders slumped and a trace of guilt in his eyes, like a bounty hunter with the corpse of a man the sheriff wanted alive. Total impotence gnawed Harry's guts as part of his life and heritage was hauled out like garbage. He wanted to scream. He wanted to destroy something. He sat motionless, stone-faced, giving away nothing.

They were released half an hour later, after being ticketed for disturbing the peace and creating a public nuisance. They could pay a stiff fine and avoid going to court. Outside they filed silently past the cops and waited until they were out of earshot. "Don't be afraid," Harry forced himself to say. "It's all right now."

Marisol's lip curled. "Don't patronize me, Harry. I'm *not* afraid. And it's *not* all right."

Mauricio sucked on a cigarette like a pacifier. The smoke stung Harry's nose. The only copies of the songs he had written in Chile were in that guitar case. He wanted to help, to be part of Chile's return to freedom — but he did not want to go to wherever it was they took Godoy. He put his arm around Marisol, and felt an almost imperceptible tightening.

He tapped Mauricio on the shoulder. "Got an extra cigarette?" he asked.

19

The streets near the majestic old Teatro Caupolicán were packed, but still people pushed to get closer. New bodies jostled for better spots, squeezing through spaces that eventually refused to open, and the human knot fanned outward. Harry hadn't seen such a crowd since an outdoor Grateful Dead concert the summer before he came to Chile. The riot police kept stepping backwards, to avoid getting trapped in the throng. A few *pacos* on horseback had tried to assert authority, but the street in front of the theater was impassable now without risking a riot, so they pranced around the outskirts and did their best to look in control. Harry lifted Marisol's wrist to check her watch. Twenty minutes until the speech of Eduardo Frei, Chile's president before Salvador Allende was elected in 1970.

"I hope Frei hammers the bastards," Harry said. "Too bad Lalo couldn't fly in today." He looked at the expectant, hopeful faces surrounding them, and smiled grimly. "Pinochet must be squirming," he said, and the smile widened.

Marisol's fingernails dug into his arm. "You know

there are spies," she whispered. Harry stared off at the theater, at the big loudspeakers mounted atop the stone steps. His smile hardened.

"*Sí*," he said. He was thinking about the ballot for the upcoming plebiscite: a red, white and blue star for *Sí*, approval of the new constitution and eight more years of Pinochet as president; a black box for *No* if you disapprove and, as the government's propaganda insisted, want to throw the country into Communistic anarchy and violence. Pro-*No* groups were not allowed to campaign in any of the mass media, while *Sí* advertisements bombarded the populace every day through TV and radio, newspapers and magazines.

"Three cheers for democracy," Harry had said when he saw how it worked.

He turned to Marisol. She bit her lip and shivered, hands stuffed deep in her coat pockets. The mid-June air was already crisp with winter; Marisol's breath formed faint wisps of steam. A full moon shone. As he occasionally did, each time with surprise, Harry suddenly noticed how short Marisol was. Her view ended with the sweatered shoulders of the man in front of her.

"Frei! Frei! Frei!" Scattered voices began the chorus as the time for the speech drew near, and more and more people joined in, thrusting their fists in the air as confidence grew. But few of those in back near the police dared to do anything. On their skittish horses, the stern riders towered over the crowd.

An elfin man in a black stocking cap pried his way through the mass of bodies, passing out small yellow leaflets picturing a downturned thumb. DOWN WITH THE DICTATORSHIP! they read. Harry flipped his over. NO TO THE FASCIST BUTCHER CONSTITUTION! FREE SPEECH IS A RIGHT NOT A PRIVILEGE! The Pinochet constitution had no provision for freedom of speech or of the press, yet was daily hailed by the government as a triumph for liberty and democracy.

Harry scornfully thought of Steve Castle. As Chilean residents, Peace Corps volunteers were allowed to vote, but Castle had prohibited it. Stay completely out of politics, said the memo in their mailboxes, and steer clear of this speech tonight. Not that the actual tally mattered, because the military counted the votes and no one could challenge the results, but Harry had made up his mind to vote, anyway. He couldn't forget the bruises dark as eggplant on Jorge's arms and back, when he was released from jail four days after the raid. Black and blue and Harry's smashed guitar spoke far louder than a bureaucrat's memo.

"Do you smell it?" Marisol said.

Harry raised his nose and sniffed. She had a much better olfactory sense than he did, but soon the odor of burning marijuana was unmistakable. His skin tingled. Gooseflesh formed, but not from cold. Meaningless in itself, in some tiny way the pot represented a challenge. He took a long hit off the joint when it came by.

"Harry!"

"What?" he croaked, holding the smoke deep in his lungs.

"Use your head."

"I am. Have some." He thought that would make her laugh. It didn't. He gave her the *pito* but she passed it on without smoking.

232

"How is smoking *hierba* going to change anything? It's just asking for trouble — for no reason."

"I'm through being afraid," he said, and immediately felt like a melodramatic idiot. But he swore he could feel the vibrations of the crowd, an unstoppable ground swell. Things *could* change, if good people conquered their fears.

A shrill whistle blew, piercing, painful. Bodies collided and entangled, surged around them. Harry lost his balance and stumbled backward against Marisol, but people were clumped so thick she didn't go down. A mounted cop barely restrained his horse at the fringe of the excitement, but two others on foot swung billy clubs as they bulled through spectators. One *paco* grabbed a fleeing man by the collar and yanked him back like a roped calf. The captive's hand flew up and a cloud of yellow leaflets shot into the air. No one tried to catch them. The man kicked and struggled until the other cop clubbed him on the temple. A black stocking cap slumped over the man's strangely accepting face, then fell and was trampled underfoot. The crowd filled in the gap like water. After cautious glances, people stooped to pick up the leaflets. Most read them furtively, then dropped them again; some slipped them into their pockets.

Frei's speech began and the crowd fell silent. Most had no idea of the incident with the leaflet man. That's the way it always is, Harry thought. It's hard for people to know the truth in the first place. Arrests don't make headlines here. News is women in skimpy bikinis, and soccer scores, and the international song festival.

"The election is a farce," orated the bodiless voice,

233

distorted by loud volume and echoing off the buildings. "This address is prohibited from even being broadcast on the radio. If the government is so confident of its policies, what is it afraid of?" The audience burst into applause, drowning out the next sentence. Marisol, listening intently, clapped too, but her gloves muffled the sound. Harry could tell she was surrendering to the moment. He thought of her story about the 1970 mini-Woodstock outside Santiago during the heady early days of Allende, how thousands more than expected showed up to the concert, and the point arrived when they could not be turned back. So they went forward. "They had brains enough not to make us fight for the right to go inside and be peaceful," Marisol had said. She tilted her head, as if listening to her own words, and laughed at what she heard. "I danced all day and never got tired. We were starting a new way of life and together we would make it work. Nobody doubted that."

"— the blatant violation of basic human rights. How long can it be tolerated? When will 3,000 *desaparecidos* be accounted for? Where is *their* justice? Where is *their* vote?" An elbow nudged Harry's ribs; someone handed him a stack of the yellow leaflets. Upside-down as he held them, the thumb pointed skyward, toward the moon, while the words were unreadable scratches. The elbow jabbed Harry again: "Pass 'em down." He took two, Marisol took one with hardly a glance and the pile kept moving. People craned their necks to look at the loudspeakers. Harry watched the sky. He saw the man in the moon and remembered the man with no face. It must be freezing in that asylum. He wondered if Nurse Chacón still worked there, if the boy still beat his head against the wall, if the doctor was still a patient. He wondered where they had taken Tito.

Tonight, he decided. Tonight I ask her.

Wild applause followed the speech, unrestrained approval that continued for minutes, then transformed into rhythmic clapping. Harry joined in; Marisol took off her gloves to make noise. But Frei did not appear on the steps. There was no encore. Watching the mute loudspeakers and each other, the crowd began to realize that its reason for being was over. Their excuse was gone. Faces so recently flushed with victory looked to neighbors for guidance, and saw only mirrors. *Pacos* on the fringes ordered people to disperse. Slowly, not wanting to miss anything, turning around every few steps to check, they left. Those formerly hidden in the womb of the crowd became the new outsiders, and soon followed. The knot loosened.

"Just like that?" Harry said. "That's the end?"

Marisol was beaming. "To hell with the end. Maybe that was a beginning." Energized, she grasped his arm and led him along the damp sidewalk. "*Vamos, mi amor,* come see where we saved the world many a night."

A few blocks away, *El Progreso* was packed with bodies and smoke. One look told them it would be a long wait for a table. People were drinking as quickly as they were talking. Fog thickened the windows.

They leaned against a streetlight, their breath frosty clouds.

"It feels so strange," Marisol said. "I don't recognize a single face in there."

"We could get a drink somewhere else."

"I don't want a drink. Frei's speech, it made me — I

don't know, I wanted you to see where we met in the old days."

"That's OK. I did see it."

She smiled, not sadly, but wistfully. "But not the way it was," she said.

More people wedged into the bar. A subway train rumbled under the sidewalk. Across the street, lights flashed and tinny music played at a small amusement park.

"Come on," Harry said. "Let's ride the Ferris wheel."

Marisol looked dubious. "If you want," she said.

The park was practically deserted on such a chilly evening. The ride operators yawned and scratched themselves, envious of the ticket seller in her warm booth. They lit cigarettes and waited for church bells to tell them they'd made it through another fifteen minutes.

"Last ride," said the attendant, pulling the safety bar over their heads. "Don't get too scared." He pushed forward a lever.

The wheel's rusty gears creaked as it carried them higher. Suddenly it stopped, stranding them at the top. Harry leaned over the side and saw the operator grinning up at them. The man tipped his cap.

Harry's mouth was dry. "This is as good a time as any —"

"*Mira las putas!* See? By the fountain?"

Marisol leaned ahead to point. Two teenage girls, freezing in their miniskirts, stood in high heels next to an old stone fountain, talking to a pair of men in leather jackets. A minute later, the four of them walked around a corner and out of sight. At the fountain other women waited, with blank expressions and arms folded across their chests for warmth — until a man came by and they dropped their arms to advertise.

"So sad," Marisol said. "But amazing to watch from up here. It's like a dance."

Harry remembered Lalo calling *himself* a whore. The wheel groaned, and began to turn again. Harry felt more nervous than at the *peña*, waiting to go on stage. On each descent, his stomach dropped a few feet lower than the car. Harry slid closer to Marisol. The city went up and down. "Come with me to Arica for the tournament," he said. "When it's over we'll head right for Peru. We'll finally make it to Machu Picchu."

"It's less than a month away."

"Perfect. Panchy's in school, and you know your mother would love to have her for a few weeks. Arica's supposed to be beautiful, too, a nice warm place in the winter."

"Careful, *mijito*, or I might just say yes. After Frei's speech, anything is possible." She looked up at the moon, but Harry could tell she was seeing some other picture in her mind.

"Machu Picchu," she said to no one, or maybe to the moon.

The next time they reached the top, Harry searched for the right way to phrase the question. Their hands were in each other's coat pockets.

"In the long run," he said finally, "as long as we're together nothing else matters."

"In the *long* run, what does any of it matter?" she replied.

Harry stared at the moon, and the man's face seemed to change expressions. Lalo was coming home tomorrow, and they would celebrate. Up and down, around and around they went, alone together in the moonlit wheel. As their car settled to the bottom and the brake screeched, Harry decided to wait until he and Marisol stood atop Machu Picchu before asking her to marry him.

20

P~age~ nine — on the bottom." Harry flung down the newspaper. "A massive crowd in downtown Santiago and it hardly makes the papers."

"*Más cafe?*" asked the waiter, food stains already accumulating on his white jacket.

"*No, gracias,*" Marisol said. Harry shook his head. Lalo's plane was due any minute, at 10:08. It was on schedule, so Harry figured he'd have time for some catching-up and a good lunch before his two o'clock practice. Lalo had been gone for seven months. It didn't seem possible.

"Do you think he's changed, Marisol?"

"More *loco* than ever. And with more stories." She sipped her coffee, gazing out at the runway, then rapped the paper with her knuckles. "At least it was *in* there. And at least it happened."

"Still, page nine on the bottom. . . ."

"All I'm saying is it's better than before. And someday we'll win."

"Someday."

"Yes. And I'll be waiting, and ready. Will you?"

"I'll be where you are," he said.

The plane landed on time. Standing at the railing of the second-story patio, Harry and Marisol scanned the debarking passengers. They spotted Lalo halfway across the tarmac, elegant in a blue pinstriped suit under a Panama hat. Marisol laughed at the sight.

"Lalo," she whispered, and rose on her toes. Despite her arm around his waist, Harry felt a jealous twinge. She waved with her other arm. Lalo saw them, and winked as he tipped his hat. He had shaved off his beard.

Lalo was nearing the front of the customs line. He solemnly held up one finger, then unzipped his flight bag and produced a fifth of Jack Daniel's. "Tonight!" he called out in English, displaying the bottle like a trophy. He did look gaunt, but younger without his beard.

Marisol sighed. "Whiskey for his ulcer. The *loco* wants to die. Why can't he care as much about himself as his friends do?"

Harry's brain agreed with her, but another part of him argued that Lalo deserved the celebration, regardless of the cost. "Is it worth postponing death till tomorrow if you don't live today?"

"You can live without killing yourself," she said.

Lalo set his open bag on the counter. Cool as a diplomat, he took his passport from the inside breast-pocket of his jacket and passed it to the uniformed inspector, who scrutinized each page. Twice he looked up at Lalo, then back to the passport. He opened a drawer and flipped through the pages on a clipboard, then compared the passport to a point marked by his finger. He nodded to two waiting military police officers. They stepped forward and flanked Lalo. One of them said something to him, while the other grabbed his arm. Some passengers stared numbly. Some pretended not to notice. Lips parted, forehead furrowed, Marisol leaned into the railing. Harry's palms sweated on the metal.

The soldier hauled Lalo behind the counter. Lalo tried to shake him off but the grip tightened. His partner carried Lalo's bag, still open, his fingers wrapped around the bottle. They stopped to frisk him, in plain sight of everyone, and he finally exploded.

"I already went through the goddamn metal detector, you fascists!"

They shoved him toward a rear door, and he stumbled. "Lalo!" Marisol cried, but cut it short with her hand over her mouth. Lalo never looked their way. The soldiers pushed him into a room and yanked the door shut behind them like a vault.

The P.A. system announced a departure. The customs line moved efficiently again. Harry and Marisol leaned on the railing, staring at a cloud-gray door and trying not to admit how defeated they felt. Harry tasted salty blood where he'd been chewing his lip.

They waited.

"We have to do something," he said.

"What?" The word caught in her throat, and she said it again. "*Qué?*"

Harry didn't know how to comfort her. Marisol wiped her eyes.

"What if they planted drugs on him?" she said.

"— some red troublemaker itching for another chance to ruin this country."

Harry's head spun at the sound of American English. Two tall men in business suits passed by, snappy attaché cases in hand, one sandy-haired, temples graying, with gold-rimmed glasses, the other twenty years younger and thick like a fullback out of training.

"He bent my ear all flight about the immorality of doing business here. Hell, Ron, if he spent half the energy working as he does crying we'd all be a lot better off."

"You said it, Mr. Dreyer."

"*Bob*," said the older man.

"Okay . . . Bob."

Bob grinned and clapped his protegé on the back. "How 'bout a drink? The stockholders owe us one after *that* flight. Nine hours in coach? I mean, Jesus Christ."

Harry barely caught the last words as they moved away. He wondered why he didn't despise them, why he felt as much like laughing at them as he did like shaking some sense into their skulls. They were pitiful, yet they were powerful, probably more powerful than they realized. But could they begin to imagine what goes on behind gray doors? Their idea of injustice was flying coach instead of first class.

The last passenger filed through customs. Harry and Marisol stood alone at the railing. The customs official eyed them, but made no remark. No one emerged from the gray door. Marisol stared at the clock.

Morning turned to afternoon. More planes arrived, and more people passed through the gates. At 1:30, Harry knew he would miss practice. He made three phone calls, and though no one could cover for him he finally found someone to at least make it to the field and tell the boys practice was canceled. Suddenly, he heard his name over the P.A.

At the customs gate, the official inspected his I.D. and frisked him, then led him to the gray door. He walked into a cheaply furnished office, vinyl, fake wood, photos of the four members of the junta the only decoration. Another door on the opposite wall. No torture implements, no goon cracking brass knuckles. He frowned at his naiveté. What did you expect, a dungeon with a rack and an iron maiden? This is an *airport*.

The other door opened. Lalo entered with hands cuffed in front of him, the two soldiers following a stride behind. He stared at Harry like a death-row atheist confronting a priest; silently he held out the handcuffs to his jailers. They shook their heads.

"Five minutes, Garcia," said the smaller soldier, a captain. "Starting now."

Lalo's nose wrinkled. "What's it like knowing your neighbors despise you?"

The big, block-jawed soldier raised his fist, but the other stopped him with one stern "No!" The captain's mouth twisted into a smile.

"Four and a half minutes," he said. He folded his arms and leaned against the wall, whistling a mindless, irritating tune.

Lalo and Harry went to the opposite corner. "Lalo, what's —"

"Listen! Just listen. And keep it in English, got it?" He jerked his thumb at their audience. "They're sending me back. The bastards won't let me in the country."

"But how —"

"Fuck *how!* They do what they want and that's it. Fuck *how!*" His face was only inches away, his eyes wide and hypnotic, not releasing Harry for a second. His breath smelled of whiskey.

"They had me under surveillance the whole time I was in the States, and now they call me a traitor. *I'm the* traitor!" He clutched his belly, and though his face betrayed nothing Harry knew his ulcer was on fire. "In two hours I'll be flying back to New York — six hundred fucking bucks one way."

"Tick-tock, tick-tock." Guffaws from behind them.

"Ignore the scum," Lalo commanded. "Don't give them the satisfaction of seeing you burn."

"Time's almost up, Garcia. Better kiss sweet-cheeks good-bye while you've got the chance. *Maricón de mierda.*" They laughed like drunks at a stag party. "Three minutes, queer."

Harry marveled at Lalo's self-control. He realized Lalo was trying to teach him, to show him how to deal with this type of madness. Harry ached to hug him, but he held back. He loathed the mocking falsetto voices of the guards, ignorant and untouchable, and that moment convinced him that frustration is even worse than fear.

"Maybe this is only harrassment, Lalo. Someday they'll let you in again. They have to."

Lalo snorted. *"Have* to? This government doesn't *have* to do anything except someday fall by its own rotten weight. Listen. I called you in because I don't want them recording her name, if they don't have it already. A gringo cries to his embassy and gets deported at the worst, but a Chilean. . . ." Lalo wiped one eye with a finger and his handcuffs rattled.

"What I'm trying to say is watch out for yourself and take good care of her. Why's that so hard for me?"

"I will, Lalo. Trust me." Lalo offered his manacled hand and Harry shook it.

"Hurry, tell me about the speech last night. Was it —"

"One minute, time's up."

"But that's only four minutes!" Harry blurted out.

"The gringo faggot is teaching us to count," the captain said, sweet as a kindergarten teacher. He started toward them, his stooge a step behind. "Isn't that nice of the gringo faggot, Diaz?"

Diaz grinned like a redneck eyeing a skinny long-hair. "Real nice of the gringo faggot," he said.

The captain checked him with a stony stare.

Diaz's grin snapped to attention. "Nice of the gringo faggot, *sir!*"

Lalo smirked, and Diaz smacked him on the ear. He looked toward his superior penitently, but the captain gave no sign of disapproval.

Lalo glared at both of them. "Suck skunk shit," he said pleasantly in English.

Harry snickered and Diaz cracked his face with the back of his hand. The blow struck his nose, causing a few involuntary tears to spill out.

"Bawl, queer. Which one of you queers gets on top?" the captain sneered. "Get out of here, Bayliss — I'll remember you. Let's go, Garcia."

"Tell her calling out my name was stupid," Lalo said quickly. "She has to be more careful."

"I said move!" The captain punched Lalo in the kidney. Diaz prodded Harry toward the gray door with a night stick in his spine.

"So long, queer. Does Garcia have a big one, *maricón?*"

Diaz's cackling followed Harry out the door. His legs were rubber, muscles quaking as one foot fell in front of the other. The shock hit him that he might never see Lalo again, that his last, most vivid image of his friend would be in a pinstriped suit, handcuffed, stumbling toward the opposite door.

"*Hasta luego,*" the customs official said. Harry slid past without responding.

Marisol was staring at the floor, elbow on the plastic armrest and chin in her hand. He plopped into the chair next to her.

"They won't let him in. He's taking the first plane back to New York."

She nodded. They sat silently, an awkward silence Harry wasn't sure how to break. The kind of silence he'd never known with Marisol.

"He didn't ask to see me," she said finally. She licked her finger and wiped a spot of mud off her boot. Her hands trembled. She sat on them.

"He only gave them my name to protect you."

She fought for a moment, her lips quivering, then gave in. Harry kissed her hair and smelled grass and flowers. People gave them sidelong glances and hurried by. *None of them know why she's crying,* he thought. *Nobody knows.*

"Let's get out of here." He stood up, pulling her with him. "Come on. I don't want to hear his plane take off."

Marisol walked at his side like an automaton. At the car she groped for the keys in her purse, then dropped them trying to unlock the door. She kicked the door and started crying again.

Harry heard his name from a distance but didn't react at first. It couldn't be. But there it was again, insistent, undeniable. Approaching.

246

"*Gringo!* Harry! Wait up, you fucker! Yahoo!"

The pin-striped suit jogged a crazy slalom through the parked cars. Lalo leaped into Harry's arms. Marisol ran from the Citröen and they shared a joyous three-way hug.

"They let me go, gringo! The phone rang and you should have seen that prick captain's face when he answered it. I could hear someone screaming at him over the line and next thing I know he tells that fucking cretin Diaz to unlock the handcuffs. Yes!"

Lalo reached in his bag and pulled out the Jack Daniel's. "The bastards even gave my bourbon back!" He unscrewed the bottle and thrust it at Harry. "A toast, gringo! A fucking toast!"

Harry gripped the bottle with both hands, stunned. "I can't believe it," he said. "What just happened in there?"

"Buggered if I know and right now I don't give a damn! What is it you gringos say about a gift horse?"

"To a new beginning," Marisol said, and took a stout swallow without flinching.

Lalo put an arm around each of them and kissed their cheeks. "It's good to be home, amigos."

Harry drove into the sun. Traffic was light. Scum-brown smog was thickening over the city, blurring the base of the *cordillera*. A jet plane sliced the sky, leaving a ragged white scar on the blue. Harry watched the trail as it began to dissolve, then gunned the accelerator to pass a smoke-belching bus.

"Get this," Lalo said. He swigged from the bottle. "I'm fucking engaged."

Marisol hugged him from the back seat. "*You*, Lalo?"

"Congratulations," Harry said. His heart began to thump. Not faster, just harder, as if something were pressing on his chest. "Who is she?"

"I'm almost embarrassed to say. A lawyer from Washington. But somehow she's wonderful anyway."

"The world is ridiculous," Marisol said, laughing. "And I love it."

Lalo took the bottle from between his legs and sent it back to her.

"Tonight we celebrate," he said.

The neighbor's maid was sweeping the walk next door to Lalo's house. They waved and she waved back. Lalo got out to unlock the gate and Harry pulled into the driveway. Fat oranges hung on the tree in the yard. A few lay half-hidden in grass that needed mowing.

They walked toward the white stucco house. The branching cactus by the bedroom window was taller than the first red tiles of the roof. "Remember, Lalo," Harry said, "when you told me once that white was the only color for houses?"

Lalo had hardly left for the bathroom when Marisol hugged Harry so tight that he gasped. Her strength surprised him: the power in her arms, the grip in her lean, artist's fingers. Her hands rubbed down his sides, coming to a firm rest on his waist. They leaned back but remained joined at the hips, fingers intertwined behind each other, supporting each other.

"Like Siamese twins," he said. "Then we could always sleep together."

"I'd rather be together and apart, *corazón*." Her lips brushed his. "I love you, Harry Bayliss."

"That makes us even."

The toilet flushed and they broke apart. Lalo checked the refrigerator.

"We need beers!" he said. "Every homecoming needs beers."

Harry saluted. "No problem, I need to stretch my legs anyway." He took the mesh bag off a nail by the refrigerator. "I'll go to that *fuente de soda* down by the Peace Corps center."

"Take the car," Lalo said.

"Man, you've been in the States too long."

Lalo actually blushed.

Harry started walking with a light step. He felt full of ideas but tongue-tied, as if his mind were stuttering. The change had done it, the swift change from despair to elation at the airport. He adjusted his stride to miss sidewalk lines. He realized he was hungry. Time had passed. Breakfast was fuzzy. The beer would taste good. Oranges in the grass. Every step took him closer to the mountains. Snow. Oranges. Springtime in Arica in a few weeks; get out of this city for a while. Cuzco. Machu Picchu. Stuff of dreams.

A black sedan crawled around the corner. It had a long radio antenna and two short-haired men in gray suits inside. The passenger spoke into a microphone. The car crept up Lalo's street.

Then Harry heard the explosion.

Afterward he thought he must have felt the blast, but no, not a tremor. Just a huge, awful sound of disintegration, of ripping and tearing and flying apart. The sedan locked its brakes and roared down the first road away from Lalo's. Oh Jesusgod. The moment of denial exploded; the prayer got no further.

Arms pumping and lungs on fire, he ran. Two blocks, three blocks, four. The world bouncing. A hundred yards from Lalo's driveway he heard a scream, a horrible, animal shriek. He sprinted to the gate and turned the corner like third base, slipping on the driveway gravel and cracking his knee on Marisol's bumper. Blood oozed from his torn pants leg. The house's front windows were blown out, but he saw no other damage.

"Marisol!" he yelled, never so afraid. "Lalo! Answer me!"

His feet crunched on glass. That smell, what's the word — is it cordite?

Voices. A siren. Running so hard that he took a wide turn around the house, not flaring out early to cut the angle like he taught his players. Vision blurred by smoke, tears, disbelief. The studio wall, the window wall facing the mountains gaping like a messy wound, roof collapsed, tiles and glass shattered, twisted earthquake rods protruding like worms, a singed canvas impaled on one of them. Rushing closer, Harry trod on a tube of red paint and splattered his shoe. He had no time to swear. He saw. His stomach vomited while his mind still refused to register. His legs wilted as if hamstrung and he stumbled to the ground, retching up nothing. A shard of glass stabbed his palm, and bit deeper as his fist slammed the turf again and again.

A naked arm, twisted the wrong way at the elbow, stuck out of the rubble near a smashed tennis racquet.

Voices closer now, surrounding him.

"*Madre de Dios. . . .*"

"He must have been right next to it."

"Dig him out."

"Help him."

"Don't touch anything!"

Harry retreated to a world of mountains and oranges.

He heard his name as if underwater. Marisol embraced him just as he opened his eyes, and he tasted the blood on her face. It flowed from a two-inch gash on her temple.

Marisol sobbed against his chest. "Lalo went into the studio to see my painting and I got water in the kitchen for the plants. Then everything blew up. I fell and hit my head. I screamed when I saw him, God he was all. . . ."

Harry was too numb to cry — pure, dumb luck was the only reason he and Marisol were alive. How did an ambulance get here so fast? Suddenly, sickeningly, he knew why that phone call had released Lalo at the airport. Ambulance attendants rushed by with the battered body on a stretcher. Shutters clicked. It was the kind of photograph that wins awards, and it appeared on the front page of every Santiago newspaper the next morning.

21

Steve Castle scowled when Harry walked into his office. "Close the door," he said. He threw down the newspaper on his desk and jabbed a finger at the picture. It was stained by a brown coffee-cup ring. The caption called Harry a *"norteamericano no identificado."*

"I want an explanation, Bayliss, not bullshit, and it damn well better be good."

Harry had spent a bitter night. His bandaged hand throbbed. He and Marisol had woken each other with violent nightmares; they hardly slept, and got up at dawn. Castle's secretary called Harry at 9:05 and told him to report to the Peace Corps office immediately. He didn't have to ask why. He'd bought the morning paper at seven.

"Good? Sorry, it can't be good because it can't get much worse. Lalo Garcia died and my girlfriend barely survived a bomb planted to kill him."

"Planted by who?"

"By the fascists who run this country. Who do you think?"

"That's a very strong charge, Harry."

"You wanted the truth, not bullshit. You want bull-shit, read the papers."

"Radical Communist Lalo Garcia, 32," read *El Mercurio*, "was killed when a homemade bomb detonated in Garcia's La Reina home. Police say the device was similar to those involved in several other recent bombings in Santiago."

"Marisol Huerta, 31, longtime associate and lover of Garcia, was slightly wounded in the incident. An unidentified man, a *norteamericano* according to some witnesses, was also present at the scene. He appeared distraught and refused to answer questions. Police are investigating, but no charges have as yet been filed."

"They know my name," Harry said. "They made me show my I.D. But they don't want trouble with the American embassy, so they didn't let it out. They know we had nothing to do with that bomb, except as fucking targets."

"This is certainly far-fetched." Castle bit a fingernail. A Peace Corps director could get the Braniff Award for something like this.

"I *saw* them, for Christ's sake! Heading toward the house, showing up right after the explosion. How much proof do you need?"

Castle lit his pipe. He shook the match twice but it stayed lit; finally he blew it out. "Harry, Garcia's dead." Castle looked out the window, avoiding Harry's eyes. "Nothing will bring him back. But your girlfriend is all right. Why kick up a ruckus? No good will come of it."

"What 'ruckus' are you talking about? What are you so afraid of?"

"I have the welfare of an organization of the U.S.

government to worry about. I won't see it jeopardized by personal vendettas."

"What's that supposed to mean?"

"It means that as a representative of your country, you have a responsibility to more than yourself."

"Like a Chilean soldier has the responsibility to blow up innocent people if his government tells him to?"

Castle sighed and rubbed his eyes. His forehead was corrugated and a crooked furrow formed between his eyebrows. Harry looked at the wall map of Chile. The green pushpin that represented him was gone from Santiago, leaving a barely visible hole. His stomach flip-flopped; he felt dizzy and trapped. The heat was suffocating. Why was Castle running the *estufa* full blast?

"You've been one of our most successful volunteers. Nobody denies that."

Harry waited for the "but".

"But there's more to being a Peace Corps volunteer than doing good work. You of all people should be aware of our policy on drugs, and avoidance of political activity is no secret either. Yet you flaunt these restrictions by living with a suspected drug peddler and openly allying yourself with leftist causes. This is obviously counterproductive to our purposes here."

Castle folded his arms on his desk, as if bracing for a barrage. But Harry was too amazed to answer. Marisol a drug dealer! It was too absurd.

Harry took a deep breath, and tried to speak calmly. "Marisol is not a 'drug peddler', and I'd laugh at the accusation if it wasn't more vicious than it is absurd. And I'm not 'allied with leftist causes' either. I'm just on the side of anyone trying to help the people of this country — the real people, not a few rich ones. Last I

254

heard, that's what we're supposed to be doing. Have you put out a memo notifying us of a change in policy? Where did you *get* those lies, anyhow?"

Castle leaned forward over the desk. "Your attitude's gonna get your fanny in deep crapola, pal. Don't play games with me, because the ball's in my court. I know you defied my memo and attended the Frei rally. You sang at a clandestine Communist meeting and were arrested —"

"That was a *peña*, not a Communist meeting!"

"Semantics. You're here to do a job, not play politics."

"And my conscience?"

"An asset within the parameters of your job. This organization is a team effort, and one rotten apple can spoil the whole barrel. The topper was going out to the airport, getting involved with the police, then this bombing garbage. Front page, Bayliss! This sort of publicity could scotch our whole operation. I'd call it a damn selfish stunt."

Castle has power over me, Harry thought, and he knows it. But I still have one chance.

"How did you know about the *peña*? How could you know what happened to me at the airport yesterday? The papers never mentioned me and the police."

Of course, Harry thought. It would have been the Braniff Award for sure if Castle had known about the *peña* when it happened.

"Someone told you about me between yesterday and today. Who was it? Or don't I get to tell my side?"

The wrinkles deepened in Castle's forehead. His face sweated, and he bent to turn down the *estufa*. He loosened his tie.

"I'm not at liberty to divulge that information."

Harry stood up. Finally, he was beyond fear. He wanted to punish, to give back some of what he was getting.

"Are you sure that's your final answer, Steve? Because that's the one I'm going to relay to the Peace Corps in Washington. The newspapers too. You want a ruckus, I'll give you one."

He turned his back on the director and walked to the window. The Braniff Award, he thought. This is actually happening.

Castle cleared his throat. "Regardless of my answer, your actions have given me no choice but to terminate you."

The Peace Corps terminology sounded so morbid, as ominous as the Spanish verb when soldiers "controlled" you at a checkpoint. Or when people were "disappeared". Harry knew Castle meant it. Marisol and I will take Panchy to the States and start over, he thought. It just happened sooner than I planned, that's all. It's not the end. Then he thought of Lalo. His knees wobbled and he had to sit down again.

"Who told you?"

"I shouldn't say," Castle said. "But as a personal favor, and to put your mind at ease that my information is reliable and there's no sense pursuing the matter further, I'll make an exception in your case. It was Captain Uribe of Internal Security, the officer who questioned you at the airport."

"Gringo faggot" crawled in Harry's ear like an itch.

"Stop blaming everyone else for your problems and start assuming responsibility for your actions, and maybe you'll learn something from this unfortunate experience. Live by the rules and you won't have to die by them."

"Are you through?"

"You've already collected this month's full living allowance, and I won't ask you to return the balance. Termination takes about a week. Make an appointment with Dr. Correa as soon as possible."

Harry got up with an acid taste in his mouth. He was glad Castle didn't offer his hand.

"If you think it would help, I'll authorize a session or two with a psychiatrist."

Harry detected no sarcasm in Castle's voice, nor in his solemn expression.

"I'm not the one who's crazy," Harry said, and opened the door.

Lalo's funeral was three days later; two days after that Harry was terminated. The next week, though they knew what the results would be, he and Marisol cast their "No" ballots in the plebiscite over support for Pinochet and the new constitution. Soon all Chilean media proclaimed a glorious triumph for *"Su Excelencia"* General Pinochet, 79%–21%. On election night, a dissident labor union leader was found floating in the Mapocho River with his throat hacked open. The police had no leads. The following weekend Harry and Marisol got off the bus in Arica, after a grueling two-day slog through the desert. Memories rode with them, but Harry had come too far with the kids not to see them play in this tournament. Lalo would have wanted it that way.

And from Arica he and Marisol would travel to Machu Picchu.

Arica was a sunny oasis on the shining blue Pacific, a springtime city in the dead of winter. They stayed in a clean — and quiet but for the parrot in the lobby — *pensión* for five dollars a night, and made love to forget. Not that it really worked. The first night they had dinner with Ray and his jewel-covered *ariqueña* girlfriend, who drove them to a superb seafood restaurant on the beach in her father's new Oldsmobile. Ray didn't ask about Veronica.

"So you got shit-canned, Rookie. That sucks moose cock." The girlfriend chattered about becoming a model and an actress and living in New York. Harry didn't offer his address.

Harry's team lost to Ray's in the championship game, 11–8. Without Barata, Harry hadn't expected to even reach the final, so he wasn't disappointed. Only the somber faces of his kids made him feel bad, as Ray's players mobbed him after the victory. Ray held aloft the trophy and grinned for the local news photographers. Harry bought his team ice cream and took them to the beach. They removed their uniforms and the black armbands they had worn for Barata, and drowned defeat in the waves.

The tournament ended on Sunday, and Harry and Marisol planned to cross into Peru on Tuesday or Wednesday. To insure plenty of leeway against bureaucratic bungling, they had left their safe-conduct passes, needed to exit the country, at the Bureau of Investigations for stamping on Friday. Monday they went for a picnic in the Lluta valley, on the road to Bolivia, lush green vegetation along the river stopping sudden as a border at the base of the desert hills, so dry not even a cactus could survive. It was perfect and peaceful along the gurgling stream. But Harry kept thinking of Lalo, and knew Marisol was, too. For a long time they silently watched the desert rise forever into the Andes.

They caught a *colectivo* taxi back into town, then a rattly orange #2 bus to *Investigaciones*. They climbed the stairs past a plainclothes guard in a black tie, feet planted wide apart, submachine gun like a giant wasp in his arms. A scrawny man in a ripped shirt shuffled by, head down and hands cuffed behind his back, escorted by two soldiers. Harry presented his passport at the counter and received the *salvoconducto* pass from a young woman who would have been pretty if she smiled.

"*Gracias,*" he said.

"Request denied," she said to Marisol, and slid back her passport.

"Denied?" Marisol turned an ear toward the woman as if hoping she'd heard wrong. The new scar on her temple flushed red. "All I want to do is go on vacation."

"Denied. No authorization from Santiago. Security risk." She rolled a form into an old manual Underwood and started typing, efficiently ignoring them.

"What do you mean 'denied'?" Harry's voice rose. "She's no more of a security risk than I am." That's not the way to put it, he thought immediately. "Who can we talk to?"

"*Investigaciones* in Santiago." The woman threw across the carriage. "Now leave before I have you removed."

The guard at the door watched them through mirrored sunglasses, scowling, probably grateful for an incident to snap his boredom. Several people arrived behind them in line. Harry and Marisol drifted to the side, awaiting a bureaucratic miracle. The guard yawned. Finally, they walked to the bus stop in silence. At the corner Harry scuffed the sidewalk with his sandals, shifting his weight from one foot to the other. "There's got to be a way," he said. "We'll figure out something." The orange bus arrived, brakes squealing. In a vacant gravel lot kids played baseball without gloves, some without shoes. At the final stop along the beach, they were the last two passengers at the end of the run, sitting together in the rear seat — like Benjamin and Elaine, Harry thought, at the end of *The Graduate.*

The tide was going out. Harry still had no plan. The sun was sinking toward the water, and a breeze kicked up. The salt air smelled fresh, healthy. They walked on slick rocks, recently submerged, coated with barnacles and seaweed. Marisol dipped her hand underwater and came up with a hermit crab living in a corroded bullet shell. Its oversized claw snapped blindly.

"Carrying your house on your back has its advantages," Marisol said. A fishing trawler crawled in the distance. Harry wrapped his arms around Marisol's waist. What was it Jean had said, that long-ago day in Viña? "In California the beach is for fun. Back East you guys take it too seriously — the beach is for volleyball and surfing, not heart-to-heart talks. Get your priorities straight, boy." Then she had tickled him and they ran splashing along the shore.

Harry didn't tickle Marisol. A pelican knifed into the water, and surfaced with a wriggling fish in its beak.

"Marry me," he said. Marisol swayed from side to side. She took a deep breath and exhaled in a long sigh, then raised his clasped hands to her lips and kissed them.

"I can't."

It was the one response he hadn't foreseen. "What do you mean? Say you don't want to, but don't tell me you can't. I *love* you."

"I can't because *I* love *you*." The sun dipped below the water, its fire now a dying glow. Marisol shivered. "Please, let's walk. I have to keep moving."

"Marisol, we love each other. Isn't that why people get married?"

She shivered again. "You've never been in love before, and you've never been married. You're twenty-three, I'm thirty-one. I have a six-year-old daughter. And I've already lost one husband. I don't take marriage lightly."

"I take it seriously."

"Then take the consequences seriously. How will we live?"

"We could go to the States."

"When I can't even get a safe-conduct pass to Peru?"

"We'll live in Chile, then." But even as he spoke, he realized how hard it would be to live permanently outside his own country. Family, friends and freedom were so much to give up. He thought of Lalo, the exile — and saw a limp, twisted arm in the rubble.

"What would you do for a job, sell caramels on buses?"

"I could give English lessons, or teach at that American private school."

"Maybe. Twenty-five percent unemployment in this country, but maybe something would come up. And how long would you be happy teaching irregular verbs, or babysitting rich American kids? I refuse to be the reason you give up your dreams."

"You're my dream. I need you."

"What about your plans to travel? To see the world?"

"We'll go together, after we've saved some money."

"On a Chilean teacher's salary? I love you because you're so sensible," she said.

They came to a rocky peninsula, and clambered up a boulder to the top. Suddenly salt spray jetted from a nearby crevice; dense mist peppered their skin.

"Bufadora!" Marisol laughed. "Blowhole, like Moby Dick!"

Harry sat glumly. Stars flickered in the darkening sky. A lone seagull cawed overhead. Waves washed the shoreline, lapping like tongues. Harry couldn't see how the pressure built up for a blowhole, but without warning the geyser erupted again. Salt mist sifted through the air.

"We could move to the States in a few years, or whenever this blows over and they let you leave. You didn't do anything. They have to let you go!"

"What sort of job could I get? My English is not so good."

"Your weaving. Your knitting."

"Maybe. So much could go wrong, and Panchy would be caught in the middle. I'm thinking of her most of all."

Harry had no answer to that. He helped her to the sand. They strode double-time in the chill, shirts buttoned and sleeves rolled down. Her arguments made sense, like a chess master anticipating every move. Hatred surged inside him, violent, ugly hatred. Lalo's torturers and murderers had damaged his life, too, stepped on his dreams and ground them into dirt. Without even getting their boots muddy. Machu Picchu, the States. What a joke. Grow up, naive little gringo.

To their right loomed the famous Morro, the rounded cliff captured by Chile from Peru in the War of the Pacific a century earlier, and ever since a symbol of victory and national pride. The soldiers who stormed the hill had fired themselves up by chugging *aguardiente* laced with gunpowder.

"Harry, please say something."

"I was thinking about battles."

"If I didn't love you so much, I'd marry you tomorrow."

"I know. Just like I know that everybody on earth will be dead someday."

On Maipú Street, teenage prostitutes made up like debauched dolls eyed him with disappointment.

"Too bad," one said.

"Come with me, *lindo*. That *vieja* is too old for you."

Harry pretended not to hear. "So," he said, "when should we head back to Santiago?"

"No!" She shook her head. "You've looked forward to Machu Picchu for years. For most of your life! Harry, I will *not* be the reason you don't go."

"Why? Someday we could go together — next year, maybe, or the year after."

Blood rushed to her face; her scar flamed red. "Someday? Be serious. Did Lalo have 'someday'? The only day you're sure about is right now. Take it or leave it — and if you leave it you're not the man I thought you were."

She left him no choice.

"OK, but I'll miss you. And I'll take pictures. Photos as good as the puzzle. Better."

Her mouth softened. "I hope they won't have two pieces missing." The Machu Picchu puzzle, which they'd finally finished the day of Frei's speech, had a hole in the sky and another bare spot in the Temple of the Sun.

"You'll be the only piece missing." He touched her hand.

"Harry. . . ." Marisol took a deep breath. "Don't come back unless you're sure it's best. Probably you should travel, then go home. That would save us the pain of saying good-bye again."

"What are you saying? That's crazy!"

"No. Crazy is ignoring reality. Go home. Live without me, then decide. Harry, do you really want to play this scene again someday?"

"Now who's talking about 'someday'?"

"It's better that you leave, *mijito*. It tears me up to say so, but it's the truth."

"I love you too much," he said. "Way too much."

They walked sad streets until after midnight. The next day Marisol flew to Santiago. Harry took a *colectivo* taxi to Tacna, the border city in Peru. He was on his way to Machu Picchu, alone.

22

The darkness smelled wet. No moon at five A.M., and even a mountain sky dizzy with stars did not light the earth. Harry picked his way along the railroad tracks, stumbling on the loose stones between the ties. Despite the sweater Marisol had knit for him, he was cold: he hugged himself to rub some warmth into his stiff body. He had left the grubby little hotel in Aguas Calientes half an hour before, and now the deeper blackness on either side of him was dense forest, jungle almost. He recoiled when an unseen leaf, dank and slippery, brushed his face. The rushing Vilcanota River crashed loud as a waterfall, reverberating in the narrow valley so Harry couldn't even be sure on which side of him the water ran. Trying to orient himself, he tripped on a spike and went down, scattering rocks as he landed.

"*Qu' est-ce que c'est?*" someone shouted.

Harry sucked the scrape on his wrist and tasted salty blood. He looked into the weak outer edge of a flashlight beam that bounced as it approached.

"*Está bien?*" asked a voice in a French accent.

"*Sí.*" The light showed a torn patch in the knee of his jeans but only a trickle of blood.

"You are the American in the train," a woman said.

"Yes."

"Good, we are speaking English better than Spanish. You are going to Machu Picchu, I think so? You may use our torch with us."

"Thanks," he said, but he didn't sound grateful, even to himself. This trip had become a pilgrimage, a compulsive journey impossible to deny. He had wandered the streets of Arequipa, seen Lake Titicaca and the floating islands of the Uru Indians, roamed the Inca ruins of Cuzco, Sacsayhuamán, Ollantaytambo. But he thought always of Marisol. At night he would slink back to his empty room and lie awake on the inevitable concave mattress, dreaming of her and Machu Picchu.

They hiked three abreast, the woman in the middle holding the light. Laurent and Lydia Bessat, from Fribourg, Switzerland. He was lanky; she was short, with red bangs. They smelled of cigarette smoke.

"We were here ten years ago, before we were married," Lydia said. "And now we have finally a chance to return."

Laurent hawked and spat. "It is magnificent. You will see."

Harry kicked a stone and sent it skittering into the darkness. He thought of the lonely time in Arequipa two days after leaving Marisol, when he had explored the cloister of the Santa Catalina convent, where thousands of nuns had spent their entire adult lives hidden from the world and its temptations. Time hung heavy within those walls.

"I've seen pictures," Harry said.

Lydia lit a cigarette. "Ah, but it is not the same."

Dawn came to the valley long before the sun did.

Black was melding to gray by the time they had tramped the mile and a half to the foot of the mountain trail. Mist shrouded the heights, prehistoric fog hiding the mountaintops.

Harry didn't notice the moment of transition, just suddenly realized that the night was gone. He sweated in the chill, climbing vigorously with Marisol's sweater now tied around his waist, his hair damp beneath his stocking cap. Laurent and Lydia led the way but he soon chafed at their heels, tired but anxious to push himself and reach the top. When, panting, they stopped to rest and light Gauloises, he forged ahead up the steep trail. He had to do this alone.

Sometimes he needed his hands to clamber up rocks slick with dew. Eyes heavy from nervous, fitful sleep last night in Aguas Calientes, Harry paused and took out a bag of coca leaves. Twice he had woken terrified from dreams: in one Marisol had rolled over in bed to kiss him, but had no face; in another, he was sprinting to warn Lalo of the bomb, only to hear the explosion and see Lalo's body hurtle through the air and out of sight.

He stuffed in a mouthful of the dry, bland leaves and worked to moisten them into a pulp, then bit off a small piece of the ash ball needed for the leaves to take effect. The vile taste nearly gagged him, but the leaves were supposed to give energy and he forced himself to keep chewing. They numbed his mouth. He climbed, up toward the fog but never into it, jagged green peaks slowly emerging from the darkness. What a photograph, he thought, and cursed again his carelessness at the Arequipa train station, where his camera had been stolen — sliced right out of his pack while it was on his back. Now he couldn't take the pictures he had promised Marisol. Not enough light anyway, without a tripod, or a lot steadier hand than I've got. The leaves were working.

He reached the top a few minutes before the gate opened at 6:30. The small white tourist hotel was still asleep, dark and dead quiet. Harry leaned over a stone wall, cold on his elbows, watching the switchback road snake down and disappear into the valley, far below. A coca stem lodged between two teeth and he picked it out with a fingernail. They have this figured out, he thought. You can't see any of Machu Picchu unless you're inside the grounds. He caught a glimpse of Laurent's red cap fifty yards below. The gate opened, and he and five other waiting hikers, none of them Peruvian, paid their fee and went in.

The stone city did not spread out beneath him, as he had expected — as the puzzle and photographs had led him to believe — with jutting Huayna Picchu mountain in the background. Instead he found himself level with the roofless buildings, a participant as well as a spectator. Narrow stairways, low doors — these were small people who had lived in the clouds. The river's roar never ceased, a constant reminder of its power. If you lived here long enough you'd probably stop noticing it, like street noise to someone from Santiago. Or New York.

A tentative gleam, then the sun flared over misty mountains. Birds swooped through slanting rays of dawn. And everything is indifferent to its own splendor, Harry thought, dreaming about the forgotten people who called this mystical place home. He looked for a condor, knowing he wouldn't see one, wondering if the nearly extinct birds were as common as sparrows to Incan eyes. Awestruck and alone, he leaned against a smooth-hewn cornerstone that had lain motionless and unyielding, in earthquake country, without mortar, for over five hundred years.

Eight days ago we said good-bye.

Harry found the famous snug-fitting stone with thirty-two angles, locked in a wall like a jigsaw puzzle piece. He had wanted to touch that stone since seeing a photo in the encyclopedia as a kid. This early in the morning he had the grounds practically to himself. He tore off a chunk of bread, then spat out the leaves and climbed up the hill behind the ruins.

Day-old bread tasted a lot better than the leaves. He came upon a huge "bowlder" (as Hiram Bingham spelled it, in his book on Machu Picchu that lay contorted in Harry's pack), higher than he was tall, and boosted himself up with the help of a smaller rock. No *bufadora* by this boulder, he thought. The stone was cool but the sun shone warm on his back, and he loosened the buttons of his flannel shirt. Below him lay the lost city, dominated by the spire of Huayna Picchu, the same view in the puzzle he and Marisol had put together. For many minutes Harry dreamed with his eyes open.

The opening line from *A Tale of Two Cities* — "It was the best of times, it was the worst of times" — stuck in his head and wouldn't let go. *Is*, he told himself, not *was*. It's not over. Marisol's arguments flooded his mind. She was right, completely right, yet nothing could be more wrong.

Nothing? He heard the bomb blast, saw Lalo's lifeless hand. Pain and frustration gnawed his guts. You want to go back to that?

"Chee, chee! Chee, chee!"

On the trail a few yards away, a caravan of Peruvian porters, loaded like packmules, raced down the slope faster than Harry would ever have dared — even with nothing on his back. "Chee, chee!" they panted in headlong rhythm, rubber sandals made from old tires scuffing on worn stone, earflaps flopping on their alpaca caps. Their eyes were as wide as racehorses', their bare calves dark brown and thick with muscle. Harry contemplated the mess if one of them took a spill. In minutes the men were out of sight.

"Tell those kids to get their fingers out of their asses, Diego."

Strolling down the same trail came a silver-haired man in a ten-gallon hat and western-cut shirt with pearl snaps instead of buttons. His Levi's looked ironed. At his side, barely reaching his shoulder, walked a young Peruvian guide.

The guide looked puzzled. "Sir?"

The man twiddled his mustache. "I said get those guys moving, I'm already behind schedule. Do you want a good recommendation or not?"

"Yes, Mr. Barnett." Diego jogged back up the trail, where two twelve-year-old Peruvian boys, wearing *mantas* and blank expressions, lagged behind. One lugged a bulky, multi-colored knit sack. The other hauled an oversize blue pack with an American flag sewn on it.

Diego berated the boys in rapid-fire Quechua. Barnett pulled a can of snuff from his shirt pocket and took a big pinch. He seemed in halfway decent shape, pretty soft in the gut but not fat all over. Harry shifted his weight and the cowboy noticed him.

He chuckled to cover his embarrassment, and had trouble fitting the snuff lid back on. "These damn people'd fuck up a High Mass." He nodded uphill. "Gotta be firm with 'em or they'll never do a thing right, if they do it at all. Take you to the fucking cleaners."

Harry stared at him in stony silence.

"Don't speak English, eh? Funny, you *look* like an American." The cowboy doffed his Stetson and wiped his brow with his sleeve. He spat and turned away.

"Carry your own pack, asshole," Harry said in Spanish, using the derogatory informal form.

"Spanish, huh? You don't look like one of them. Say it slower, buddy. *Más lento, por favor.*"

"I'll say it as fast as you want those kids to move, you obnoxious prick."

"Hey, slow down! I'd get it if you'd just slow down! A bridge, right? Something about a bridge."

Diego and the boys caught up, breathing hard. "Hey, Diego, ask this guy what he's trying to tell me. I understand most of the Spanish, but can't quite make it all out."

Harry nearly laughed in his face. "What did you say, *señor*?" Diego asked regretfully.

"I said that your boss is an insufferable jackass and I'm ashamed to come from the same country. Please don't think we're all like that. And do me a favor — ask this jerk if he knows his wife's been screwing the Mexican gardener since the day he left."

Harry delivered the spiel with a straight face, but Diego couldn't suppress a grin. Terror shone in the boys' expressions.

Barnett cracked his knuckles. "Well?"

"And tell him he looks like a horse's ass in that hat."

"Mr. Barnett, he say your hat remind him of Ronald Reagan."

"That's *all* he said?"

"He wishes also you a nice day, and hopes that your family in the United Estates is well and happy."

Barnett tipped his hat to Harry. "Well, thank you kindly. It's an honor to be compared to our next president." He guffawed and slapped his thigh. "At least he didn't take me for a goddamn peanut farmer!"

The party started off. "We see now Temple of the Sun, Mr. Barnett? Very famous."

"Is that where they cracked the virgins? We were born too late to get in on what this place *really* had to offer!" His laugh echoed.

Harry was weary, bone weary. He slowly chewed his last piece of bread.

Up here, on this rock. This is where I would have asked her to marry me.

A thousand feet below, the jungle-green Urubamba River wound away into the valley. Climbers were a handful of colored specks, on the sheer slope of Huayna Picchu. Harry felt tiny within the immensity, face to face with forever. For the hundredth time, he raced around the corner of Lalo's house, his knee throbbing. He told himself again that the memory of Lalo's death would pass, that back home his life would renew itself. Except. . . .

He was alone.

He reached under his shirt and pulled out the leather pouch hanging from his neck, the one his dad gave him before he came to Chile. It left a patch of sweat on his chest. The two snaps clicked open. Passport, traveler's checks, Peruvian tourist card, a couple of bucks in cash . . .

Stuffed behind everything else was a photo and a wrinkled newspaper clipping. Lewis had sent the photo when he heard of Harry's termination. It was of the two of them knee-deep in a crystal river at the bottom of the world, an arm around each other and laughing at being alive. Lewis's Minneapolis address was on the back, along with BEST FRIEND, BEST TIME, NEVER FORGET. Harry looked down over the ruins. Mid-morning had arrived, and with it more people. He could no longer pretend to have the lost city to himself. Soon, the train from Cuzco would screech into the station, and buses would ferry hundreds of tourists up the mountain. Harry put back the photo.

He carefully unfolded the paper; it was tearing at the creases like an old road map. Once again he saw himself on the front page of *La Tercera*, two inches above a photo of a goalie futilely diving for a penalty kick. His mouth still contorted, his fists, one leaking blood, still clenched behind Marisol. The dark hole of Lalo's blasted studio framed him perfectly, and with admirable depth of field the photographer caught the lumpy bag on the stretcher and kept it in sharp focus. COMMUNIST BOMBER PERISHES BY OWN HAND, proclaimed the blazing red headline.

Harry ran a finger along the pink streak of scar on his palm, slicing the lifeline. Of course the Peace Corps had paid to stitch him up — you're very lucky, *señor*, no muscle damage. Not deep enough. Whistle shrieking, brakes screaming, the Cuzco train chugged into the station; minutes later, the first busload began the looping climb.

He stared at the imposing peak of Huayna Picchu, a green steeple jutting high above the city, and realized he had neither the energy nor the inclination to struggle up it. This was as high as he'd get, this time. Harry's eyes burned, then closed; he melted into a twitching sleep, his pack for a pillow.

When he woke, the sun was directly overhead. Bizarre light patterns danced in the darkness behind his eyelids. He sat up, squinting, one hand shielding his eyes, scanning in amazement the spectacle below. Tourists swarmed Machu Picchu like ants cleaning a skeleton. The mysterious lost city at dawn had become a crowded museum by noon.

The clipping! He arched his legs — nothing underneath him. He cursed himself for nodding off without protecting it. Harry jumped off the boulder and a minute later was peering down a steep mountain wall at the clipping, snagged by bushes twenty feet below. His face stared up at him. It was a brutal drop, all the way to the crashing river. But there were plenty of bushes to grab. He took a step back. "It's a piece of paper, Bayliss," he said out loud. "A piece of paper, and a hell of a long way down."

He left the paper to flutter. Suddenly his plan of burning the clipping on Machu Picchu and scattering the ashes seemed ridiculous. Stupid, romantic, the kind of thinking that convinces young men to fight wars they want no part of, and die. It was better this way. As he descended, a fat man in a green leisure suit complained in English of aching feet; a French woman with hennaed hair barked at her children to stand still for a Polaroid. A teenage Peruvian girl, face and toenails painted, pants form-fitting, pouted because the inconsiderate Incas had not designed Machu Picchu for her spike-heeled shoes.

Some shuttle buses were already heading down the mountain. Harry watched people boarding like commuters at rush hour, angling for position so they wouldn't have to wait for the next one. Others lounged on the hotel terrace. The bus gunned its engine, and Harry inhaled a cloud of diesel fumes. He set off down the trail that had been barely visible on the way up at dawn.

Hiking down was a lot easier, but Harry walked carefully. *"Chee, chee!"* Harry stepped off the trail and a boy sped by, wearing the same used-tire sandals and wild-eyed look of the porters he'd seen earlier. The boy reached the road below and waited till the bus approached, tires kicking up dust. "Good-bye!" he shouted in English, waving at the passengers as the bus rolled by.

Harry had heard about these kids. They ran down the trail so swiftly that they could meet the buses on every level of the switchbacks to wave and holler "good-bye", hoping to earn some tips at the bottom for the entertainment. Then they climbed up and did it again. And again and again.

Harry stood on the road, halfway up or halfway down the mountain. The sky was a blanket of translucent cotton; jungle green surrounded him; the brawling river surged forever. One last, unrewarded search for a soaring condor.

"Chee, chee!" Another boy ran up next to him, no taller than Barata, round-faced and surely not as old as he looked. Harry smiled, wondering if he'd ever seen a baseball. The boy eyed him warily. A bus appeared around the bend.

"Good-bye! Good-bye!"

Harry waved and shouted along with the kid. Fingers pointed at them. Faces distorted, pressed against window glass.

"Good-bye!"

Then gone. Dust hung like smoke. A quick, competitive glance and the boy shot off. Harry watched him disappear.

He touched two fingers to his buttoned shirt-pocket and felt a reassuring crinkle. He took out Marisol's letter, three lines on a sheet of onionskin paper: "Do what's best for you, *corazón*, because that's what's best for both of us. For all of us." He wasn't sure what was best anymore, but he knew what he had to do. He was tired of losing people and things: Dad, Lalo, his grandfather's guitar. He slipped the letter back into the pocket over his heart, and buttoned it tight.

Standing alone below the lost city, he had no lofty thoughts of Incas and immortality. His mind was full of Marisol dancing, dancing alone, wildly dancing to "Satisfaction" before the lights went out. While Harry waited outside in the dark.

This time he wouldn't wait. Not ready to disappear, not ready at all, Harry picked his way down the mountain, heading south for the winter.